ILLEGAL HOLDINGS

A VALENTIN VERMEULEN THRILLER

—•—

Michael Niemann

coffeetownpress

Seattle, WA

coffeetownpress

Coffeetown Press
PO Box 70515
Seattle, WA 98127

For more information go to: www.coffeetownpress.com
www.michael-niemann.com

Cover design by Sabrina Sun

Illegal Holdings
Copyright © 2018 by Michael Niemann

ISBN: 978-1-60381-591-8 (Trade Paper)
ISBN: 978-1-60381-588-8 (eBook)

Library of Congress Control Number: 2017961012

Printed in the United States of America

For George,

whose kind invitation

opened my eyes to Maputo

ACKNOWLEDGMENTS

——◆——

MY THANKS TO THE "MONDAY MAYHEM" writing group, Jenn Ashton, Carole Beers, Sharon Dean, Clive Rosengren, and Tim Wohlforth, for encouraging writing discipline and alerting me whenever the story became too convoluted. Fred Grewe deserves credit for a suggestion that triggered my thinking of the final plot twist. Herb Rothschild read the entire first draft and helped clean up the manuscript prior to submission. Jennifer McCord and Catherine Treadgold at Coffeetown Press shepherded this book to publication with their expert advice and meticulous editing. Pam Dehnke and Darrell James opened Nightingale's, their lovely B&B, for salons where I read the first chapter of the novel. Bobby Arellano and Ed Battistella, my co-host for Literary Ashland Radio, are always good for inspiring conversations. Our dog Stanley has trained us to take him on four walks a day, one of the best things to do when the writing doesn't go so well. My gratitude to my partner Joanna for being there, always. I couldn't have done it without all of you.

Part of this story was inspired by the work of the *União-Geral das Cooperativas*, a women's cooperative that helped feed Maputo during and after the civil war. The "new scramble" for African land has been underway for some time and continues apace. More information on this collusion of international investors and unresponsive or hapless governments can be found at the Oakland Institute (www.oaklandinstitute.org), and Grain (www.grain.org).

Full-Length Valentin Vermeulen Thrillers

Legitimate Business

Illicit Trade

Valentin Vermeulen Short Stories/Novellas

Africa Always Needs Guns

Big Dreams Cost Too Much

Some Kind of Justice

CHAPTER ONE

AN UNCANNY SENSE

———— ◆ ————

IT WAS JUST ANOTHER TUESDAY MORNING in late January, the warmest and rainiest month in Maputo. Acacia pods littered the streets of Mozambique's capital, and its million-and-a-half residents were looking forward to winter.

The email, which arrived at the Nossa Terra office at eight thirty, hit Aisa Simango like a fist in the stomach.

She was looking out the window. That much she remembered afterwards. Looking at the Avenida Vladimir Lenine, thinking that the street seemed forlorn in the watery morning light. Why she was looking out of the window, she didn't remember. She should have been printing the agenda for the nine o'clock staff meeting, steeling herself for the chaos that erupted when her staff barged into the office.

Instead, she was standing by the window, pensive. Maybe she'd stopped to straighten the picture of her children, Alima and João, on the windowsill. Sometimes the vibrations of a heavy truck driving by nudged it closer to the edge. Or perhaps she was thinking about the Sofala Project, wondering if it stood any chance of being completed on time.

In any case, her computer dinged, she sat down and opened the message.

It came from the Maputo office of Global Alternatives, the Swiss foundation set up by hedge-fund billionaire Vincent Portallis. The foundation was a newcomer to the development-aid field. It undertook big, flashy projects, lured famous actors to its causes, and dispensed a trickle of the millions of dollars it leveraged to local subcontractors like Nossa Terra.

The message itself started with the usual noncommittal niceties—Greetings, Aisa. How are things? It's been a while—but got to the point quickly. We've emailed Helton Paito repeatedly regarding a discrepancy in the disbursements. We've received no reply. Would you kindly review the numbers in the attached spreadsheet and supply the proper documentation, or alternatively, remit the specified amount to Global Alternatives?

She wasn't worried yet. Not then. The message sounded more pro forma than anything. Just dotting the i's and crossing the t's. Making sure all the numbers added up, *accountability* and *efficacy* being big buzzwords in the donor community. Most likely, Helton was already dealing with it. Her first glance at the spreadsheet also didn't raise any suspicions. Yes, they had proposed to spend those sums for those purposes. She knew, because she had personally reviewed the project proposal before submitting it five months ago.

It was the last column that sent her reeling. She rubbed her eyes, focused on the street outside, then back on the screen. The numbers were still there, including the last one, bold and in bright red. Like dabs of blood left on the screen. The number was too large, too ghastly to imagine. Five million dollars. Unaccounted for, missing, not properly documented. No matter what phrase she came up with, it still meant trouble, serious trouble.

Of course, it was all wrong. Five months ago, when they'd been notified that the project in Sofala had been accepted, everybody had clapped. But so far, they'd only received a small disbursement. Enough to set up the infrastructure and hire personnel. Certainly not five million dollars.

She got up. Went to the window. And back to her desk. She grabbed her mobile. *Call Global Alternatives, ask if there has been a mistake, if this is someone's idea of a joke.* She didn't. Obviously, Global Alternatives didn't make mistakes or joke around.

There were documents, receipts, invoices for the hundred thousand they'd received. They could account for all expenditures. She dialed Helton's number. He would know where the mistake lay, which numbers had ended up in the wrong column, projected expenses instead of disbursements, or vice versa. He was her second in command and usually the second one through the door in the morning. He answered after four rings.

"*Bom dia*, Helton," she said. "Where are you?"

"Just got off the *chapa* at Julius Nyerere. Be there in fifteen."

"I need you here now."

The *chapa* stop, where the minibus taxis dropped and picked up passengers, was close enough, one of the reasons they had chosen an office so far from central Maputo. But Helton liked to check out the wares of the hawkers along the roundabout connecting Avenida Vladimir Lenine and Avenida Julius Nyerere.

"I still need breakfast. Why the hurry? *Tudo bem*?"

"No, everything isn't okay. Where are we with the Sofala Project?"

"We completed the first phase. We rented a space, hired a local manager, did the registration and all that. Next phase is community meetings. Then comes the big stuff—land acquisition."

"And we've spent what, a hundred thousand?" She hated the guessing game. A sheet of paper, better yet, an old-fashioned ledger with dated entries for every *centavo* would have calmed her.

"Yes, about that much."

"And you have documentation for every expenditure?" She held her breath without meaning to. Helton had been good for Nossa Terra, even if she didn't always get along with him. He was the accountant who'd made it possible to land projects like the one with Global Alternatives.

"Of course. I'll be there soon. *Até já.*"

He sounded both upset and defensive when he ended the call.

She went back to the window. The melancholy she felt when looking at the Avenida Vladimir Lenine in the rain was more bearable than the dejection evoked by the stark office. When Nossa Terra first moved here after their big expansion four years earlier, the soulless space had weighed on her. But the rent was cheap, and Nossa Terra had no money. Since then, new employees had tried to spruce it up. They affixed posters to the walls and brought in all sorts of plants. In the end, they all surrendered to the futility of the makeover, giving in to the cement walls, impervious to any improvement.

Before the move, Nossa Terra had been a scrappy community organization fighting for land so its members could farm. It had taken Aisa in thirteen years earlier. She had just given birth to João sixteen months after having Alima. Their father up and left, unwilling to face raising children. She was desperate for food, shelter, companions. She wasn't much of a farmer, but she had an uncanny sense of the limit beyond which the authorities would abandon any pretense of accommodation and just call the police. That skill helped her get concessions, then leases, and eventually, land titles.

By that time, the global aid complex had fully embraced Mozambique. Nossa Terra was noticed. Graduate students from Scandinavian universities came to study it. A documentary filmmaker from Brazil shot enough footage to put together an hour-long feature.

When the foundations came knocking, Aisa, the single mom, was ready. She hired three staff not knowing how she'd pay them at the end of the month and drew up a proposal to expand the work Nossa Terra had done near Maputo to the next province. After submitting the proposal, she landed her first project, worth a hundred thousand dollars, three days before payroll came due.

Helton barged into the office. He seemed to compress the air in any room he entered. The others called him "Hilton," not because he was as refined as a luxury hotel, but as big as they imagined a Hilton to be. It wasn't just his size. With his shiny face, wooly hair, spotty beard, and big smile, he exuded maleness, not in a primordial sense, more in a *here's-a-guy's-guy* sense. Men liked him automatically. Many women did, too. Even some who worked at Nossa Terra. Aisa wasn't one of them.

"What's the matter with the Sofala Project?" he said, stopping in the open door.

"Have they contacted you?"

"Yes. Routine stuff. Why?"

Closing the door, he walked to his desk, took off the blue suit coat, and hung it over the back of the chair. Helton always wore a suit, shirt, and tie. Since he only had the one suit, time had taken its toll on the garment. Aisa thought a simple shirt with tie would look far better, but the suit was part of Helton's guyness.

"So far they've disbursed a hundred thousand?" she said.

"Yes, yes. I told you."

"I received an email from Global Alternatives. They mentioned discrepancies. They say they have repeatedly sent you messages."

"Oh, yes. I've gotten requests for documentation," he said. "I sent them."

"Well, the discrepancies are still there."

"What discrepancies?"

"Five million dollars' worth of discrepancies," she said.

"Impossible."

She turned to the computer, thinking that Helton's protestation made him look like he knew more.

"Look at the spreadsheet."

He plopped into Aisa's chair, which squeaked under his weight. He jiggled the mouse. The picture of Maputo's beachfront disappeared, and the columns and numbers reappeared, the last one still a blood-red punctuation mark. Helton followed the numbers, his right index finger moving down the screen. He mouthed each number silently. As the finger approached the red number, he started shaking his head.

"No," he said so quietly she barely heard it. "No, no, *no*." His voice became louder with each "No." Whatever defensiveness Aisa thought she'd noticed was gone. The Helton before her was a man utterly shocked.

"This can't be," he said. "They're basically saying we've accepted five million and submitted no expenditure reports, no receipts, nothing. As if we took the money and socked it away in a secret account in Jo'burg."

"But we didn't, right?"

He gave her a withering look. "Do you have to ask?"

"I'm sorry, but I do. For the record."

He looked away, his body taking up less space. They each waited for the next word.

"What do I have to do to earn your trust?" he said finally, looking at her again. "It wasn't my fault."

She knew he wasn't talking about the five million. He was talking about the past, a past that linked them. When she was twelve, her village in Sofala was attacked by soldiers of the Mozambican National Resistance known everywhere as RENAMO. The long civil war between RENAMO and the government had ground to a halt. A ceasefire had already been agreed to. Still, her village was attacked. Her father was killed. She saw him bleed to death because the soldiers burned the clinic and killed the nurse first.

After she hired Helton, she found out he'd been a RENAMO soldier in Sofala. He never denied that. By his account, he'd been kidnapped and forced to fight for the rebels like so many other kids. They made him and the others attack their villages and kill as many as they could. After the kids had become killers, they couldn't go back.

During the attack, Aisa had seen children, their ragged uniforms held up by sisal ropes, their rubber boots intended for adults, the AK47s too big for them. But they pulled the trigger and killed just like adults. After the war finally ended, villages held reconciliation sessions. Bringing the children face-to-face with the families whose members they'd killed. Teaching them to ask for forgiveness. Her own village had held one. By all accounts, the event had helped many cross chasms of anger, fear, and hurt. She'd missed it, having moved to Maputo well before.

"I know it wasn't your fault," she said. "You have my trust, but five million dollars is too much money. This isn't a personal thing. If those numbers are correct, it will be the end of Nossa Terra."

"We never got five million," Helton said.

Aisa nodded. That much money she would've remembered. "What is the disbursement schedule for the rest of the money?"

"Phase two? Just seventy thousand. Enough to buy a four-wheel drive and pay travel expenses to the community meetings. The big disbursement was to come in phase three, land acquisition. But we're at least a half year away from that."

"So it has to be a data-entry error."

"Naturally. Somebody over at Global Alternatives got their wires crossed."

"So a simple phone call should straighten this out, right?"

Helton shrugged. "Naturally."

"Before I call them, show me everything you have. And I mean everything."

Helton opened the first file cabinet. One of his jobs after joining Nossa Terra had been to bring order to the paperwork. Most of the staff didn't care much for paperwork. The filing system was a mess. Helton had changed that. He'd pushed for the purchase of a scanner to store paperwork electronically and kept the hardcopies as backup in designated folders, clearly labeled and stored in file cabinets in the order in which they were completed.

Aisa looked on as he yanked open drawer after drawer, fingering folders, pulling out one or the other only to put it back again. Ten minutes into his increasingly frantic search, the rest of the staff started drifting in. Neither Aisa nor Helton greeted them, so they went to the kitchen and started the morning tea ritual.

"You can't find it, can you?" Aisa said.

Helton pulled open one last drawer. His fingers crawled over the folder tabs, stopping here and there, but he didn't pull anything out. He stood up and wiped sweat from his forehead.

"They're not here," he said quietly.

"Are you sure there is no other place it could be?"

Helton nodded. He went over to his computer. He clicked on folder icons and closed them again equally fast.

"This is impossible," he mumbled. His clicking grew more desperate, as if tapping the mouse button fast enough would reveal the missing files.

"Talk to me, Helton."

He didn't. More and more windows filled the screen. He cycled through them faster than she could comprehend.

"Talk to me. Please." It was more a whisper than a command.

"It's gone. Everything is gone," he said finally, his skin ashen.

* * *

"WE RECEIVED SOME TROUBLESOME NEWS," AISA said to the staff, who had stood there, tea cups in hand, puzzled, while Aisa and Helton looked for the documents. "Kindly take your seats and pay attention."

Raised eyebrows, murmurs, shuffling feet, and scraping chairs followed. Everybody had their spot. Helton's was across from Aisa. He'd said it balanced the table. She thought it was a power play. Zara Nyussi, a slight woman with close cropped hair, took the chair on his right, as if trying to disappear next to his bulk. She kept to herself but made sure their computer network functioned without a hitch. She was the go-to resource for anything technical below the level that required a consultant.

Bartina Macie took her seat next to Aisa. She was a big woman with an unruly afro and a face that made people think twice about contradicting her. Aisa had hired her, not sure what, if anything, she could do at the office. Bartina had stopped her on the street and asked if she had a job cleaning, washing, cooking, anything. Having no space or money for a maid, Aisa had waved her off. But Bartina wasn't easy to get rid of. She just followed Aisa from the *chapa* stop to the office. By lunchtime that day, Bartina had a job cleaning the office and making tea. By evening, she'd fixed the eternally leaking toilet and her job at Nossa Terra was secure. In the three years since, she'd worked her way up to project assistant and was forever loyal to Aisa. "You heard the woman," she bellowed across the room. "Sit on down and listen up."

The chair pulling and murmurs stopped.

"As you know, Global Alternatives is funding the Sofala Project and we work as their local partners on the implementation," Aisa said. "This morning, we received an email telling us that we've failed to submit the necessary documentation for the expenditures. They've asked us to send that information or return the funds."

The silence engendered by the curt announcement lasted almost a minute.

"How much?" Tendai Cunha, manager for a vocational training project at the outskirts of Maputo, said. Tendai was the living embodiment of average. Average height, weight, face, and clothes. Even some of the regulars at his favorite bar forgot his face the moment he left. Many concluded therefore that his averageness also extended to his mind. More than one had found they were wrong after being reduced to embarrassed silence by his sharp tongue. Only Bartina was impervious to his slights.

"Five million dollars," Aisa said.

A collective gasp faded into silence. Not everyone working for Nossa Terra was familiar with all budgetary details, but they knew five-million missing dollars meant serious trouble.

"There is no reason to worry. Helton and I will sort out what happened and we'll get to the bottom of it. I ask that the rest of you continue your work. Thank you all. Zara, would you join Helton and me in the meeting room?"

Aisa waited until Helton and Zara had entered the room and closed the door.

"Zara, Helton can't find the electronic copies of the Sofala Project paperwork. Please double-check. Were they accidentally deleted? Moved to a different place?" Helton opened his mouth. "Quiet, Helton," she told him. "I know you looked everywhere. But we need a fresh set of eyes. And, Zara, if they're really gone, can they be retrieved? If not, I need to know what happened. Do you think you could do that in an hour?"

Zara nodded and left the room.

Aisa sat down. The shock and worry on the faces of her employees, her colleagues really, brought home the magnitude of the threat. The knot in her stomach tightened. All she could do was hope, hope that Zara found the documentation, hope that Helton remembered the special place where he'd stored the folder, hope that it had all been a silly mistake.

"When was the last time you saw the files?"

"The hard copies? I don't know. It's been a while. I work with the electronic copies."

"And when did you work with them?"

Helton shrugged. "Last week?"

"Please try to be precise."

"I don't know. I think I worked on it last Thursday. That's the best I can remember."

* * *

At eleven, Zara tapped Aisa on the shoulder. Aisa had been staring out the window again and spun around, annoyed at having been caught daydreaming.

"I can't find the files," Zara said. "Usually when files are deleted, they don't disappear, the system just deletes their directory entry. But I didn't find any stray files on Helton's computer."

"Let's talk in the meeting room," Aisa said.

After she closed the door, she didn't sit down.

"I'm not sure what you mean, Zara. Helton assures me that he had them last Thursday. Are you saying they were never on his computer?"

"I can't find any trace of them."

"So he never had those files?" Aisa remembered his cagey behavior when she first told him about the email. She'd been right to mistrust Helton.

"I'm not saying that," Zara said. "Those disk sectors could have been overwritten by new documents. Once a file name isn't in the directory anymore, the computer thinks the space is available for new data."

"And were they?"

"Maybe."

"So we don't know if the files were ever there or not."

"No. But I did find one odd thing. A part of the disk was overwritten with zeroes."

Aisa had no idea what that meant. Zara must have seen that.

"An empty hard disk has nothing on it," she said. "It's just empty space. Nothing there, not even zeroes."

"So how did those get there?"

"One possibility is that someone used secure erase."

"Please, Zara, speak to me in terms I can understand."

"Oh, sorry, of course. Secure erasing is meant to make sure that nobody can find a deleted file. So, in addition to deleting the directory entry, secure erase overwrites with zeros the space where the file's data was. It's meant to make sure the data are unreadable."

"Could Helton have done that by accident?"

Zara shook her head. There was sadness in her face. "No, the system asks you specifically if you want to choose that option. It was deliberate."

The magnitude of that statement dawned on Aisa only in stages. *Deliberate.* Someone did it on purpose. It wasn't just an innocent mistake. Someone meant to do it.

"Is it possible to tell who did that?"

Zara shook her head again.

"So anyone could have done it?" Aisa said.

"Anyone who knows the password to access that computer. Which means everybody here."

Each machine had its password taped to the monitor.

"Could someone from the outside have done that?" Aisa said, desperate now. She couldn't conceive of anyone on her staff being the culprit. There had to be someone else, an outsider.

Zara shrugged. "It's possible. But how did they get inside? The doors are locked when we aren't here. You made sure we understand that policy. There are grates over the windows."

"How about over the internet. Could someone have broken in that way and done it?"

"Again, it's possible. For hackers, it's not difficult. But who would hack into our computers? We don't have anything worth stealing."

"Could you find out?"

"No. A good hacker wouldn't leave any traces."

Chapter Two

Without Resistance

———◆———

AT THREE FIFTEEN THAT AFTERNOON—AISA HAD just corralled the staff for another unscheduled office conclave—the door to the Nossa Terra office opened and a visitor entered. That was the first anomaly. Visitors didn't just show up. They made appointments. He was tall but not big and wore a dark-gray jacket over a beige shirt, tan slacks, and brown leather shoes. He was also white, another anomaly. White visitors meant important visitors—heads of foundations, funding agencies, European development NGOs. They never arrived without prior announcement and they never arrived alone. Aisa looked out of the window and saw a taxi drive away. That was the final anomaly. White visitors usually had a car and driver.

The man nodded and scanned the room with his pale blue eyes. He was clean-shaven, mid to late forties with a northern European countenance. Not so much British as continental. Looking tense, he pushed back a lock of blond hair that had fallen down his forehead. He was probably wondering whom to address. Aisa waited. Would he pick one of the two men in the room to speak to? Helton was the most likely candidate because his blue suit appealed to the Western sense of hierarchy.

The man didn't get his chance to make the wrong choice because Bartina stood up and said in her rudimentary English, "*Bom dia.* We help you?"

The man relaxed a little and smiled.

"*Bom dia.* Yes, you may. My name is Valentin Vermeulen. I'm with the United Nations and I'd like to speak to Aisa Simango, please."

The room fell quiet again. United Nations? They'd never had a visitor from the United Nations. Aisa rose from her chair. Why had no one called to schedule the visit? Even though a large part of the money Nossa Terra received originated with the United Nations, by the time it reached them, it had gone through three or more organizations. Getting a visit from the very top was a big deal. And it couldn't have happened at a worse time.

"I am Aisa. What can I do for you?" she said.

He stretched out his hand and walked toward her. Aisa shook it. He looked around.

"Is there a space where we can speak in private?"

He sounded solicitous, eager to lessen the tension in the air, which stood in sharp contrast to his request for a private conversation. The knot in her stomach tightened again. She suppressed a wince.

"Please, come this way."

She led the man to the meeting room, which was littered with folders, left after the unsuccessful search for the Sofala documents.

"Please, excuse the disarray," she said. "We didn't know you were coming; otherwise we would have been prepared."

Bartina, as usual tuned into her boss's internal turmoil, stuck her head into the room.

"Tea, coffee?"

"Yes, coffee please. Thank you," Vermeulen said.

"Aisa?"

"Tea. Thank you, Bartina."

She picked up a stack of files from one end of the table and dropped them at the other end. Vermeulen followed her example. They sat at the cleared side of the table.

"I understand that unannounced visits are rather unorthodox," Vermeulen said. "I apologize for that. Ordinarily, we would have sent an announcement of my visit. This case, however, is urgent, and I decided to skip the formalities. I hope I didn't trouble you unduly."

Why did his calm demeanor and friendly words have the opposite effect on her? She hadn't done anything. She wasn't guilty. Yet telling herself didn't make it so. Something had gone terribly wrong in her organization. Maybe it was a simple error; maybe one of her staff had had a hand in it. It didn't matter. Files were missing, and she didn't know what to do next.

"No troubles at all," she lied. "Please tell me why you are here."

"I'm with the Office of Internal Oversight Services. We're auditing Global Alternatives' UN-funded projects. You are listed as a subcontractor of Global Alternatives and there is a discrepancy in the accounts."

If the email seven hours earlier had been a punch to her stomach, the words from the visitor were the long-delayed follow-up jab that sent Aisa reeling. She had no memory of the moment afterwards. Did she gasp? Cover her mouth? Slump down on the table? She only remembered Bartina slamming down the tray and rushing around the table and patting her cheeks.

"What you do?" she yelled at the visitor.

Aisa ran her hands through her hair and took deep breaths.

"*Tudo bem*, Bartina, *tudo bem*." She turned to the visitor. "My apologies, Mr. Vermeulen. We have had a difficult morning."

Bartina hovered by the door, with a look on her face that threatened physical harm to the visitor, should he even think of harassing Aisa again. Aisa waved her out of the room.

"I gather from your reaction that this isn't news to you," Vermeulen said.

It was a heartless thing to say, but it made Aisa sit up and reclaim her composure.

"We received an email message alerting us to that discrepancy only this morning. We are investigating the claim and will respond soon. We'll supply all the necessary documentation. There was no need for Global Alternatives to send a UN investigator so soon. It's a simple bookkeeping error."

She didn't like her defensive tone. It made her sound as if she had things to hide, just like Helton did earlier.

"I'm sure it is," Vermeulen said. "Global Alternatives didn't send me. I was at their offices, and seeing that they've contacted you repeatedly, I decided to follow up on my own. I was in town and thought that a quick check would clear it up. After all, one doesn't misplace five million dollars. Can you show me the books?"

There it was again. That friendly smile and calm demeanor paired with a sharp demand. No, she couldn't show him the books because she didn't know where the bloody books were.

"I'm afraid that is not possible right now," she said. "As you can see," she pointed to the pile of files, "we are in the middle of reorganizing our documents. You caught us at a bad moment. If we had had a little more notice, we would have gotten everything you need ready. If you wouldn't mind coming back later … uh … I would be more than happy to show you the books."

Aisa wasn't a good liar. Not enough practice. She'd never had the need for subterfuge. Being straightforward, telling it like it is, especially when dealing with people in power, had always worked for her. This was different. The survival of Nossa Terra was at stake. Being straightforward meant telling the man that all the files were gone. Her gut told her that would be a bad idea.

Vermeulen looked at her, his face kind, understanding, but his eyes piercing the veil of her lies. At least that's what it felt like to Aisa.

"Okay," he said after a moment. "When would be a suitable time?"

How about after we find the files? she thought. But she didn't say that. Instead, she remembered to smile and shrug.

"Would tomorrow afternoon work for you?" she said. "About three?"

Vermeulen nodded.

"I've never been to Maputo," he said. "Could you recommend a nice place to eat? I'd prefer something other than my hotel."

He was finally behaving like the other Europeans who came to Nossa Terra. Aisa usually sent them to one of the bigger hotels, because she knew that, despite the professed interest in local cuisine, they ultimately preferred more familiar surroundings and their food toned down. She was about to ask him which hotel, when she remembered that he'd come on his own in a beat-up taxi and that he might indeed be up to the local fare.

"Do you like prawns?"

He nodded.

"Follow Avenida Lenin all the way to the port. It'll stop at the Hotel Tivoli. From there, go to the Twenty-Fifth of June Park and follow it to the water's edge. You'll find a little shack, no sign. You will smell it before you see it. They have the best piri-piri prawns in Maputo."

* * *

BACK IN THE MEETING ROOM WITH Helton and Zara, Aisa paced. The files were still piled at one end of the table. The more she thought about it, the uncannier this day seemed. First the email, then the frantic search for the documents, finally the visitor from the UN. All that couldn't be a coincidence. There was something orchestrated about it. She said as much to her colleagues.

"You mean we're being set up?" Helton said.

"Doesn't it feel like that to you?" Aisa said.

Zara had grabbed the backrest of a chair and propped herself against it. She kept shaking her head as if trying to wake up from a bad dream. Aisa looked at Helton, wondering. Could he have deleted those files? No matter how much her mind told her to let it go, the nagging doubt remained. In a perverse way, it would be the easiest explanation. Helton took the money. He covered his tracks. He'd disappear in a couple of days, taking with him more money than she could imagine. The alternative was too complicated.

"Helton, I need to know. Did you delete those files on your computer?" Aisa said.

He slumped into a chair and buried his head in his hands. Zara let go of the chair and backed away from the table as if seeking a blast-proof spot.

"It's your computer, Helton. Nobody else uses it. Zara found parts of the disk overwritten with zeroes. She didn't find any evidence of internet activity overnight. I need to know."

Helton raised his head.

"Goddamn it, Aisa. Will you ever let it go? No, I did not delete the files. No, I did not hide the documents. No, I did not take five million dollars. No,

I am not RENAMO scum. I am Helton Paito. I'm an honorable man. If you don't believe me, I can't help you. Pester your own goddamn demons but leave mine the hell alone."

He was right to shout at her. Aisa knew that. She leaned against the wall and closed her eyes. What next?

"We need to look at other possibilities," Zara said in a firm voice. "You are right, Aisa. This isn't a coincidence. The hardcopies and electronic files can't just disappear at the same time. Somebody must have taken them. We need to check the locks on all the doors. We need to contact the police. Something has happened here. We better get on it."

Aisa looked at her. Was that really Zara? Quiet, mousy Zara? Helton must have had the same reaction because he raised his head and stared at her.

"Well," Zara said with an apologetic shrug, "that's better than accusing each other." She opened the door of the meeting room and went back into the office. She said something to Tendai and the two went to the front door, opened it, and examined it carefully.

Except for the steel bars over the windows, there were no special security provisions, no alarms, no private security patrols. And the bars had been there when they moved in. Nossa Terra was a community organization. Its ethos was to be with the community, not to keep it out. And Aisa was certain that if there had been a burglary, it hadn't been committed by a random burglar.

She went to the rear. There was a short hallway with two doors, a wooden one to the office and a steel one to the alley. The outside door was always locked, with the key hanging on a hook next to it. Nobody ever used it. Aisa didn't know when it had been opened the last time. The corridor itself was empty except for a shelf with cleaning supplies and a broom and mop hanging on the wall. She headed for the door, but Helton tapped her on the shoulder. He pointed at the floor. There was something there. A smudge, no, two, on the concrete floor.

"It rained last night," Helton said. "Maybe somebody came in with wet shoes and left footprints."

She went to the door, took the key from the hook. It slid into the slot without resistance and turned easily. That was odd. She remembered the lock being obstreperous. Opening the door, she stepped outside. There was nothing there. Just a cement-block wall separating the plot from the next one. The space between the building and wall was narrow. Some trash had blown in from the alley.

After pulling the key out of the slot, Helton wiped the blade between his thumb and index finger. He held them up to show her the oily sheen.

"The lock has been oiled. Somebody has definitely come in here."

They followed the stone path along the wall to the alley that ran parallel to the Avenida Vladimir Lenine. Halfway along the path, there was a patch of dirt where the stones were missing. In that patch was a footprint. No doubt remained. Someone had stepped into the wet dirt and left a clear print. The size indicated that it had been a large shoe, which eliminated the kids that sometimes ran in here playing.

"Are you satisfied that someone broke into our offices?" Helton said. "Can you let go of your idea that I had anything to do with this?"

Aisa nodded.

"Yes. Someone broke in. I accept that. Sorry, Helton. I'm not myself today. Please accept my apologies."

She tried her best to push away the thought that Helton could have left the footprint himself.

* * *

THE STAFF HAD ASSEMBLED FOR THE third time that Tuesday. It was time to go home, but everybody lingered. The turmoil and tension had kept them from doing their regular work. Aisa, exhausted and at her wits' end, had no energy left to keep up a brave façade. She told them that the office had been burgled. That the hard copy files related to the Sofala Project had been stolen. That the electronic versions had been deleted and were irretrievable. That the demand from Global Alternatives to produce expenditure records or return the funds combined with the unannounced visit of a UN investigator left her no alternative but to think that Nossa Terra was being set up. She told them that she had no idea why it happened or who was behind it, and most importantly, what she and the staff could do to stop it.

When she was done, she sat down, not sure she would ever be able to get up again. The silence lasted a minute or so. Bartina was the first to speak.

"I'm not accepting this." She gestured to the pile of folders still lying at one end of the table. "Our work is too important. We call the police and tell them to investigate this burglary. We call Global Alternatives and explain what happened." She looked around for support. There was only a pall of silence. "Come on," she said. "Are we not fighters? Fighters for justice? This is unjust. We didn't take the money. We have to fight back. We have to right this wrong."

The others moved in their seats and looked at each other. Still stunned, but also with a hint of a smile. That Bartina. Leave it to her to rally the troops. But it was Tendai who lifted the cloud of despair by asking what everybody afterwards called the obvious question, "Shouldn't there be a bank record of us receiving five million dollars? I mean, Global Alternatives didn't deliver it in suitcases."

CHAPTER THREE

MILK RUN

———◆———

Vermeulen looked out the window of his hotel. It had rained overnight, and the puddles on the street reflected the tentative rays of the sun. Three stories below, taxi vans trawled for customers. An old woman was selling bags of oranges. Business was slow. The louvered windows of his room didn't close all the way anymore. He could hear the taxi touts whistling and shouting out destinations. The damp air had blistered the paint on the window frame. Some of it had peeled, leaving the aluminum crusty with salt. He went back to the table, where the room service waiter had left a tray with an ancient thermos and chipped cup. He poured the coffee. At least it was hot.

Back at the window, he looked at the waves on Maputo Bay, gray like the clouds racing in from Madagascar. The Catembe ferry struggled against the swells of the estuary. It didn't seem to make any headway. He knew the feeling. The view of the ocean brought back memories from his childhood, his dad's farm by the North Sea in Belgium, the ocean vistas with low clouds and whitecaps. Good memories. Even during the winter gales, he knew he was safe. Too bad he couldn't conjure up that feeling now.

Maputo had its share of street crime. But he didn't think about that. You couldn't spend your time worrying about being in the wrong place at the wrong time. Besides, he was six feet tall, which made potential muggers think twice. No, that wasn't the source of his disquiet.

The job, too, had sounded like a milk run. Go check the books at several foundations and NGOs in Maputo that are spending a lot of UN money. After the mess in Vienna—while fighting for his life, he'd shot a corrupt UN bureaucrat—his boss at the Office of Internal Oversight Services didn't know where to hide Vermeulen. He was fully cleared, but the shooting didn't sit well with those who were more concerned with the good name of the organization than putting a crook away. Sending Vermeulen off into the field seemed like a good idea. So, Maputo it was. And summer in Mozambique sounded way better than winter in New York. Of all the places to be in late January, Maputo was pretty close to the top.

The other upside was that Tessa Bishonga, his long-distance lover, had hinted that she might land a job in Mozambique when he told her of his assignment. A freelance journalist, Tessa rarely could make long-term plans. Her destinations were dictated by her assignments. With the implosion of the traditional news business and the ever-increasing army of people with smartphones reporting for obscure websites, seasoned professionals like Tessa had to hustle to get jobs. The result was a four-month stretch of not seeing each other. Too long even for Vermeulen, who'd used Tessa's unpredictable schedule to ward off conversations about a more settled future. An odd impulse, really. He was as monogamous as they came.

It didn't help that the milk run had turned complicated when he checked up on Global Alternatives. A recent arrival on the global-aid scene, the foundation pooled the resources donated by its founder, hedge fund mogul Vincent Portallis, with those of various UN agencies for big, splashy projects, the kinds that generated photo opportunities with A-list stars, grateful local politicians, and black children showing white teeth.

Vermeulen had dealt with plenty of aid organizations. Many had been founded during the seventies. They were staffed by graduates of Third World volunteer projects bitten by the aid bug. These battle-scarred veterans had come up against repressive governments, venal politicians, cruel international financial agencies, and starry-eyed do-gooders without losing that spark that made them get into the field in the first place.

Global Alternatives wasn't like that. It was … what? He couldn't quite put it in words. Too shiny? A silly word to use, but somehow it summed up his feeling. Too many new laptops, tablets, and expensive phones. Too fancy an office for a country that was among the world's poorest. The executive director of the Maputo office, Isabel LaFleur, couldn't have graduated from her MBA program more than a week before Vermeulen showed up. The entire staff was a little too hip. He felt like he'd stepped into a Silicon Valley startup, not an organization that was supposed to address agricultural development in Mozambique.

His interactions with LaFleur had been predictably complicated. He spoke the language of accountability. She spoke the language of innovation. Maybe that's where his sense of dealing with a startup came from. LaFleur seemed to think that burning through a mountain of cash was no problem. Since Global Alternatives' mission was to help people, any money was well spent.

So what if some of it came from the pockets of the UN? *Trust us. We're on the same side, doing the right thing.* She was fluent in the humanitarian lingo—stakeholders, efficacy, deep impact, sustainability, broad-based equity, best practices. Vermeulen wondered if it meant anything to her.

At least their accounting was in line with regular standards. They hadn't figured out a disruptive way of stating the numbers yet. That didn't stop Paolo Gould, the accountant, from obfuscating the numbers every time he opened his mouth. Keeping track of the foundation's own funds and those of the UN proved to be the primary challenge. More than once, Gould mixed up which money was used where, only adding to Vermeulen's impression of the flip attitude at the foundation. The bird's-eye view seemed fine. Revenues and expenditures matched. But then, he'd never seen a balance sheet where they didn't. The problems, if there were any, always showed up in the details, which meant digging. At least Gould provided access to all the necessary documents without putting up resistance. He may have been flip, but he didn't act like he was hiding anything.

Vermeulen didn't have to dig very long. Global Alternatives' signature project in Mozambique—expanding agricultural exports through innovative land use—showed the first problems. A large amount of UN funds had been dispensed to a subcontractor without any evidence that the monies had been properly spent. At the same time, the foundation had partnered with an investment company to acquire land titles in the same area. Which seemed a duplication of effort.

Vermeulen knew well that in a country like Mozambique, receipts for expenditures weren't always possible. A donation to a chief's village-improvement fund was a courtesy, like bringing a bottle of wine to a dinner party. Asking for a receipt would be impolite. But Nossa Terra, the subcontractor in question, couldn't have spent five million on the equivalent of host gifts. Something else was going on. Which had prompted his unannounced visit there yesterday afternoon.

The people at Nossa Terra were the exact opposite of those at Global Alternatives. They were the folks struggling in the trenches of aid work—nothing slick about them or their office. Their equipment looked several generations behind the tech curve. Sitting in the office with Aisa Simango, he knew he was in the presence of a woman whose life was dedicated to changing the fortunes of her compatriots. Of medium height, with short hair showing the first tinges of white framing her brown face, she had a no-nonsense demeanor that told him she'd get things done. But that didn't change the fact that she had lied to him.

Just entering the office, he'd known that something was wrong. The tell was their startled faces and the long pause before someone greeted him. His suspicions grew stronger talking with Simango. Despite her honest face, or maybe because of it, he knew she was being evasive. Then she'd flat out lied to him about reorganizing the files. The pile lying on the conference table could have been there for a month, as far as he knew. Say what you like about Global Alternatives, at least they knew where their files were. Either Nossa Terra was really sloppy about their paperwork, or they indeed had something to hide. His gut told him it was the latter. And he would find out this afternoon.

* * *

AISA SIMANGO HAD WOKEN THAT MORNING in better spirits, though the knot was by no means gone. Her meeting with the manager of Banco Terra did not settle the turmoil in her stomach. No, there hadn't been a deposit of five million dollars or a withdrawal of that amount. So far so good. But she didn't like the frown on the man's face as he viewed the account on his computer screen.

"Is something wrong?" she said.

The manager didn't answer and kept staring at the screen.

"Uh, no. Not as such," he said after a minute of clicking his mouse at regular intervals.

"What does that mean?"

"I see some unusual activity in the logs. Do you bank online?"

"No, we don't. We receive deposits that way, of course, but we only disburse funds via checks, not online transfers. Most of our clients don't have bank accounts in the first place, never mind a computer to do their banking."

The manager shook his head and clicked the mouse some more.

"Well. There's a record of two wire transfers arriving five months ago. But the funds from the second one disappeared again without so much as a credit or debit elsewhere. That's very unusual."

"What amounts are you talking about?" Aisa said. She remembered only receiving one transfer.

"Both were for one hundred twenty thousand dollars. Let me put one of our tech people on this."

"But you are certain that there hasn't been a deposit of five million dollars?"

"Yes. Your balance isn't even close to that amount. Call me this afternoon; we'll know more then."

Her panic returned with a vengeance. Had whoever stole the documentation at the office also accessed their account? Someone was out to undermine Nossa Terra. She had no doubt about that. She just couldn't fathom who'd do that. Or why.

Providing land for landless peasants wasn't the kind of project that would generate opposition. Especially not the Sofala Project. They had targeted a swath of state-owned land. The provincial directorate of agriculture had cleared the land as free and available, meaning there were no competing claims, no villages or individuals with traditional rights to the land. The majority of the funds from Global Alternatives were used to pay for the cadastral survey, mapping, registering, and the *Titulo do DUAT*, the title to use and enjoy the land. The rest was to provide extension services for the new farmers and some infrastructure upgrades. Once they had completed the community consultations, they'd submit the proposal to the directorate for its final approval. Nossa Terra had done this before, albeit on a far smaller scale. The Sofala Project was its first step into the big league.

* * *

AISA GOT BACK TO THE OFFICE shortly before noon. Bartina was busy proofreading the first draft of a progress report. Zara fiddled with Tendai's computer. The rest of the staff was busy, as if yesterday had never happened. Aisa knew the calm was deceptive. The tension in the room was palpable.

"Where's Helton?" she said when she noticed him missing.

They looked up at her, then at each other. Puzzlement. As if nobody had noticed. Which was unlikely. Helton's absence was as noticeable as his presence.

"*Anda desaparecido*," Tendai said. "Probably roaming the stalls at Julius Nyerere for his second breakfast."

"Or his third," someone said from the back of the room.

"Did he say anything? Call in?" Aisa said.

A collective shrug was the response. She wasn't surprised. As enamored as people were of Helton when they first met him, that feeling often gave way to reserve after working with him. His brash tone and manner, always couched in a big smile, could be grating after a while. He had little capacity for empathy, which was odd, given his choice of work.

"He didn't call the office," Bartina said, "if that's what you're asking."

"Did any of you try to call him?"

Again silence. It wasn't their job to keep track of Aisa's second in command. She went into the meeting room, took out her phone, and speed-dialed his number. The call rolled over to voicemail. She told him to call as soon as possible. *What a time to not show up.*

All her doubts from the previous day flooded the void left by his absence. Helton had to be behind this. No one else had the wherewithal to pull this off. Whatever *this* was. Who outside this office even knew of Nossa Terra's contract with Global Alternatives? The project was still in its early stages. Maybe he didn't hatch the plan, but he'd participated. Why would he do it? For five million dollars? She couldn't even imagine that much money. Those numbers in their proposals and projects were just that, numbers. They were too unreal to be a temptation. Clearly, they weren't for Helton.

Three years ago, he'd stood right in this meeting room, explaining the positions he'd held prior to applying for the job at Nossa Terra. Junior, then senior planner at the directorate of agriculture in Tete province. Before that, some unspecified position at a trucking company. Education at the *Politécnica de Manica* and a Christian school in Tete. He was effusive when explaining the help he'd gotten from good teachers at both places. He praised his co-workers at the directorate who helped him excel there and move up in the ranks. He was modest when it came to his own achievements, but explained that he had a lot of experience working with foreigners, be they investors or NGOs. In all, he was by far the best candidate for the job. And he seemed personable, easygoing. A good fit for the office. Then he told her about being a child soldier for RENAMO. She didn't ask. He volunteered that information. A sign of his openness, she thought. Not hiding anything. Good for him. One couldn't blame the kids for what happened to them at the hands of the rebel commanders. They were children, after all. Only later did she remember the cold hatred she'd seen in their eyes during the attack. Had they really been so innocent?

It was a moot point then, because she'd hired Helton on the spot. And he turned out to be the best thing that could have happened to Nossa Terra. He'd brought in new contracts. He had that disarming way of talking with foreigners, that combination of competence and joviality that put donors at ease. Aisa envied him for that. Her interactions with the same people were formal, distant. She had her expertise. She knew more about the lives of landless peasants than anyone in the office. She'd been one herself. That authenticity shone through, convincing the donors that she meant what she promised. But Helton was more fun to be with.

Until now. Three years of putting on a façade. Who could be so duplicitous? The sheer energy required to keep up the front, to pretend to be one of the team .... She couldn't imagine herself being able to do it. You had to really hate somebody to be able to lie to them for so long. Was it the same hatred she'd seen in the eyes of the kids who'd killed her father?

Chapter Four

Chargeback

———————◆———————

AT TWO THIRTY IN THE AFTERNOON, Isabel LaFleur had her assistant bring cappuccino and biscotti. It was her daily ritual. A smart-ass boyfriend once told her that real Italians don't drink cappuccinos after ten in the morning. "I'm not Italian," she'd said. Then she threw him out. The assistant placed the tray on the coffee table by the leather chairs near the windows of her fifth-floor corner office. To the west was the botanical garden. To the south, the waters of Maputo Bay lapped against the seawall and the pier of the ferry terminal. The view was unbeatable, even on a gray day.

"Is there anything else?" the assistant said.

"Send Paolo Gould in."

"Yes, ma'am."

She watched him leave the office and enjoyed the way his fluid walk made his ass sway. He was almost as bright as he was good-looking. If you had to have someone around all day handling the annoying stuff, he might as well be easy on the eyes. Of course, he was off-limits. Intra-office affairs inevitably ended in a world of hurt. But looking was just fine.

She sat in one of the leather chairs, dipped her biscotti into the cappuccino foam, and nibbled on it. The dark clouds racing across the sky sent a shiver down her back.

Maputo. Of all the places in the world to end up. Two years ago, in New York City, she'd never imagined being here. But staying in the City hadn't been an option. She kept telling herself that. She just hadn't seen the warning signs soon enough. When she finally recognized what was happening, it was too late. Too late to send Mark packing. Because he was a nice guy. Way too nice. But she didn't want a nice guy. She wasn't looking for flowers, candlelit dinners, two-point-five children, the house, and the picket fence. So, she told him she was sleeping with another man.

It crushed him, as she knew it would. He moved out. That first evening alone was heaven. She could breathe again. Mark came back the second evening, ready to forgive and forget. She told him that there'd been a third man, too. She even went so far as to pay a guy to kiss her in front of her apartment when she knew Mark was looking from the shadows of a garage entry. It only made him more fervent in his need to absolve her. She didn't need absolution; she needed space. Running away seemed the only solution. A friend pointed her to Global Alternatives and she got the job.

The job turned out to be a dream. Executive director for the Mozambique office of Global Alternatives. Working for hedge fund mogul Vincent Portallis. Who wouldn't jump at that opportunity? The pay was amazing. She got to talk to Portallis himself once a week. And after her stint in Maputo, there'd be more opportunities back in the States. So things were good, really. Except that the coffee here sucked. It had taken her three months to train her assistant to make a decent facsimile of cappuccino using coffee flown in from South Africa. The biscotti had to be flown in from New York City.

There was a knock on the door and Gould came in. He took the other seat.

"Looks like more rain," he said.

That just about summed up Gould. He was almost as wide as he was tall, with a round face, a comb-over that stuck to his sweaty pate, and a rumpled thousand-dollar suit. And he talked about the weather. All the time.

"What did you make of Vermeulen?" she said.

He kept looking out the window, his gaze fixed on something far away. "Should be sunnier tomorrow. About time."

He finally turned to her.

"Vermeulen?" he said. "Competent. Knows what he's doing. Kept asking the right questions."

"The right questions?"

"For an auditor. He wasn't interested in the big picture, because you can't tell anything by looking at those numbers."

"What was he interested in?"

"He seemed unhappy about our mingling foundation resources with UN funds."

"That's his problem, isn't it?"

Gould looked out the window again. "Might be. Might not be," he said.

"Why?"

"He spotted the missing five million at Nossa Terra right away. If he says it's our money, not the UN's, it's our problem."

"But he can't say that. We got the money from the UN for the project Nossa

Terra is implementing. So if they can't account for it, it's the UN's problem."

She finished the last of her biscotti. The cappuccino was cold, and she pushed the cup away.

"We didn't write Nossa Terra into the proposal. We contracted with them after the UNDP approved the project. So, he could have a point, theoretically."

"And practically?"

Gould patted his comb-over again.

"Not a leg to stand on. We determine how we spend the money along the guidelines of the proposal approved by the UNDP. If I say Nossa Terra got UN money, they'll have to accept that. Don't worry. Vermeulen is a minor functionary in a small office that was created only because the U.S. wanted to stop the UN from wasting its money. They're not gonna let him turn on Vincent Portallis."

Vermeulen wasn't half bad-looking either, she thought. For a UN bureaucrat. She'd seen more than her fair share of those in the past couple of years, and as far as she was concerned, the world would have been a better place without them. Busybodies, every last one of them. Stuck in a twentieth-century mode of thinking that went out of style with the Soviet Union. Sixty years of plowing billions of dollars into "development" and nothing to show for it. Zilch. Any company performing that poorly would have been bankrupt decades ago. But not the UN. No, they kept coming with that holier-than-thou attitude, preaching yesterday's gospel and pretending they actually had an impact.

"Good," she said. "Let's keep it that way."

"Will do. Anything else?"

"Let me know when the report is done."

"The Nossa Terra report?"

"It's the only one that matters at the moment."

Gould got up and headed for the door.

"And Paolo," she said, prompting him to turn around, "keep track of Vermeulen. I need to know if he becomes a problem."

* * *

Vermeulen was early for his three o'clock appointment. He asked the cab driver to drop him at the traffic circle connecting Vladimir Lenine and Julius Nyerere. It was a busy intersection. Hawkers had set up their stands just past the roundabout where Julius Nyerere inexplicably stopped being a grand boulevard and devolved into a dirt track. City funds had obviously failed to keep up with planning quite some time ago. The hawkers' stalls had as permanent a quality to them as a hammered-together wooden structure can be permanent.

Everything one could imagine was for sale. One stand sold Vodacom top-up cards and SIMs. Next to it was a cloth on the ground covered with heaps of onions, tomatoes, and something that looked like squash. Next to that, sneakers tied together by their laces hung from a rack, the seller wisely only displaying the left shoes, keeping the rights stashed away. *Calamidades*, used clothing, hung from the racks of the neighboring stall. Smoke from a small brazier made his eyes tear up. A woman was searing pieces of fish over the coals. Chewing gum, individual candies, cigarettes, matchboxes, batteries of any conceivable size, shoelaces, glue, sticky tape, and more vegetables—they were all displayed for the throng of shoppers who examined each stand with discerning eyes. Vermeulen wondered why anyone would need a store. He was tempted by the guy selling individual cigarettes. He'd quit smoking, mostly, six months earlier. His daughter Gaby had been nagging him about it. Still, a nice smoke and a cool beer were the best way to relax. The hawker didn't have his favorite brand, Gitane Papier Maïs, and there was nothing unfiltered on the table. Just as well.

He ambled down Vladimir Lenine and knocked on the doors of Nossa Terra at one minute past three. This time, they were expecting him. Simango opened the door. The rest of the staff pretended to be busy at their desks. She led him to the conference room, where a tray with a hot-water carafe, two cups, and a beaker of milk already sat on the table. The big woman—Bartina, if he remembered correctly—loitered by the door of the conference room, still ready to protect her boss.

"Welcome, *Senhor* Vermeulen," Simango said. "Have a seat."

They settled into chairs across from each other. Bartina spooned instant coffee into one cup and dropped a teabag into the other, adding water. He thanked her, and she left the room.

The table was clear. The pile of files had been removed. Maybe the reorganization was over, although he doubted that there had ever been one in the first place. It was time to sort out why they had lied to him. On the wall was a large map of central Mozambique. It showed a meandering river reaching the Indian Ocean near the city of Beira. One of the oxbows created by the river was marked with a red outline.

"So, Ms. Simango," he said, "can you show me the documentation for the project you contracted with Global Alternatives?"

She took a sip of tea as if to strengthen herself and said, "No. I'm afraid I cannot."

He sat up straighter. That wasn't what he'd expected. He'd anticipated all kinds of deflection, including false documents to get him off their backs. But Simango coming straight out and refusing his request?

"May I ask why?" he said.

"They have been stolen."

"Stolen? Not just missing, stolen?"

"Yes." Simango sat there, erect and with a stony face. He could tell it took all her energy to maintain that appearance.

"You've got to do better than that. We're talking five million dollars here. First you lie to me, saying you can't show me the documentation because you are reorganizing your files, and a day later you tell me that those files have been stolen. Excuse me, but I can't help thinking that this is yet another lie."

"I apologize for lying yesterday. We had only just realized that something was wrong when you walked in the door asking to see the very files we could not put our hands on. But I am not lying now. The files were stolen."

"What about digital copies? I've seen the scanner in your office. I'm sure it isn't just an expensive paperweight."

"They are gone, too."

"So you're telling me that you've spent five million dollars of UN money and that all the evidence that the money has been spent on what it was intended for is gone? I'm sorry, but that's unacceptable. If you refuse to provide such evidence, I will turn this case over to the police. I can assure you that the UN will pursue all legal means available to retrieve those funds."

Simango got up, pressing her palms against the table. She leaned forward and said, "I am not refusing to provide evidence. The evidence we had was stolen. Therefore, I cannot turn it over to you. But most importantly, we never received the five million dollars in question. Global Alternatives never transferred that much money to our accounts. So far, we have only received funds for stages one and two. That was a hundred twenty thousand dollars."

He'd gotten up, too. If there was going to be a shouting match, he'd make damn sure he'd win it.

"Global Alternatives' books say otherwise. I checked them as part of a routine audit. It is clear that those funds were transferred to you."

"Then their books are wrong. I talked with our bank manager, and he tells me there was never a deposit in that amount."

"I'll need to see those records," he said, curbing his anger. "Who stole the documents? You must have some suspicion? A staff member?"

She looked at the door and then back at Vermeulen. The energy she'd mustered to face him left her. She sank back into her chair, deflated.

"Yes. One of our staff could have been involved."

"Who?"

"My deputy. Helton Paito. He was in charge of the Sofala Project. The documents were on his computer before they were deleted and overwritten with zeros. He could have come in during the night to take the hardcopies."

"Where is he? Did you speak with him?"

"He didn't show up today. He doesn't answer his phone. I don't know where he is."

* * *

THE BANK MANAGER CALLED THE OFFICE at three thirty. She told him that Vermeulen would be listening to the conversation and that he might have questions as well. The manager didn't see any problems with that as long as Simango was fine with it. She wasn't, but what could she do? She tapped the speakerphone button on her phone.

"What can you tell me about our account?" she said.

"As I said this morning, there has been some odd activity. You told me you don't do online banking, right?"

Aisa said they'd never done online banking because they didn't see the need. All deposits were made automatically and all disbursements were via check or cash.

"Good," the manager said. "My tech man looked at it and came to the same conclusion I did. There's nothing wrong."

"So, there was no deposit of five million dollars?" she said.

"No. Just as I said this morning," the manager said.

She nodded, looking at Vermeulen, eyebrows raised. *See, this is what I've been telling you.*

"But," the manager said, pausing a moment, "you received a wire in the amount of one hundred twenty thousand dollars five months ago."

"That is correct," Aisa said. "Those funds were to pay for the first two stages."

"Shortly thereafter you received another one for the same amount. The reason it didn't show up in your balance is because there was also a chargeback, which took the money out again. That happened two minutes after the deposit. That's why your balance stayed the same. My tech thought that the chargeback was simply a correction, like someone had mistakenly wired the money and pulled it out again right away. Because you had gotten that same deposit earlier."

"Who originated the wire and the chargeback?" Aisa said.

"Global Alternatives. Same as the earlier transfer."

"Did it come straight from Global Alternatives' bank?" Vermeulen said.

"No, it came via Mauritius Bank and Trust. Their branch here acted as the correspondent bank."

"Why didn't it come straight from the U.S. bank?" Vermeulen said.

"We don't have a SWIFT account, so we need a correspondent bank to act as our intermediary for international wire transfers. Usually it's the

Mozambique Commercial Bank. Sometimes, we get them via Mauritius Bank and Trust."

"How long will you be in your office today?" Vermeulen said.

"Until four thirty."

"Good, Ms. Simango and I will be coming before then and you can show us what you just told us."

CHAPTER FIVE

FURTHER CREDIT

————◆————

T HEY HAD TO HUSTLE TO MAKE it to the Banco Terra offices near the port. His taxi was gone and there weren't any others waiting this far from the city center.

"Do you have the number for a taxi service?" he said.

"That would not do any good. The metered taxis take a half hour to get here and then we would be too late. We will take a *chapa*."

Vermeulen didn't know what a *chapa* was, but on the way back to the traffic circle, he realized it had to be one of those minivans he'd seen congregating there. Sure enough, Simango flagged down a red and green Toyota van coming down the Avenida Vladimir Lenine. The sliding door flew open and a boy— the *cobrador*, Simango explained—waved for them to climb in. The van was about half full and Vermeulen had to fold his six-foot frame into a suitable crouch to fit into the back row. Simango seemed used to the gymnastics and got in much faster. She handed the boy money before Vermeulen could get his wallet out of his pocket.

He nodded to his seat neighbor—a toothless, haggard man wearing a straw hat. The man looked at him as if he were an apparition. Apparently, whites didn't frequent *chapas* for their transportation needs. He did nod back but didn't take his eyes off Vermeulen. Simango was too tense to make conversation. Being squeezed next to her, he noticed the sheen of her hair. Her scent reminded him of lush forests.

The *chapa* lumbered down the street, stopping at intersections where the boy yanked the door open and hollered the destination. More people crowded into the van. When Simango pushed against him firmly, he realized that the rear bench, intended for four, wasn't filled up. A fifth person, a woman with a big plastic bag, squeezed in. After another stop, the *cobrador* must have decided that the van was full. He said something to the driver and the van accelerated. Including the driver and the *cobrador*, Vermeulen counted sixteen people in the van. The smell of compressed humanity filled the air and the boy opened the sliding door to keep the breeze flowing.

As they neared the city center, more and more people got out. Since no new ones came in, Vermeulen could spread out again. They got off at the botanical gardens, passing some tennis courts, flowerbeds, and an astonishing variety of trees to a half moon-shaped island with a tall statue of Samora Machel, the first president of independent Mozambique.

"That is the Casa de Ferro," Simango said, finally breaking her silence and pointing to the right across the semi-circular drive. "It was designed by Gustave Eiffel."

Vermeulen looked at the gray two-story structure. Indeed, a house made of iron with balconies along the top story. It seemed out of place in a city marked by Mediterranean pastels.

* * *

THE MANAGER WAS NONE TOO HAPPY about the visitors showing up five minutes before closing time. He'd already packed his briefcase, slipped into his jacket, and put on his trilby. The cashiers had closed their windows. A last customer hurried to the door.

Vermeulen pulled out his UN ID and showed it to the man. Not that it gave him any authority, but the blue-on-white logo had often persuaded reluctant officials, bureaucrats, and mid-level administrators to cooperate. The trouble with being an investigator for the OIOS was that Vermeulen's jurisdiction was limited. He could investigate UN personnel and contractors. What he couldn't do was walk into a bank and demand to see the accounts of some NGO. But he made up for that by acting as if he had all the jurisdiction he needed. Usually, it worked.

"We are very sorry to come in at the last minute," Simango said. "But this is important. We cannot put our hands on some of our files to clear up a misunderstanding with the UN. So, it would really help me if you could show us the things you talked about earlier."

"You could have just logged on to your account and seen it there," the manager said.

"I told you already that we aren't set up for online banking. Would we have seen the incoming wire and the chargeback you mentioned?"

The manager shook his head in the direction of his office. They followed him. The manager turned on his computer. They looked at the screen waiting for the startup to finish. It was astonishing to Vermeulen that in this day and age, it still took so long for a computer to start. His phone was as powerful as that computer.

Eventually, the logo of Banco Terra filled the screen and the manager tapped on his keyboard to enter his credentials. A few more clicks and keystrokes later and a new window popped up, showing a column of numbers and dates.

"This is your account history for the past six months. As you can see, there are the normal withdrawals and salary transfers. And here are the two wire transfer in question, each for a hundred and twenty thousand dollars. And there is the chargeback. Just a couple of minutes later."

Vermeulen was satisfied that there had never been five million dollars in the account. Unless Simango was running a major scam and had paid off the bank manager to show him a fake account history. He dismissed that notion. If Simango or this fellow Helton really had planned to defraud the UN, bribing the bank manager was a bad strategy. The man would just come back for more money.

"You said that the wire transfer came to you from a Mauritius bank."

"Well, from the local branch of Mauritius Bank and Trust. As I explained, we're not set up to process international transfers. The correspondent bank sends it to us for further credit to our client's account."

"What do you know about Mauritius Bank and Trust?"

The manager looked puzzled. He shrugged. "It's a bank headquartered in Mauritius with a branch in Maputo. That's about all I can say. I haven't really dealt much with them before. We get wire transfers from multiple banks, but mostly via the Mozambique Commercial Bank."

"Can you be certain that the sender was Global Alternatives?" Simango said.

"Well, their name is on the paperwork, so I assume it came from them. But that's just what some clerk typed in. The sending bank has to verify the sender's particulars. As long as the transfer is properly credited to our accounts, we don't really care. Our responsibility is making sure it goes to the proper recipient."

"Can I speak with you privately?" Vermeulen said to the manager.

The man arched his eyebrows. But Vermeulen's face was clear. This wasn't a request. They went into an empty office. Vermeulen closed the door.

"I'm going to ask you one question," Vermeulen said. "It is vital that you answer this question truthfully. And let me tell you, I have plenty of experience telling when someone is lying to me. So here's the question. Is this the sole account Nossa Terra has at this bank?"

The man looked confused.

"Yes. Yes. They don't have another account here. Why should they?"

"I'm just checking that there is nowhere else those five million dollars could have gone."

"No, sir. Not in this bank."

Vermeulen nodded, opened the door again and went outside.

"Thank you," he said, turning his head to the manager. "I appreciate your taking the time to clarify this for us. Have a good evening."

He was halfway to the exit when he noticed that Simango was not with him. He turned and saw her standing by the door of the office, staring after him. He wanted to say, "What?" but didn't. Her lips were pressed together, her eyes ablaze.

"How dare you treat me like your minion?" she said when he'd walked back. "I have extended you every courtesy to help you sort out this mistake. I run Nossa Terra. Whatever problems crop up are my problems. You may ask your questions, you may rifle through our papers, because we agreed to that when we took UN money. But you may not cut me out of the loop. This is my organization."

A familiar sensation flooded Vermeulen's body. It was hot and mean, getting him ready for the looming fight. *You started the whole thing. You lied to me. Where do you get off telling me how to conduct my investigation?* He got as far as opening his mouth when his brain kicked in and stopped the flash of anger. Yelling wasn't an option. He had to work with Simango, especially now. The case wasn't a milk run anymore. The money could have leaked at Global Alternatives, or somehow been siphoned off by this Helton Paito guy. For all he knew, it could have ended up in Mauritius.

"I apologize, Ms. Simango. I acted rashly, but without intending to undermine your position or that of Nossa Terra in any way. I think we got off to a bad start. Can we try again?"

She'd better accept that her behavior helped set the stage; otherwise he couldn't see how they could work together.

She nodded and pointed to the door.

* * *

BACK ON THE STREET, SIMANGO DIRECTED Vermeulen to a *pastelaria* around the corner from the bank. They took their seats, and she ordered two coffees and two slices of something called *bolo polano*. It was a peace offering, but after the confrontation at the bank, Vermeulen was loath to start the conversation. Simango seemed content to be quiet. So he looked around. The pastry shop had seen better days. Display cases and store fixtures reminded him of New York cafés that spent enormous amounts of money to mimic the 1930s. Here it was authentic, to the extent that a colonial-era institution could ever be authentic. The stainless steel of the cases was dull from decades of merciless cleaning.

The glass had a film for the same reason. The iron tables and chairs were a bit wobbly but sturdy. The place felt like a pair of comfortable slippers—a little frayed around the edges, but you wouldn't trade them for new ones.

A waitress brought their order. The *bolo polano* looked like a dense pound cake.

"It's a cashew cake," Simango said. "Cashew nuts are an important export of Mozambique."

He tried a bite. It was sweet and lemony and as dense as it looked. Not a cake you'd have seconds of.

"What else is in it?" he said.

"Cashews, potatoes, butter and eggs, and lemon. Do you like it?"

"Yes, the flavor is nice, but it's very filling."

Simango laughed. "That it is. It's good for breakfast the next morning, too."

He drank his coffee and took another bite of cake.

"What happened at Nossa Terra?" he said. He wanted to add qualifiers, explanations, but decided to let her talk.

Simango blew across the top of her cup, then swallowed a sip. Her eyes focused on a place well past the window of the café.

"I really don't know. Everything was going along fine. We were getting the Sofala Project off the ground. It's our biggest yet. Land for many peasant families. I came to the office yesterday morning and there was that email. It was like everything came crashing down. Five million dollars. We are all still in shock. But we never got it. You saw the bank records."

"What about this Helton Paito? You said he could have deleted the paperwork."

"Yes, but so could I. Everyone at the office can access all of the computers. Now that I know the money was never in our account, I do not think Helton had anything to do with this. Why would he steal the paperwork when there was no money to be had in the first place?"

"But you think he would have if there had been money."

Vermeulen could tell that she was uncomfortable with the question. He didn't press and focused on the cake and coffee instead.

"Helton and I share a painful history," she said after a moment. "Sometimes I let that cloud my judgment. He has denied having anything to do with the theft of the documents or the missing money and I have no proof he did."

"But he didn't come to work today."

"No."

It was as flimsy a lead as he'd ever had. Who could resist the lure of UN money? In a poor country, the temptation was huge. Often the sums were small, just enough to pad one's paycheck and help with expenses. Compared to the numbers of the UN budget, they were minuscule, but that didn't make it right.

This case was different. An employee disappears and takes with him the paperwork related to a UN-funded project. There was money missing, but it never made it to the place where it could have been stolen. There was a mistaken deposit that was canceled, but the deposit didn't amount to the missing money. It just didn't add up.

"I think I'll go back to the other end of the trail, Global Alternatives."

"I'll come with you," Simango said.

"Why? There's nothing you can do there."

"It is important that I clear our name. Global Alternatives has accused us of squandering so much money. That isn't true. We did not. I have to tell Isabel LaFleur."

"Suit yourself, but please do it after I talk with them. In the meantime, try to find Paito and the paperwork. It's better to have everything in hand when you confront them."

CHAPTER SIX

DUE DILIGENCE

———◆———

SHOWING UP UNANNOUNCED FIRST THING IN the morning was one of Vermeulen's favorite strategies for surprising reluctant witnesses. It had worked often enough for him to try it on Paolo Gould. If anyone had things to hide, it would be the accountant. The receptionist at Global Alternatives tried to keep him waiting at the front desk, but since he knew where the man's office was, he marched right to it. When he opened the door, he saw Gould hang up his phone. The receptionist had alerted him.

"There's no need to barge into my office this way, Mr. Vermeulen. I'm always happy to help a representative of the UN."

Gould gestured toward two black-leather chairs standing on opposite sides of a wooden coffee table. They looked well worn. The entire office had a lived-in look. Add some dark-wood paneling, and it could have been a minor club in London that had seen more prosperous days. Gould's office didn't have the stunning views LaFleur's did. The sole large window faced east. Only a sliver of the Indian Ocean was visible between the buildings crowding the view.

"Show me Nossa Terra's accounts again," Vermeulen said and sat down. The leather felt hard and brittle. "I want to see everything you have."

Gould brought his laptop to the coffee table. Its screen displayed a spreadsheet. Vermeulen scooted closer. And there, in red, was the number. Five million dollars. Just like two days earlier.

"When did you transfer these funds?" Vermeulen said.

"About five months ago. That's why we've been contacting them about paperwork and expense reports."

Five months ago was when the two wire transfers from Global Alternatives had arrived in the Nossa Terra account. Except they didn't amount to five million dollars.

"Didn't you send two wire transfers?"

"No." Gould pursed his lips. "Oh, wait, yes. There was a clerical error. Someone in the accounts department made a mistake. We reversed the second transaction immediately."

"Where did the transfers originate?" Vermeulen said.

"Our main account in New York. Why do you ask?"

"And the Global Alternative bank is …?"

"International Commercial and Industrial Bank."

"Any intermediary banks?"

"How would I know? We just instruct the bank to wire the money."

Gould was all solicitous, the competent accountant explaining the complexities of international money transfers to a naive outsider. Vermeulen didn't disabuse him of that idea.

"Nossa Terra never received five million dollars. I checked with their bank. Not five months ago. Nor any other time. They received startup funds amounting to one hundred twenty thousand dollars. That's all. How do you explain that?"

Gould arched his eyebrows and ran his hand across his comb-over.

"I can't," he said. "It doesn't make any sense. I have the paperwork that says we sent five million, which is why I entered it on the spreadsheet. They didn't get the money? Why in the world did they start work on the project?"

"Because they received the startup funds. Besides, how would you know whether or not they'd started work on the project? You just told me they weren't responsive to your requests for information."

"Initially, they did send a couple of progress reports. I assumed the proper accounting would follow, but it never did."

"I'll need to see those reports."

"No problem."

Gould got up, went to his desk, picked up his phone and requested the paperwork. He sat down again.

"This is indeed puzzling," he said.

But he didn't look puzzled. More like someone trying to work himself up over something he couldn't care less about. As if he'd already written off the five million dollars. Maybe it wasn't a large amount for Global Alternatives. He hadn't seen all the books, but if Isabel LaFleur's attitude was anything to go by, money wasn't an issue. Except that those five million weren't the foundation's money. They came from the UN.

"You don't seem concerned that the money appears to have vanished into thin air," he said.

Gould shrugged.

"We sent it to them; we have the records to prove that. At this stage, it's not really our concern anymore. Whatever is missing is Nossa Terra's issue. You take it up with them. Or their bank."

"It's not that easy. You have a contract with the UN and you are accountable to the UN for the funds you received. You can't just pass that responsibility off to a contractor."

"Of course we can. We exercised due diligence in selecting Nossa Terra. We followed all UN guidelines regarding the selection of contractors. Nossa Terra fit the bill. They had a solid track record. They're local and have a female executive director. I don't have to tell you how much the UN is pushing for women's empowerment. We had no reason to assume they would mismanage UN funds."

Gould seemed happy to blame Nossa Terra and move on to his next project. And that bugged Vermeulen. He'd dealt with plenty of organizations that received UN funds. If there was anything they all had in common, it was a sense of solidarity, even camaraderie, a *we're all in this together* spirit. Its utter absence in Gould's demeanor just didn't fit.

"We're not yet at the stage of assigning blame," Vermeulen said. "I want to get to the bottom of this, and as the primary contractor for the UN, you are expected to give us your full cooperation. You can begin by getting me all the paperwork associated with the wire transfer in question. Your spreadsheets are just numbers on a computer. I want to see documents that show me the money was actually sent. By the way, what do you know about Mauritius Bank and Trust?"

Gould hesitated a moment. "It's a bank in Mauritius?"

"And you don't know anything else?"

"Uh, no. Should I?"

"Never mind, just get me the paperwork showing the wire transfer and all reports you received from Nossa Terra. Call me when you have them."

* * *

"DID I JUST SEE VERMEULEN LEAVE the office?" Isabel LaFleur said, leaning against Gould's door frame.

Gould looked up from his laptop.

"You did."

"That was rather early. What did he want?"

LaFleur came in and perched on the corner of his desk, a habit he disliked, if only because she would never have tolerated his doing the same in her office.

"To find out if it's going to be sunny today." He paused a beat. "What do you think he wanted? More information about the transfer. He knows the money never arrived. He knows about Mauritius Bank and Trust."

"He does? That was fast. Any idea how he found out?"

"Probably went to Nossa Terra's bank and checked the paperwork. The transfer documents aren't a state secret."

"And will he cause problems?"

"Not sure." Gould smoothed his comb-over. "Right now, he's got nothing. But he struck me like a dog that's picked up a scent. If he starts digging, he'll be a problem."

"And will he?"

"Start digging?" Gould shrugged. "I don't know. I would if I were him. He's got to account for five million dollars. The people at Nossa Terra probably told him their sob story. Remember, as far as they are concerned, they haven't done anything wrong."

"What about the guy who started snooping. What's his name ... Paito? We set it up so they would suspect him, right?"

"Only if nobody finds his body."

"I thought you took care of that."

"I made that clear. But human nature being what it is, the guys doing the job might not have followed through. There are no guarantees."

LaFleur stood up and leaned across his desk. "That was your job."

"My job was to hire the right people, not to supervise them. If you feel so strongly about it, why didn't you go along and make sure?"

"I don't need any lip from you."

"And I don't need you to second-guess my actions," he said. "As far as I know, Paito's body is floating to Madagascar. But I didn't get where I am by hoping for the best. Worst case scenario, they find the body before enough fish have eaten away its extremities. It's unlikely to happen, but we should be prepared."

*　*　*

THE SMILING WOMAN AT THE CUSTOMER service desk of Mauritius Bank and Trust passed Vermeulen on to someone well above her pay grade. Mr. Pai, mid-thirties and of Indian extraction, was the deputy branch manager. He invited Vermeulen into his office, a plain modernist affair—steel and glass. The desk was a mess of papers, folders, and magazines. Pai offered him tea and coffee. Vermeulen declined, eager to get to what he really wanted, insight into the transfer of five million dollars. Mr. Pai was polite to a fault. Yes, their branch routinely acted as a correspondent bank for international wire transfers, as did many other international banks in Maputo. No, he didn't have access to the information Vermeulen wanted to see. That would ordinarily be the purview of the branch manager, who, alas, was out all day. If Mr. Vermeulen wanted to wait a moment, he'd make a call or two to see if someone else had been deputized to reveal that information in the manager's stead.

"All I want to know is the total amount of that transfer. That's all."

"I understand, Mr. Vermeulen. But this is a privacy issue. When people transfer money, they don't necessarily want the rest of the world to know about it."

"But I already know. I've spoken with both the sender and the recipient. I have their cooperation. The only missing piece is Mauritius Bank and Trust. So, you wouldn't be revealing any private information."

"My apologies. I didn't mean to insinuate that you were just someone walking in off the street. Still, we have our procedures and I am bound by those. Just let me make the call."

Pai left the room, which was odd, given that there was a phone right on his desk. So he didn't want Vermeulen to hear the conversation. Understandable? Maybe not. It was just a simple question—can someone give this man the information he wants? The answer would either be yes or no, not an agonizing decision requiring a lot of back and forth, which would be unseemly in front of an outsider. That meant Vermeulen's visit and request were unexpected, requiring consultations with people in charge, even concocting a plan on the fly.

Vermeulen studied the mass-produced art prints on the wall for fifteen minutes. None of them depicted any scenes from Maputo, or Mauritius, for that matter. Just random patterns of pastel colors meant to imitate modern art. Finally, Mr. Pai came back.

"I'm terribly sorry, but we can't help you right now. You'll have to come back tomorrow when the manager is in. Only he can reveal the information you seek. I know it's not what you were hoping for, but it's all I can do. If you come back tomorrow around ten thirty, the manager will be able to help you."

* * *

PAOLO GOULD PUT DOWN THE RECEIVER and hurried into LaFleur's office.

"Vermeulen went to Mauritius Bank and Trust. Pai called, asking what to do," he said.

"So we have to deal with Vermeulen?"

"Yes. Pai told him to come back tomorrow. He can probably stall him again with some excuse, but that'll just make Vermeulen more suspicious. We need to stop him before we lose control."

"Okay. Make it happen."

Gould went back to his office and closed the door. He dialed Vermeulen, who answered on the third ring.

"Where are you?" Gould said. "I have the paperwork for you."

"Just send it to my hotel. You have the address. I'll be there shortly."

"Will do."

Gould ended the call. He went to the IT manager in a part of the office that didn't have windows. A man with skin the color of black coffee sat behind two huge monitors occupying a large desk.

"Mustafa, can you get me a picture from the security camera? The guy who came in just a little while ago."

Mustafa looked up, nodded, and started clicking away. A moment later, he said, "This good enough?" It was a frontal picture of Vermeulen as he stormed into the office.

"Can you crop it to just the face?"

Mustafa did just that. "You want it printed?"

Gould asked him to email it. Back in his office, he closed the door again and opened the bottom drawer of his desk. In it lay several mobile phones still in their packaging. He had to use his scissors to cut the plastic open and extricate the phone, but he still nicked his left thumb on the sharp plastic. He put the SIM card in, registered the phone, and texted a code to a number in South Africa.

The reply code arrived almost immediately. His computer dinged. He checked and the picture of Vermeulen appeared on the screen. Using the phone to snap a picture of it, he texted it with instructions. Five minutes later, the return message arrived with the okay and information for the money transfer.

* * *

VERMEULEN LOOKED UP AT THE HAZY sun. The rain from the day before had added to the humidity. There wasn't much he could do until tomorrow's appointment. He slung his jacket over his shoulder and walked back to his hotel. This would be a good time to file an interim report with Arne Bengtsson at the Nairobi OIOS office. Let him know what had happened so far.

Missing funds were the institutional nightmare of the UN. Such reports only reinforced the prejudice against the organization in Washington and the capitals of other main funders. Though there wasn't as much mismanagement as the detractors charged, any time fiscal irregularities happened, they became a cause célèbre for the ones who, in the words of one U.S. ambassador, thought that the headquarters in New York City could lose ten stories and it wouldn't make a bit of difference. Five million dollars, although merely a tenth of one percent of the total budget, was a large enough amount to become such a cause.

He sat down at an outdoor café next to his hotel and ordered a coffee and something that looked like a doughnut. The waiter, eager to practice his

English, tried to explain the origin of the pastry. Apparently, Arab traders brought the recipe to Beira several hundred years ago. From there it came to Maputo. He took a bite and had to agree that the Arab take on it was better than the U.S. version. Cardamom made all the difference. As they talked, a black Land Rover with darkened windows drove by and pulled up to the hotel. The waiter stopped mid-sentence. Vermeulen saw the man's face and knew something wasn't right.

"What's happening?" he said.

"Trouble. Black car like that comes, is trouble."

Vermeulen had long ago learned to trust local knowledge. He got up and stepped toward the entrance of the café. At the door, he stopped and looked back. Three men, all African and wearing black clothes, had gotten out and were scanning the area. One of them looked in the café's direction, checking the street, then the customers sitting outside. His gaze came to rest on Vermeulen, continued, then returned. Vermeulen knew then that he shouldn't have stopped to look. The man had recognized him. Vermeulen was sure of that. What he didn't know was how or why.

The waiter must have sensed that Vermeulen was connected to the black car. He coaxed him past the display case into the rear, where there was a kitchen with several ovens, prep tables, electric mixers, bowls, and wire whisks. A woman was stirring white paste in a bowl. Another woman dabbed jam on rounds of dough arranged on a baking sheet. They looked up and went back to their work. The waiter opened another door.

"Stay here," he said and closed the door behind him.

Vermeulen looked around. A store room. Sacks of flour were stacked in a corner. Shelves with jars and bags full of dried fruit and baking ingredients covered one wall. Another shelf unit laden with baking implements covered what looked to be the emergency exit. So much for building codes.

Being in a room where the only exit was the way the bad guys would come in was not good. Vermeulen pushed against the shelf blocking the other door. It didn't budge. There wouldn't be time to empty the contents and move it. He had to get out *now*. Before the men from the black SUV came into the café.

Chapter Seven

Milk Tart

———◆———

Vermeulen opened the door of the storage room and peered into the kitchen. The two women were still working. One was dusting a baking pan with flour. The door to the café was closed. He inched into the kitchen. There had to be some kind of weapon there. But he didn't see anything. This was more a bakery than a restaurant. No blocks with twelve-inch chef's knives. There were no nooks, cupboards, or other hiding places. He looked for anything useful. A baker's outfit—white pants, smock, and chef's hat—hung on a hook. Dressing up like a baker? Not really an option. His skin color would be the giveaway. Or would it? The hands of the woman prepping the ban were white with flour.

He grabbed the clothing. The outfit was made for a far fatter man, but he didn't have time to worry about that. The women stared at him. The one dusting the pan giggled. He stuffed the top of the pants into his own waistband and slipped into the smock. The chef's hat had an elastic band. Vermeulen pulled it as far down as possible to cover his blond hair. A jar of flour stood on the workbench. He grabbed a handful and tossed it on his face. Another handful covered his hands. Eyeing a stack of empty baking sheets in a rack on the wall, he grabbed one and looked around for something to put on it. Four milk tarts stood cooling on a rack in front of the kitchen. He put two on the sheet and opened the door to the café.

The three men from the SUV had just come inside and were scanning the patrons in the room. Vermeulen held the sheet with the tarts high to conceal his face. He stepped over to the display case, keeping his back to the three men. The server behind the counter looked at him with wide eyes. Nobody had ever pulled that kind of stunt with her. She was about to say something, but Vermeulen put his free index finger against his mouth, and she stayed silent. The curved glass of the display case reflected a distorted image of the café. He could tell that one of the men remained by the door. The other two moved from table to table. The atmosphere in the café had become leaden. The customers and staff knew the men meant trouble. The waiter talked to them in rapid sentences. They ignored him.

The woman behind the display case must have understood that Vermeulen was the target of the two men. She whispered something in Portuguese that Vermeulen didn't understand. But she also pointed to the edges of the curved glass. Apparently, one could lift the glass to place items in the case. A good suggestion. The longer he stood there with the milk tarts, the more suspicious he'd be. He put the sheet on the counter, lifted the lid. The hinges clicked into the open position. He took a tart from the sheet. The disadvantage of having opened the case was that he couldn't follow the progress of the men anymore. But the waiter took care of that. He pointed to the kitchen door, continuing to speak to the men. The two men opened the door and entered the kitchen.

This was Vermeulen's only opportunity. He put the milk tart into the display case, took the tray with the other tart from the counter, and marched toward the front door. The man guarding the door even moved aside to let him exit. That courtesy didn't last any longer than the flash of recognition. Vermeulen knew it was coming and slammed the tray with the tart against the man. He stumbled backward. Pushing the door open, Vermeulen ran out. The man, milk tart smeared all over his clothes, raced after him.

Vermeulen dodged the tables and chairs in front of the café. No way could he reach the safety of the hotel. He grabbed one of the chairs, a flimsy bistro thing, and spun around, swinging it like a bat. That turned out to be a smart move, because the guy behind him had just aimed a pistol at him. The leg of the chair connected with the assailant's outstretched arm at the moment he pulled the trigger. The blast of the shot rang across the street, the bullet shattering a window of the hotel. The blow hadn't dislodged the gun from the assailant's hand and the chair wasn't going to stop a bullet. Attack was the only option. Vermeulen jabbed the chair legs against the man's chest. It was barely enough to slow him down. And he still had the gun. Holding on to the chair, Vermeulen stepped back. Sure enough, the guy fell for it and followed. Vermeulen waited until he had one foot in the air and lunged forward, using the chair like a battering ram. The guy went down. His head hit the concrete hard as Vermeulen tumbled on top of him. The guy was out cold. Vermeulen grabbed the pistol from his hand and patted the man's jacket pockets. There was an extra clip for the pistol, which he pocketed, and a folded piece of paper. On the paper was a picture of Vermeulen's face.

* * *

BY THE TIME VERMEULEN GOT TO Nossa Terra's office, it was past five o'clock. Simango didn't strike him as someone who'd leave her office at the stroke of quitting time. The office was the only safe place he could think of, and even that was dodgy. His hotel was off-limits. The gang had arrived there looking for him. It was only by accident that they'd recognized him at the café next door. They'd also know that he'd been to the office on the Avenida Vladimir Lenine. He just hoped that they'd search elsewhere first.

The paper with his photo worried him. Sitting in the taxi, he'd tried to sort out where it might have come from. It wasn't as if his likeness was easily found on the internet. He'd googled himself not too long ago and was delighted to find very little information. For obvious reasons, OIOS didn't publicize the names of their investigators. The only real clue as to his activities was an article in the Newark *Star-Ledger* recounting an incident in which he'd played a role. And his picture on that website was blurred, not at all like the paper he'd taken from his assailant. No, that picture had been taken in Maputo. He could see the collar of his jacket, which was new. It was also clear that the photo was taken indoors. Which really left only four places where it could have been taken: the two banks, Global Alternatives, and Nossa Terra.

Aisa's organization hadn't invested in a surveillance system. Their hand-to-mouth existence was obvious. Why spend scarce cash on equipment that had limited utility? That left the other three. The banks were the obvious candidates, since they had video cameras everywhere. But he'd only just left the Mauritius bank; it'd be quite a feat to pull a picture from the feed, print it, and get it into the hands of the gang all within an hour. Besides, nobody there knew his hotel. The Banco Terra was a possibility, but the background of the picture on the paper was the wrong color, and they didn't know where he stayed either. Which left Global Alternatives. And that was a frightening thought.

* * *

SIMANGO WAS STILL IN THE OFFICE when Vermeulen knocked at the door. She seemed surprised to see him.

"I apologize for the second unannounced visit," he said, "but I just escaped an assassination attempt, and I couldn't think of any other place to go."

That greeting made Simango sit down on the closest chair.

"A what? What happened? Where?"

"I had just come from Mauritius Bank and Trust and was sitting at a café next to my hotel when a black Land Rover drove up to the hotel. Three men exited and started looking around. One of them saw me at the café and they came after me. I escaped."

"How did you know they were after you?" she said.

He pulled out the paper with his photograph. "One of them had this in his pocket."

She gasped. "In his pocket? How did you get it?"

"Well, I had to escape and that man didn't want me to leave. There was an altercation."

She looked at him, eyebrows raised. "I see."

"Have you heard from Paito today?" he said.

"No, Helton did not come again. That tells me he is involved. I also found out he has a bank account with Mauritius Bank and Trust. Even more damning evidence. But there is no indication that the missing money is or ever was in his account."

"How do you know that?"

Simango looked a little sheepish before telling him how she'd searched his desk and eventually found his passwords on a sticky note stuck to the bottom of a drawer.

"I'd asked Zara if she could hack into his account. She was rather upset about the request, telling me that I'd lost my mind and that she wouldn't do it even if she could."

"I don't know if that is important," he said. "At the moment we have a bigger problem. Look at the picture. It was taken here in Maputo. And I'm pretty sure it was taken at Global Alternatives."

Simango's eyes widened. "Are you sure?" She took the paper and examined the background. "Many places have white walls."

"Yes, but I haven't been to those places. No, this was taken at their offices."

"But what does that mean?"

Vermeulen shrugged. "I don't know yet. Someone there clearly wants me out of the picture. I just asked that smarmy Mr. Pai at Mauritius Bank and Trust about the paperwork of the wire transfer. He told me the manager was not available. Then he left to find someone else in charge. When he returned, he told me to come back tomorrow."

"Whoever they are, they could have worked with Helton," Simango said. "I can't see how such a swindle could happen without someone in our office participating."

"Maybe. The much bigger question is the motive. Why would a foundation as rich as Global Alternatives be involved in stealing five million dollars? Can you give me more detail on what the money was intended for?"

Simango went to a desk and came back with a folder. She pulled out a map showing a meandering river. Partially enclosed by an oxbow and stretching a ways beyond the river was a swath of land demarcated with a red line.

"The money was supposed to pay for this land," she said. A resettlement project for landless farmers, people who have always been at the margins of rural society. First they were forced laborers under the Portuguese, then they got caught up in the collectivization cooked up by the newly independent FRELIMO government after 1975. Simango became animated. "Please do not misunderstand me. I support the revolution. I support FRELIMO, even with all its problems. The East German and Soviet advisors simply didn't know about tropical agriculture." At least that's what her father had told her. What he hadn't told her was how bigoted those advisors were. She had to learn that herself. They implemented foreign schemes and completely ignored the fact that FRELIMO had already pioneered alternative models in its liberated zones. The advisors simply didn't want to listen to Africans. And FRELIMO's leaders decided to please the foreigners without whose support the revolution would have been overthrown by South Africa and Rhodesia.

"It took us a long time to get past that and focus on those who wanted to work the land, if only they had some."

Vermeulen began to see the map in a different light. As no longer a cadastral survey, but a sign of hope. "What's going to happen now?"

"Without the money? I don't know. Global Alternatives had partnered with us to see this plan through. We did similar work around Maputo and in the next province, but on a much smaller scale. For us it was joining the big league. We're talking enough land for two hundred families, with titles and everything."

Vermeulen looked at the map again. His only frame of reference was his father's farm by the North Sea, where he'd lived until he was five. That was when his father threw in the towel. He couldn't make a go of it anymore, milk and cheese from the rest of Europe competing with his dairy cows. He knew how hard it was to make a living on a farm. And yet, for landless Mozambicans, it had to be a better option than becoming beggars in Maputo.

"How was dealing with Global Alternatives?"

"Isabel LaFleur was nice enough during the initial negotiations. But she didn't really seem engaged. Then the fat man took over. Less friendly, but still supportive. What struck me was the way they were less concerned with our strategy than with our reporting. They kept saying to make sure and file regular reports."

Vermeulen nodded.

"I had the same feeling. There's something strange about this foundation. How else could a photo taken in their office end up in the hands of a hit squad? Worst case scenario, LaFleur or Gould ordered the hit themselves. I can't fathom why, but I have to consider that possibility. More likely, someone hacked their system and got my picture. Or somebody bribed some tech guy there. But for what?"

"Maybe it had to do with your visit to Mauritius Bank and Trust. Could somebody there be involved?"

Vermeulen considered that option.

"Yes. Global Alternatives might not be involved at all. But how can a correspondent bank make that much money disappear? There'd be a paper trail."

He stared at the screen saver on Simango's monitor. A colored line snaked its way across the screen, changing its colors from one lurid hue to the next.

"Tomorrow Isabel LaFleur will be the keynote speaker at a symposium on agricultural development," Simango said. "I plan on going. Do you want to join me? You might get some insight."

"I'm not sure I should be out and about. Someone just tried to kill me."

"Then you shouldn't be here either. The gangsters surely know about us."

"You're right. And I can't go back to my hotel. Do you know a place where I could stay around here?"

Simango thought for a moment.

"Yes, there is a *pensõe* not far from here. But I have to warn you, it's rather basic and caters to local travelers."

"Don't worry about it. I've slept in all kinds of places. But my suitcase is still at the hotel."

"I can send Bartina to pick it up in the morning. You have the key?"

He handed it to her.

"Tomorrow, we will go to the symposium. Nobody will expect you there."

Chapter Eight

Grande Hotel

———◆———

KILLBILL THRUST HIS SWORD FORWARD. IT sliced into his opponent right below the armor. He pulled the sword back and side-stepped, anticipating the counterattack. There was none. The wound was fatal. He stepped back and spun around, acutely aware that where there was one *ninja*, there were more. They always lurked in the shadows. He spun around, fell into a crouch. They stayed hidden. Cowards. Every one of them.

"Show yourselves!" he said.

They remained hidden. Wait. There was one. He could see the shape in the darkness. The shape came forward. He assumed the warrior stance, the sword ready to parry. The shape came into the light. It was only Maria, the girl from Block B.

"*Você é malouco, pah,*" she said.

"I'm not crazy. I'm practicing." Maria didn't understand—she was just nine. She didn't know about warrior discipline. "Warriors practice all the time. That's how they get good at fighting."

"There are no *ninjas* here."

"I know that. But I have to be ready, *né?*"

"And that's no sword. It's just a stick with a knife tied to it."

The stick looked a little like a samurai sword. But it was no good for slashing. Acceptable for stabbing, though, which was therefore his preferred method for dispatching his opponents.

"Why do you want to fight?" Maria said.

"You never know. One day people are your friends, the next day they aren't. Just like in the movie."

The movie was, of course, *Kill Bill*. He'd seen volumes one and two. They were badly pirated copies, and it didn't matter that it was a woman who defeated her opponents with her sword. What mattered was that she was disciplined and taking no shit from nobody. KillBill didn't take no shit either. He was fast with the knife. He did pushups and ran on the beach. He was fifteen and a good warrior.

He looked out toward the ocean, vast and gray. Clouds raced toward him. Five floors below, some kids played in the weeds next to the tiled hole in the ground. The old man in Block B had told him it used to be a swimming pool, full of water once, and that rich Europeans had played in it. Rich whites playing in dirty water? KillBill didn't believe that. No, it was full of clean water then, up to the rim. Sparkling clean water. KillBill couldn't picture it. The brown puddle at the deep end looked poisonous. But the old man had showed him an old picture of a splendid building, all shiny and white. It sort of looked like this one. The building was once the *Grande Hotel Da Beira*. A fancy place where Europeans stayed.

The old man had worked here for the Europeans, wearing a white jacket and black trousers and carrying silver trays with food that smelled so good. KillBill tried to imagine what kind of food smelled so good that you could remember it fifty years later. Maybe cassava with chicken and piri-piri.

KillBill heard a loud whistle. Raul was calling his gang. Time to earn some money.

* * *

THE MAP DIDN'T SHOW PEOPLE. MAPS never do. It's not what they are about. Maps are all about lines. Which troubled Lionel Sukuma to no end. The lines he was looking at were clear, delineating a large swath of land, land that was supposed to be empty. Except that it wasn't. He knew this because a couple of dozen of the people who weren't supposed to be on the land were outside his office on the Rua Major Serpa in Beira, shouting and holding up signs.

Sukuma looked out of the second-floor window again and swore under his breath. He recognized the man inciting the small crowd. It was the guy from Nossa Terra, a big man with a black beard, a goddamn rabble rouser. He filled clueless peasants with crazy ideas, like having land. Land for what? To grow a little cassava, a little maize, a few beans? Never enough to sell anything and often too little to live on. And yet, those foreign donors still gave them money. It made no sense. The country would never achieve food security with a bunch of peasants mucking about on an acre plot, eking out a living. As if all those donors had never heard of economies of scale. But they had, because agriculture in their countries was exactly what he envisioned for Mozambique.

The protesters had been there for an hour. Nobody had come out to speak to them, not even some low-level flunky. Ignoring them was the best way to deal with them. Far better than calling out the police. Once the cops showed up, the media did too, and next thing you knew, there was a large picture splashed over the front page with some officer's baton smacking a hapless peasant in the back. That usually resulted in a phone call from *la governadora*. The trouble with this crowd was that they came back. Sometimes more, sometimes fewer. They'd staged this protest for a week now. Each time, they attracted more attention. Passersby stopped, listened, even nodded in support. They interfered with traffic and created a commotion. Any day now, the papers would write about them even without the police cracking down. And *la governadora* would call anyway.

He picked up the phone and dialed. The number wasn't in the official directory. As far as he knew, it wasn't in any directory. But the call was answered after the second ring.

"Yeah?" a toneless voice said.

"There are people outside my office, carrying on. They've come for days now. It's bad for everybody's business. Better if they're cleared before they cause more trouble."

"Okay."

Sukuma hung up, got himself a cup of tea, and moseyed back to his window, waiting for the action to unfold. Thirty minutes after the call, two vans stopped some distance from the protesters. The men and women holding up signs didn't notice the vans. Neither did the passersby who were watching. The vans were blue and generic. Plenty of those on the streets.

A gang of youths spilled from the vans. They carried sticks. Some had covered their faces with bandanas. A tall man pointed them toward the protesters and the melee started.

* * *

KILLBILL HAD NO PROBLEM FIGHTING. HE was a warrior, after all. But that meant he'd only fight *ninjas* and other evildoers. That was the warrior code. The other directive was that his master's command had to be fulfilled. That's where the rub lay. Not all of Raul's targets seemed to be evildoers. The police were obvious enemies. So were the members of FRELIMO, the government party. But more and more often, Raul sent them to fight opponents that seemed like regular people, protesting for or against something the government had done. If the government were evildoers, how could the ones protesting against it also be evil? But those were the orders.

He left the van with the rest of the gang, grabbed his stick, and got ready to attack. He'd taken the knife off the stick and stuck it under the piece of rope he used for a belt. It was okay to beat people bloody with a stick, but Raul had told them no knives or guns.

The gang started infiltrating the crowd of onlookers. As soon as they saw the sticks, they disappeared. They knew what was going down. The first row reached the protestors and started whaling on them with their sticks. KillBill hung back, observing his buddies. The enemy crumpled under their blows. Women fell to the ground, screaming. The men did, too. They weren't fighters. Few men were, in KillBill's experience, when they were faced with a bunch of teenagers out for blood. This operation would be over before he could even test his skills. It was too easy.

Until the man with the bullhorn in front turned. He was a giant. He deflected the first stick, hit the kid with his bullhorn, jabbed the second kid hard against the chest, and kicked the third one in the balls. After only a second, three were already out of commission. One of the women on the ground took a page from the giant's book and grabbed the stick of the next guy, yanked it out of his hand, and thrust it in his gut. Four down. The next guys in line slowed. They weren't used to people fighting back.

The surprise was gone. The protestors rallied. Only ten minutes later and twelve of the guys who'd come with KillBill were either on the ground or limping back. Not KillBill. Blood flowed from his eyebrow down his face. It didn't matter. The warrior code demanded that he stand his ground until the bitter end. A flurry of fists and sticks hit him all over his body. He screamed, more from adrenaline than pain, and kept pushing forward. At last he stood facing the giant. He raised his stick, but the giant just grabbed it, held it, and asked him in a weirdly quiet voice, "Why are you doing this?"

"I was ordered," KillBill said.

"You follow all orders?"

"A warrior always does, *né*?"

The giant smiled.

"Listen, kid. You ain't no warrior. Warriors fight for justice. They don't beat up poor folks who just want to keep their land."

KillBill let go of the stick. He didn't mean to, but the doubt he'd been feeling about Raul's targets burst into the open. Which part of the warrior code should he follow? Serving one's master or fighting the just fight? The answer was clear.

"So are you going to stop fighting?" the giant said.

KillBill nodded.

"Come with me. I can see you have discipline and follow principles. Let's put that to good use."

"I haven't gotten paid yet by Raul."

"So Raul is the gangster who put you up to this. I doubt he'll pay you. We're still here. You haven't achieved your objective. Where do you live?"

"Grande Hotel."

"Well, I doubt you can go back there. My name is Chico. What's yours?"

"I'm KillBill."

"Really? I didn't like that movie much. But come with me. I could use a skinny kid like you."

* * *

"WHERE HAVE YOU BEEN," RAUL SAID. "We got back hours ago."

"The giant kept me." Sticking as close to the truth as possible was always the smart thing. Besides, warriors like KillBill told the truth.

"What did he want?"

This was the moment a warrior might have to lie. Raul was already wasted. KillBill saw his sleepy eyes and the slack lips. Raul took a swig from his bottle of *Laurentina Preta*. A few drops of dark beer ran down his chin.

"He wanted to bring me to the police." KillBill and the giant—his name was Chico Chipenda—had agreed that this would be the best excuse for his lateness.

"And did he?"

KillBill smiled.

"I'm a warrior. The *ninjas* have no power over me. They can't hold me."

"Then why are you so late?"

"I jumped out of the giant's car when he stopped. Then I had to hide until it was safe to come out. I had to walk all the way here. I didn't have money for a *chapa*. Where's my money?"

Raul pulled a few bills from his pocket but didn't give them to KillBill.

"Did you tell him anything about me?" he said.

"Nothing. I'm a warrior, *está a ver*?"

"Stop it with the warrior shit. Did you tell him where I live?"

"No, I didn't." Technically, he wasn't lying. The *Grande Hotel da Beira* was a big place and he didn't tell Chico in which room Raul lived.

Raul eyed him, took another swig, and looked again. KillBill could see that the man's desire to get wasted had won out over his suspicion. Raul handed him the money.

"Next time, be more careful," Raul said.

"As careful as you?"

"Yeah." Raul hesitated. "Whaddya mean?"

"I didn't see you in the battle. A good general leads his troops."

Anger flashed on Raul's face. But there was no fight in him.

"Oh, fuck off," he said and turned away

KillBill made his way to the top floor of the hotel and then clambered onto the roof. It was his favorite spot. The ocean was huge. Way bigger than anything he could imagine. He liked looking at it. It was good for a warrior to know his place in the world. He pulled out the mobile Chico had given him and dialed his number.

"*Que se passa, pah?*" Chico said. "You okay? No problems with Raul?"

"No, everything's fine. He's drunk already."

"Good. Be careful. Better hide the phone, too."

"I will."

He ended the call.

"Who you talking to, *meu*?" a voice said from behind him.

Maria again.

"Nobody."

CHAPTER NINE

STAKEHOLDERS

———◆———

VERMEULEN STRETCHED OUT IN HIS BED. His feet hung over the end. The bed didn't quite accommodate his six-foot frame. Other than that, the night had been as comfortable as a night at a place away from home could be.

The pension Chicari—named after the hometown of the proprietor, as Vermeulen found out—was without pretensions. The walls were white-washed, the floors swept, and the bedding cool. There was plenty of business at the *barraca* attached to the guesthouse the night before, and Vermeulen, still riled up after the escape from the gangsters, wanted to be among people. The company at the informal bar was mixed, some men traveling on business that Vermeulen couldn't figure out, a few couples, and single women. Communication was difficult, and therefore animated. Gestures and facial expressions ended up doing most of the work and everybody was the happier for it. The proprietor's wife offered him a bowl of stew, which he devoured. When he fell into his bed, he was content, even without his suitcase.

He got up and did a quick wash-up at the sink in his room. It would have to do. He got his pants from under the mattress, a trick he'd learned on one of his first UN trips. Pressed trousers always looked good. They didn't quite match his shirt and jacket. Wetting the towel, he brushed the jacket and slipped it on. The mirror was too small to tell him much.

The bar had been converted to a breakfast room with the addition of three tables. A cup of tea and two slices of white bread with butter were all he had time to eat before Simango came to fetch him.

"Did you have a good night?" she said.

"Splendid. And nice company too. Thanks for bringing me here. If I'd known about it, I'd have moved here right away."

"Glad to hear it. I felt bad about leaving you here. But my house is small, and I have my children."

"No need to apologize. It was perfect. Let me book another night before we leave."

"Good. I've already met with Bartina. She's on her way to your hotel to get your things. I told her to pack anything there. Let's go to the office. Bartina should be there soon. You can change and then we have to leave for the symposium."

* * *

THE SYMPOSIUM WAS HELD AT THE ministry for agriculture adjacent to the Praça dos Herois Mocambicanos. The Heroes Square was a vast traffic circle with a memorial in the shape of a five-pointed star at its center.

"This is where our first president, Samora Machel, is buried," Simango said, as their *chapa* drove around the circle.

They got off near the ministry, but Aisa took Vermeulen across one of the streets leading to the circle to show him an undulating wall over a hundred yards long and taller than Vermeulen. A mural covered it in its entirety. Aisa stopped near the western end of the wall.

"The history of Mozambique," she said.

Vermeulen saw depictions of struggle and suffering. Stylized barbed wire wove through sections of the wall. There were black men in chains, a policeman arresting a black man, men and women with anguish in their faces, guns and explosions, the face of Eduardo Mondlane, the leader of the anti-colonial struggle, and fighters carrying AK-47s. They stood in silence, together tracing the violent path of time toward the present.

"We'd better go," she said. "It's hard to blend into the crowd when you're late."

The symposium was held in a large conference room on the first floor of the ministry. A small crowd was milling about in the foyer. Simango nodded hellos to several people and stopped to greet a dark-skinned man.

Vermeulen scanned the crowd. Being out in public, knowing assassins were after him, put him on edge. Moving around, not staying in a predictable place, was his best protection. Bartina had been adamant that nobody saw her take his luggage from his room. But he took that with a grain of salt. She would have blended in as hotel staff, but it only took a few bills to the right people for the assassins to have eyes and ears in that place.

A young man in suit and tie urged the people to take their seats, as the program was about to begin. Simango chose seats in the rear by a cluster of representatives from some European aid organization. A wise choice. It let Vermeulen blend in, and a support column there provided some cover.

The proceedings began with a welcome from some functionary of the ministry of agriculture. He wore a stiff suit and welcomed everyone in accented English. He then introduced the moderator, a woman with cinnamon skin, dressed in a flowing outfit with large, abstract, yellow, red, and green shapes, reminiscent of traditional patterns but also thoroughly modern. She also welcomed the attendees and outlined the agenda. Vermeulen settled in for the long haul. He'd been at enough of such gatherings. Patience and a tough rear end were the key to surviving any symposium.

About a half hour into the proceedings, the emcee finally announced the keynote speaker, Ms. Isabel LaFleur, local head of Global Alternatives. The screen behind the dais displayed the logo of the foundation. LaFleur took to the stage and began her presentation without preliminaries.

"We have failed Africa," she said. "Sixty years of so-called development aid, and we have nothing to show for it. We all know the failures of the past: industrialization with all its white elephants, the basic needs campaign that didn't address poverty, the lost decade of the 1980s, the persistence of conflict even after the end of the Cold War."

The screen behind her displayed the bullet list of the failures. The aid workers near Vermeulen yawned. One of them shook her head as if to say, *same old, same old.* LaFleur didn't spend too much time on rehashing the failures of the past. Instead she switched to what she considered the cause of the failures—inflexible governments and international bureaucracies. "We need to leverage the private sector. Yes, right now markets don't work for poor people, but we can make markets work for everybody. To do so, we need to tap into the creativity, the capability, and the innovative potential of the private sector. We need to catalyze multi-stakeholder discussions where we can bring together foundations, governments, and the private sector to figure out how to use our resources to really tackle the big problems of agriculture, to open up markets for companies, and solve problems for people."

On the screen behind her, several slides appeared. Their colorful shapes and arrows were mean to provide visual aids for her suggestions. One of the aid workers near Vermeulen hissed "*Merde!*" under her breath. Her colleagues just shook their heads.

LaFleur continued by addressing land access. She rejected small-scale land distribution schemes because small plots didn't benefit from economies of scale. The accompanying slide showed crude icons and despondent farmers with empty bushels.

"Why did they support the Sofala Project, then?" Simango said. "That's all about small plots."

Vermeulen had stopped paying attention to LaFleur, focusing more on the reaction to her speech among the group next to him. Clearly, they didn't approve of her remarks. Simango's aside drew him back to the speech.

"Large-scale agriculture holds the promise of increased rural non-farm employment, the efficient use of new seed varieties, including, yes, transgenic seeds, irrigation, and fertilizer, and finally, increased export earnings. Market-based approaches can flourish, and Global Alternatives, together with its partners in the philanthropic world, the private sector, and government, will make it happen. I'm excited to announce today a major project in the Sofala province. The project will encompass two hundred fifty thousand acres and offer many new employment opportunities. The government has just approved the legal paperwork and implementation can begin immediately."

The slide behind her depicted a map with a large tract of land marked by a red outline. There was applause from the front rows. LaFleur concluded her remarks with the announcement that Global Alternatives had partnered with a U.S.-based investment fund, GreenAnt Investments, for the implementation phase of the project. There was no mention of any local partners.

The rest of the room remained quiet. Vermeulen glanced over to Simango, who sat in her chair, thunderstruck. She turned to him, her face ashen. Vermeulen looked back at the screen and recognized the oxbow of the river he'd seen on Simango's map the day before. Except on this map, that oxbow constituted only a small part of the total.

"I can't believe it," Simango said. "This is fifty times larger than the project we were contracted for. How did they even get the land titles? We only submitted applications for five thousand acres. That's impossible."

She jumped up. Vermeulen had an idea of what was going to happen. He tried to pull her down again. But Simango couldn't be stopped.

"What are you going to do with the people you've promised that land? The people who live there already? Drive them away with clubs and tear gas?" she said, her voice booming through the room.

All eyes turned toward her. The aid workers next to them nodded. One of them clapped. There was a smattering of applause elsewhere. But most attendees remained quiet. Criticism was never expressed at official occasions like this. Stone-faced smiles were the rule.

LaFleur sported just that kind of smile.

"I see we have a detractor in the audience. For those of you who don't know, this is Ms. Aisa Simango, executive director of Nossa Terra, a community-based organization working on land rights. Her organization has done yeoman's labor for land rights around Maputo. I understand that a large-scale project like the one I just announced might disturb you, Ms. Simango. But let's be frank, the food security of this country isn't going to be guaranteed by the kind of small-scale farming you advocate. You're working with a nineteenth-century paradigm. This is the twenty-first century. It's time for your organization to adapt. Let me remind you that accountability is also part of the new paradigm. And it seems to me you should account for the funds Nossa Terra has received so far instead of disparaging our project."

* * *

THE GETAWAY WAS A PROBLEM. VERMEULEN took Simango by her arm to direct her out of the auditorium. The aid workers sitting by them looked surprised and upset. They were probably looking forward to a continued exchange between Simango and LaFleur. But the show was over. The emcee had already taken the mic again and LaFleur was stepping down from the podium. Vermeulen knew they had to get out of there. Fast. But Simango wasn't done yet, and yanked her arm away from him. Vermeulen told her not to make a scene. He understood that a white man dragging an African woman from the room looked very bad indeed, but getting away from the ministry of agriculture was most important. Especially when he saw that LaFleur was talking on her phone.

"What are you doing?" Simango said in the corridor. Vermeulen could see she was livid.

"We need to get away from here. Is there a place other than your office we could go?"

"Why?"

"Don't you see how the pieces of the puzzle fit together? Global Alternatives fakes the wire transfer to ruin your reputation, then takes your project and turns it into one of theirs. You and I are just obstacles. They'll ruin you and get rid of me. Problem solved."

"That sounds crazy. Why even partner with us if that's what they wanted to do?"

"I don't know. To make you do the legwork, identify the land, and get the titles? Clearly, this is not a new plan."

They came to the *chapa* stop.

"We need to get away from here," he said. "LaFleur was talking on her phone. For all I know she was calling in the goon squad."

"The goon what?"

"The assassins. Do you know a safe place we can go?"

"Yes, the university library."

"Okay, which van do we take to get there?"

Simango shook as if from a sudden chill. "You are right." She flagged a passing *chapa*, got information from the driver, and climbed in. Vermeulen followed. They had to switch *chapas* twice before getting to the university, which was fine with Vermeulen. Instead of going into the library, they found a bench in a quiet courtyard under tall acacia trees.

"I cannot believe all this is happening," Simango said. "It is a nightmare."

"Have you ever heard of a foundation doing anything like this?"

"Something criminal? No. Sure, these big foundations are everywhere now. They have money and so they can set the agenda. Our government is poor. The bureaucrats are flattered by the attention given to them. And the UN is no help either; all they do is repeat the mantra of public-private partnerships."

"What about the project she unveiled? Is that something different?"

"She didn't say enough about it. But we've had investors come in and buy land. A lot of land. Some is used for biofuels. One company just grows rice for Saudi Arabia. You see, African land is cheap. Or 'underutilized,' as someone like LaFleur would put it. She's one of the true believers of the new way. When she says 'public-private partnership,' what she means is private profit while the public shoulders the cost."

They sat quietly for a while, each lost in thought. The silence was interrupted by Simango's phone. She answered, listened, then gasped. Her hand with the phone dropped down to the bench.

"What happened?" he said.

"They found Helton's body."

CHAPTER TEN

IFFY CIRCUMSTANCES

———◆———

THE NEWS OF HELTON'S BODY WASHING up on one of Maputo's beaches had shocked everyone at Nossa Terra. When Aisa got back to the office, her staff was dealing with his death each in their own way. Zara sat quietly at her desk, not doing anything but staring at her screen saver. Bartina looked ready to punch a hole in a wall. The wall being cement blocks, she'd resorted to pacing through the office, daring anyone to stop her. Tendai was busy checking some website for more information.

"When was he found?" Aisa said.

"The police said they were contacted around nine by someone walking on the beach," Tendai said. "They sent officers and an ambulance and brought his body to the morgue."

"How did they identify him?"

"They didn't say. Probably his ID card or driver's permit."

"Have the police been here yet?"

"No, they said they'll send an inspector soon."

"Did they say anything else about his death?"

Nobody answered Aisa's question. Her colleagues may have had differing opinions of Helton, but his death brought them all together.

Aisa went to her desk and began checking her email messages. There was the usual array of junk offering watches, more libido, and pharmaceuticals from India. A couple of invitations to participate in some conference or other. She declined those politely. It wouldn't take long before LaFleur's accusation of their lack of accountability would make the rounds, prompting the organizers to find a way to disinvite her.

The ring of her phone was a welcome distraction, even if the ensuing conversation wasn't. The call came from Chico Chipende, head of Nossa Terra's Beira office.

"*Bom dia*, Aisa. I have disturbing news. People are being told to vacate land they've been on for years. This has been going on for a couple of weeks."

"Where is this happening?"

"Just outside Tica, very close to our project. A relative of one of our candidates for land came across a 'No Trespassing' sign. One of the farmers called me, *está a ver*? That's how I found out. At first I thought it was just another local land grab—you know, some village headman expanding his holdings. So I told him to send a delegation to protest in Beira."

Aisa couldn't help but smile. Organizing a protest was Chico's default solution to almost all problems. And surprisingly, more often than not his protests were effective. Most local rackets fizzled fast once they were brought to the attention of the provincial government.

"The protests didn't work?" she said.

"No. We went to the provincial ministry in Beira. For three days nothing happened. Nobody came out. It was rather dull. Yesterday, that all changed. A gang of local hoodlums came with sticks to beat us up. They almost succeeded. But eventually we sent them packing."

"You what? Don't tell me you fought back. What did I tell you? No violence. Once we go down that road, the authorities will come down on us with all their force."

"Relax," Chico said. "We didn't fight the police. I'd never do that. But these were just teenagers commandeered by a local thug. I'm not going to run from some fifteen-year-old pipsqueak. Someone behind that land grab hired them. The government just looked the other way."

"Do you know who is behind it?"

"One of the men took a picture of one of the 'No Trespassing' signs with his phone. There was a name on that sign. GreenAnt Investments."

Aisa sucked in her breath.

"Did you say GreenAnt Investments?"

"Yes, why?"

That was the new partner LaFleur had mentioned. Aisa got up and walked toward the meeting room. She gave Chico a quick rundown of the plans LaFleur had announced at the symposium.

"Mind you, all I have to go on is what she said in the presentation. We haven't actually heard from them that our project was canceled. But the map was clear. Their project includes all the land we had targeted for resettlement."

Chico said nothing.

"Something else has come up in the past week," she said.

The explanation of the missing five million dollars took a while because Aisa wasn't clear on what exactly had happened.

When she was done, Chico said, "So, the short of it is that we're screwed. Even if we prove we never got the money, we'll have egg on our face. But it really doesn't matter anyway because Global Alternatives and GreenAnt just gobbled up the land we were going to distribute. Nice."

It was Aisa's turn to say nothing.

"Well, I'm not going to slink away like a kicked dog. None of this could have happened without collusion of the local officials. I'm going to dig into this and find out who gave them the land-use permits and leases. Somebody is lining their pockets here. I want to know who."

"Be careful, Chico. That UN investigator I mentioned? He was attacked by gangsters yesterday. He's in hiding now. And Helton—you remember Helton?—he's dead. They found his body on the beach."

"What happened to him?"

"I don't know. The police haven't been here yet. Anyway, I don't want to read in the paper that they found your body like they did Helton's."

"Listen, why don't you send that UN investigator up here? That way he can see what's going on. File a report about it, let the world know. And he'll be out of the crosshairs of the guys down in Maputo."

"Chico, I can't send him anywhere. He doesn't work for us. He's supposed to investigate us."

"But we haven't done anything wrong."

"I think he knows that."

"Then having him on our side would really help."

"Okay. I'll talk to him."

* * *

VERMEULEN WAS BACK IN HIS *PENSÃO*. It was too early to go to bed, and hanging out in the bar didn't suit his mood. His head swirled with vague notions of why he was a target and who was behind it. In the absence of any clear evidence, it was easy for his mind to start spiraling into the realm of baseless panic. Better to talk to someone who had some distance. And it was time to update his boss in Nairobi anyway.

Arne Bengtsson was still in his office. Vermeulen filled him in on the audit result at Global Alternatives, the initial assumption that Nossa Terra had mismanaged the funds, then the evidence from their bank account and the fact that the money had disappeared somewhere during the transfer.

"You mean to tell me that five million dollars just vanished into thin air?" Bengtsson said.

"No, the money is somewhere. It's just that so far, I haven't been able to track it."

"And you're sure that the folks at that little NGO didn't have anything to do with it?"

"Yes. There was one employee who went missing, but he was just found dead. I don't know the cause of death yet."

"So he could have taken the money before he died?"

"Yes, but there is no evidence to support that. His boss accessed his account and found no traces of any large deposit or withdrawal."

"Would he have been so stupid to put it into his account?"

"No, but you have to remember, the money wasn't real," Vermeulen said. "There was no suitcase with dollar bills—it was all electronic transfers."

"Good point. So do you have any suspects at all?"

Vermeulen hesitated a moment. "Yes, but iffy. What evidence I have is circumstantial. I think Global Alternatives is behind it."

Bengtsson whistled.

"You better have more than iffy circumstances. You're talking about the eight-hundred-pound gorilla in the aid field. Let me hear what you have."

Vermeulen told him about his narrow escape from being killed and his photograph in the pocket of one of the gangsters. "There were only a handful of places where I would have been filmed by a security camera, and the Global Alternatives office fits the background of the image best."

"Damn it, Valentin. The moment they let you into the field again, you end up in trouble. Correction, you were trouble even when you were in New York City."

Vermeulen was used to Bengtsson's gruff talk. The man's bark was worse than his bite. They'd become friends over the past two years and Vermeulen valued his advice.

"So, someone has pointed a gun at you," Bengtsson said. "You better get out of Maputo. Why not come to Nairobi? You can do some of the work from here. Much of that international money transfer business can't be investigated in Maputo anyway. We need cooperation from the SWIFT headquarters in Belgium."

"There's one more odd thing. The local NGO had contracted with Global Alternatives for a project to allocate land to landless peasants. Just this morning I went to a symposium where Global Alternatives' boss announced a much larger venture that incorporated all the land the NGO had slated for its project."

"Hmm, that is odd indeed. I wonder why they changed their mind. Maybe the missing money had something to do with it. Global Alternatives can pick anyone for a partner. I can see that they wouldn't want someone who isn't reliable."

"I don't think they ever wanted to do the landless-peasant project. Everything their boss said today was diametrically opposed to the idea of giving land to peasants. She's all about big agriculture. Maybe the missing money was just a ruse to discredit Nossa Terra."

Bengtsson didn't respond.

"Don't you see it? An organization that has worked to improve access to land would have been a thorn in Global Alternatives' side. One way to take the NGO out of the picture is pretend to work with them, set up a fake transfer, make them look incompetent or worse, and then go ahead with your own project."

"You really like those folks at the NGO, don't you? Enough to be grasping at straws? Come to Nairobi, get some distance. We'll get the money-transfer thing sorted out. Then we'll see what's what."

* * *

BENGTSSON WAS RIGHT. HE USUALLY WAS, when it came to being logical. Except there were occasions where logic didn't get you anywhere, when a gut feeling turned out to be more important than evidence. Vermeulen had such a feeling after ending the conversation with Bengtsson. Still, he was inclined to follow his boss's advice and travel to Nairobi. His audit was complete. Everything was accounted for, except the five million dollars. To ascertain the whereabouts of those funds required access to information he didn't have. At least not in Maputo.

His phone rang. It was Simango, and the call began as Vermeulen expected. She was reeling from all the bad news that had come her way: the Global Alternatives project, Helton's death, and—at least Vermeulen assumed so—some guilt over having suspected Helton of being responsible for the disappearing money. When she began recounting the latest bad news, Vermeulen figured she just needed a sympathetic ear. So he listened. He didn't quite understand what land the people up in Sofala province were being thrown off—their own or the acreage they were supposed to get. It didn't really matter, because the name GreenAnt Investments got his attention. LaFleur wasn't wasting any time. Her project was already in motion on the very day it was first announced.

"In any case," Simango said, "our head of the Sofala operations, Chico Chipende, thinks you should come up there and check out the situation. He is convinced that some local officials have been bribed to issue the required permits. It would also get you out of Maputo. It is not good place for you to be at the moment."

Vermeulen had to smile. Two people concerned for his safety. A rare occurrence, to be sure.

"Thank you, Ms. Simango. I appreciate the invitation. But local bribery isn't my concern. The UN deplores corruption, but leaves it to each country's institution to address it. I have no jurisdiction whatsoever to do anything about it."

"Please call me Aisa."

"Only if you call me Valentin."

"Agreed. Here's what I am thinking, Valentin. You are auditing Global Alternatives; you find funds unaccounted for. You know they did not come to us, but they must have gone somewhere because Global Alternatives showed you that they wired the money. Maybe it got diverted to bribe the people issuing the permits. Would that not be your jurisdiction?"

"There's a lot of conjecture in your chain of reasoning. We still don't know that Global Alternatives has anything to do with it. It could have been someone at Mauritius Bank and Trust without any connection to the foundation. Just because they announced a new project doesn't mean they stole the money from the old one."

She was quiet.

"I just spoke with my boss in Nairobi, and he suggested I go there and start untangling the money transfers. I might even have to go to Belgium."

"Why?"

"The headquarters of SWIFT, the organization that operates the secure messaging system that makes wire transfers possible. They would have a record of these transactions. And that would help me find out what happened."

"I understand. That must be your priority. But I have a strong feeling that the money was somehow diverted toward this new project. The way things have happened in the last week is no coincidence."

Vermeulen wanted to agree with her. She had the same gut feeling he had. But he didn't see a way to act on that feeling here or in Sofala that would move the case forward. He told her as much. She didn't agree, suggesting instead that he investigate GreenAnt Investments, since they had put up the no-trespassing signs. There had to be a connection between Global Alternatives and that company.

"I agree," he said, "but that would be easier wherever that company is incorporated than here. Maybe you could check into that. They had to have filed papers with the Mozambican authorities."

"Good point. I will do that. But if you went up to help Chico, you could learn a lot more than I could here. There's got to be a local manager. Just show him your UN ID and he'll talk to you. Same with the local officials. My country relies so much on international aid, its leadership bends over backwards to keep the UN happy. You could use that to our advantage."

CHAPTER ELEVEN

BITTERSWEET OVERTONES

———◆———

THE SKY IN BEIRA WASN'T MUCH different than in Maputo. Gray clouds racing in from the Indian Ocean with specks of blue and the occasional sunbeam lighting up the tarmac. But Vermeulen hadn't come here for the weather. Or because Aisa Simango had asked him to help Chico. In the end, he'd come to Beira for very personal reasons. Tessa had called him just as he was getting ready to book a flight to Nairobi. She'd come to Beira after all to gather more information on large land sales in Africa for her reporting assignment. He'd wanted her to come, but knew better than to get his hopes up. Too often in the past their tentative plans to meet had been sabotaged by changes in assignments and schedules. So when she called him Friday night, asking if he could come, he didn't have to think. He deleted "Nairobi" from the destination field on the airline website and typed "Beira" instead. A weekend with Tessa in Beira versus fleeing to Nairobi? No contest.

He climbed down the steps onto the tarmac. A squall of rain hit him as he crossed to the terminal building. A jetway would have been nice. He put his briefcase on top of his head and dragged his carry-on behind him. Three small aircraft stood parked to his left. The largest of them, a twin-engine model, had a green emblem on its vertical stabilizer. The emblem looked oddly bulbous until he realized that it resembled an ant. GreenAnt Investments had its own plane. Good. It means there had to be records of ownership, flight plans, and all kinds of information out there. The sight of someone waving at him from behind a glass door brought him back to the real purpose of his visit. Tessa was waiting for him.

She had changed her hair. The unruly tangle of thin braids, held together by a rubber band, was gone. And with it most of her hair. It was close-cropped, making her look a little like Grace Jones, except that she didn't have the chiseled features of the singer. With the titanium glasses and the white dusting at her temples, she looked more like a professor than a journalist.

The moment he made it into the terminal, he dropped his things and took her in his arms. The warmth of her body against his made him forget the rain outside. He could have stood there holding her forever.

She let him go, held him at arm's length, and looked him over.

"I can't tell you how good it is to see you," she said.

All he could do was nod. The depth of joy he felt was matched only by the recognition of how much he'd really missed her. He'd ignored it these past months, pretending there wasn't a hole in his life. Now it came back and brought tears to his eyes. He wiped his eyes.

"I missed you, too," she said. "It's absolutely wonderful to see I wasn't the only one."

He'd yet to say a word, but his mind was too scrambled to produce a coherent sentence. Their reunions had always had bittersweet overtones, Tessa wanting more of a commitment and Vermeulen not seeing a way to promise that. Their globetrotting lives made settling down seem like an enticing mirage. This time it was different. This time he didn't wish things were a certain way. He only delighted in being with her.

"I love you," he finally said. It wasn't like he hadn't said those words before. But they sounded different to him. Weightier. Who cared? He meant it. And that was all that mattered.

"Oh my. Are you getting all squishy with me?" she said, a crooked smile on her lips. "I love you, too. And I love hearing you say it. It's about time." She pulled him into another hug. "Okay, are we just going to stand here or should we go to my hotel?"

* * *

TESSA HAD A KNACK FOR FINDING the nicest hotels at a price she could pass on to her employers. The Beira Inn was no exception. It stood only two blocks away from the ocean and the mangroves that reached out into the estuary. Her room was comfortable. A gorgeous view of the water, the curtain billowing in a pleasant breeze. They dropped their bags and fell onto the bed, their clothes still on. Unlike their previous meetings, the impatient tugging at clothes didn't happen. They just lay on the bed in each other's arms, getting used to the idea that they had managed to get together, and enjoying having a moment to catch up.

After an hour, Tessa jumped up, declaring she was hungry. She called room service and ordered lunch. Vermeulen sat up and turned on his phone. A ding reminded him of messages and a voicemail. He was about to turn if off again, but Tessa said, "It's okay. You can check your messages. We're not on vacation, although I sure could get into that mood."

He listened to the voicemail. It was Simango asking whether he'd made a decision about Beira. Vermeulen wasn't inclined to answer her. It felt unkind, but how could he explain that he'd gone to Beira to meet his lover rather than to deal with the conspiracy that threatened to sink Nossa Terra?

His feeling must have been obvious because Tessa said, "Bad news?"

"Not really. But let's eat first before we talk business."

"I appreciate the thought, but it'll be a while before the food shows up, so tell me what's going on."

He told her his trepidation over telling Simango his reason for coming to Beira.

"And why can't you tell her that you came to meet me?" Tessa said.

"I don't know. She seems all business. I can't imagine her taking time off just for fun."

"Don't tell me you feel guilty."

Vermeulen shrugged.

"Let me tell you something. Women get the importance of relationships. You're just projecting your own doubts on her. Unless she has a thing for you. Does she?"

Vermeulen sat up straight. "For me? No way. It's been all business."

"Well, there you go. Call her later. But let's eat first."

A waiter brought the food and they sat on the balcony, eating and enjoying the view. Not even an hour later they were back on the bed. This time, their clothes lay strewn on the carpet.

* * *

WHEN HE DID CALL SIMANGO ON Sunday morning, the conversation wasn't anything like Vermeulen had dreaded. Simango was just happy that he was in Beira. She didn't care why he'd changed his mind. She gave him the phone number of Chico Chipende and said that she would search for any information she could find on GreenAnt Investments.

Breakfast with Tessa was leisurely. They took time to catch each other up on their current assignments. Vermeulen told her about the missing funds and how GA had apparently pulled the plug on a project that Simango and Nossa Terra had high hopes for. She told him that she'd landed a big assignment investigating foreign purchases of large land holdings in several African countries.

"You know when the bottom fell out of the world economy in 2008/09, food prices spiked," she said. "A lot of investment funds were looking for profitable long-term investments, and some of them discovered agriculture.

Since then, they've acquired land left and right. In Africa alone, they've bought total acreage larger than France in the last five years. I'm doing an in-depth report on how that's working out for the countries and the people."

Vermeulen pricked up his ears. "Did you by chance come across a firm called GreenAnt Investments?"

She shook her head. "No. Doesn't ring a bell. But that doesn't mean much. There are a lot of players in this game, and the layers of ownership aren't always obvious."

He nodded.

"What's up for you today," he said.

"Not much. Tomorrow I have a couple of appointments in the directorate of agriculture, getting the official perspective. So I'll see if I can hire a driver and go out to visit one of the projects and see for myself. How about you?"

"Well, I'm supposed to call this Chico Chipende and that's about it. And find out more about GreenAnt Investments. Are you doing your own camera work? Or is Sami still coming?"

Sami had done the camera work during her assignment in Dafur, where Vermeulen had first met Tessa.

"Camera men are a luxury of the past. Everybody is cutting costs. I can't afford it anymore. I record my own video now, do voiceovers later in my hotel room, and email the whole thing to the editors. It's a pain, but what can you do? Fast and cheap—that's the news motto these days. If this continues, I'll end up podcasting or curating a YouTube channel, hoping I can monetize my reporting with sleazy ads."

She got up from the table. "Time for my shower."

Vermeulen had more than half a mind to join her, but Tessa told him to save it for the evening. He used the opportunity to call Chico Chipende. They agreed to meet the next morning.

CHAPTER TWELVE

STROKE OF LUCK

———————◆———————

O N MONDAY MORNING, AN AFRICAN MAN in a suit and white shirt got out
of the cab. He was of medium height and clean-shaven. A perfect mark.
The man folded a newspaper under his arm, pulled a wallet from his jacket
pocket, and took out some bills. The driver reached through the open window
and took the money. The man put the wallet back into his jacket pocket and
took the paper from under his arm. KillBill observed the man carefully. He
worked for the government. Why else would he get out of the cab in front of
the government building?

KillBill had to hustle for money. Raul's jobs weren't regular, and the pay
wasn't that good, since Raul kept most of the money for himself to get high
and drunk. When he was hungry, KillBill stole food from the vendors in the
streets. It wasn't difficult, but he had to be careful choosing his locations. You
couldn't hit the same stand in the same week. The people recognized you, and
all it took was one alert woman to make the crowd give chase.

Since he was all alone, getting food didn't take much time. Just as well. It
gave him more time to practice sword fighting. He really needed a samurai
sword. The stick with the knife was a joke. He'd never seen a sword for sale,
but there had to be one in a city as big as Beira. All he knew was that he
needed money to buy it. To get money, he stole wallets, and to do that, he
needed to be near hotels or office buildings. That's where men in suits could
be found. Like the one who'd just gotten out of the car.

One way to lift a mark's wallet was to get near him while he was busy
with something, like answering a phone or reading a newspaper. KillBill
would lick his thumb and index finger, slide them into the pocket, take the
wallet between his moistened digits, and ease it out. Not too slow, because he

couldn't stay close to the mark for too long. But also not too fast. It was no good to interrupt the mark's focus on whatever he was doing. This worked best in crowded places where KillBill would not stand out.

This mark, though, was alone. There was no crowd. He wasn't distracted. So KillBill chose the second approach. When people are touched in more than one spot at the same time, they usually pay attention to the touch they feel the most. KillBill counted on that. He stepped from behind the tree and loped toward the man. As he came closer, he held his phone to his ear, pretending to be calling someone and not paying attention. The man was annoyed when KillBill bumped into him. He said something and took his newspaper as if wanting to swat him. That was good, because by then, KillBill had already lifted the wallet from his pocket. He raised his hand with the phone to ward off the swat, using that move to turn his body to hide the wallet from the man's view while he stuck it into his pants. He told the man to mind his own business, which made him even more annoyed and kept him from paying attention to his pocket.

At that moment, KillBill's phone rang. In his surprise, he looked at the screen and forgot to run. The man must have noticed that something was off and patted his jacket. His hand shot out. He grabbed KillBill by the arm, shouting "Thief! Thief!" That brought KillBill to his senses. He stepped on the man's foot with all his might, twisted from his grip, and ran across the street. A car squealed to a stop, grazing KillBill's leg, but he made it, raced across the lot, and found shelter among the trees behind the old exhibition halls. The sleeve of his only shirt was still in the hands of the man. This street wasn't going to be safe for him for weeks to come.

He found a quiet spot and checked the wallet. It contained an ID card and driver's permit for one Lionel Sukuma, a bank card from Mauritius Bank and Trust in the same name, and business cards. None of this was important. The only thing that mattered was the money, and there was a lot of it—ten thousand *meticais*. He'd never had this much money. It was enough to buy a sword, if he only knew where to buy one.

He took the bank card and tossed the wallet behind a tree. Maybe someone would find it and bring it back to the man. He had no use for the bank card, but knew he could sell it to people who would put new information on the magnetic strip to steal more money.

Back on the street on the other side of the park, he remembered the phone call. He checked the display. It could only be the giant, Chico Chipende. Nobody else had his number. He pressed the redial button. He liked talking to the giant. The man was kind. A far better master than Raul, who didn't know about justice at all. So KillBill had no problem telling him all about Raul.

"*Como é, meu?*" KillBill said when the giant answered. Then the giant asked him if Raul had gotten any other jobs.

"No," KillBill said. "He's drunk all the time. Must have gotten a lot of money for the last job."

"Okay. That's good to know. I have a suspicion that someone in the government hired him the last time. So I want to test this suspicion. I'm going to ask my friends to protest again, *né*? If I'm right, that man in the government will call Raul. If Raul sends you out, call me right away so we can disappear before you all come. That way, I'll know that Sukuma is behind all this."

"Did you say Sukuma?"

"Yes."

"Lionel Sukuma?"

"Yes. *Por quê?*"

KillBill hesitated. The giant didn't know he stole wallets from people. He wasn't proud of it. A true warrior didn't steal. But then a true warrior also had a master who paid him.

"I found a wallet with that name in it."

"You did? Where?"

"In the trees behind the old exhibition halls, across from the government building."

"What's in the wallet?"

"I tossed it. No good if someone finds it on me."

"But you kept the money, *né*?"

"Er ... No."

"Come on, you can't afford not to."

The giant knew him well. Almost like a master. Did he also know he needed a new shirt, new pants, and shoes? KillBill felt the giant's eye on him even though the phone had no camera.

"Can you still get the wallet?" the giant said.

"Yes."

"Get it and wait for me. *Até já.*"

* * *

THE GIANT MET KILLBILL AT THE edge of the trees. He'd brought a sweet bun. KillBill wolfed it down. He'd been scared to buy food as long as he had the wallet. The police wouldn't bat an eye locking him up if they found it on him. The giant rifled through the wallet.

"Yup, that's the same Sukuma," he said, looking at the IDs. KillBill had put the bank card back into the wallet.

"Wait, what's this?" the giant said.

He pulled out a scrap of paper with a phone number.

"Have you seen this number before?"

KillBill shook his head. He'd never had a phone, so he had no reason to remember numbers.

"Well, there's only one way to find out." The giant pulled out his phone, dialed the number, and turned on the speaker phone. KillBill could hear it ring for a while. Eventually, a woman's voice said that the call had been forwarded to a voicemail system. After that, a familiar voice came from the speaker, "Yeah. Leave a message."

"That's Raul," KillBill said.

"Are you sure?"

"Super sure. I know that voice."

The giant smiled as if he'd found a great treasure.

"I knew it. Thanks. Your find was a stroke of luck."

The way he said "find" told KillBill that the giant didn't believe his story. But he didn't seem concerned about it.

"Listen, *meu*. Be careful spending this money. I don't know if there were any large bills, but don't let anyone see you have much cash on you. And stay in touch. Anything involving Raul is important."

The giant looked at the wallet in his hands.

"I think I'll just drop this in the letter box by the post office. Maybe it'll get back to Sukuma and he'll be a little less suspicious."

CHAPTER THIRTEEN

CLUBE CHINÊS

———◆———

CHIPENDE WAS A BIG MAN, TALLER and beefier than Vermeulen, and ten years younger. At least. With his bushy black beard, dark-brown skin, and strong arms, he would have been menacing if it weren't for his smile. The kind of smile that said, *here's a man who's content in his own skin*. No matter what obstacles the world might put in his way, they wouldn't faze him.

Vermeulen and Chipende walked down the leafy Avenida Eduardo Mondlane while Chipende filled him in on what had happened in the past couple of weeks—first the "No Trespassing" signs, then the fencing, and finally, after he organized the protests in Beira, the attacks by the gang. He also told him of his suspicion that Lionel Sukuma in the directorate of agriculture had something to do with everything.

"How do you know that?" Vermeulen said.

"At first it was just a gut feeling. He doesn't care for small farmers. We also found the phone number of the gang leader in his wallet."

"And how did you get to look in his wallet?"

"An informant found it."

The way Chipende said "found" left little doubt in Vermeulen's mind that the wallet had been stolen.

"So you can't really use that information," Vermeulen said.

"Well, not to take to the police, but it's useful to know his connections."

"Who's your informant?"

"A kid from the Grande Hotel. He's part of the gang, but he lives by some weird warrior code. Calls himself KillBill. Probably has seen too many martial arts movies. In any case, I grabbed him during the attack and talked some sense into him. So he keeps his eyes open and calls me when there's going to be trouble. The gang is led by someone called Raul. According to the kid, he spends his days getting high and drunk."

"And the kid lives in a hotel?"

"Oh, you don't know, do you? The Grande Hotel da Beira is one of the white elephants left by the Portuguese. A fancy resort for rich Europeans. Never made any money, and eventually just served as a reception and banquet hall. After the civil war started, the refugees took it over. You could call it a vertical slum."

"Where did he 'find' the wallet?"

"Probably stole it. Poor kid doesn't have a family, so he has to make a living. Beating up people isn't a regular job."

"A kid like that can be useful," Vermeulen said. "Are you having him follow this Sukuma?"

Chipende looked at him, surprised. "Damn, I hadn't thought of that."

"If he's connected to the sudden change in GA's activities, it would be good to know who he meets or talks to."

They crossed to the Rua Pero de Alenquer.

"Okay. I'll ask him. But we'd have to pay him something. He probably just hit the motherlode with Sukuma's wallet, but it'd be the fair thing to do."

"I can help with that. How much would he need?"

"A hundred *meticais* a day would do it. That'd be a couple of dollars."

Vermeulen got two bills from his wallet and handed them to Chipende. "Here, that should get him started. What do you know about GreenAnt Investments? They're partnering with GA, and they're the ones who put up the signs, right?"

"Yes. I don't know anything about them except that Sukuma had their business card in his wallet. No name, but a mobile-phone number, an email address, and a strange logo of a green ant."

Chipende took the card from his pocket and handed it to him.

"I saw a twin-engine plane at the airport with the logo. Do they have an office here? A physical address?" Vermeulen asked.

"I don't know. I've never heard of them before."

"Have you tried calling that number?"

Chipende shook his head. "Not yet. It didn't strike me as a number one should call unprepared."

Vermeulen stopped and added the number and email address to his phone.

"Does Global Alternatives have an office here?"

"Yes. It's in the MCel Building. Just across the street from the provincial government where Sukuma works."

* * *

THE MCEL BUILDING WAS DEFINITELY NEW. No colonial charm here. Just a smooth façade of steel and glass. Vermeulen and Chipende stood across the street, right in front of the Embaixador Hotel—by the looks of it the most expensive hotel in Beira.

Vermeulen thought about the GreenAnt business card from Sukuma's wallet. No name, no address. Not your ordinary business card. Meant to keep visitors at arm's length. No unannounced visits, no surprises. A caller could be vetted before a meeting. Chipende was right. You shouldn't call that number without a plan.

"So, you're sure Sukuma is connected to the attacks," Vermeulen said.

Chipende nodded.

"And he might be connected to GreenAnt because of the business card?"

More nodding.

"But we don't know if Sukuma is connected to Global Alternatives, and we don't know how GreenAnt connects to Global Alternatives, except that they are partners."

"Right," Chipende said. "All we ever see is Global Alternatives. Nobody has seen anyone from GreenAnt. The first time I heard the name was when I saw the photo of the '"No Trespassing"' sign."

"How big is the Global Alternatives office here?"

"Hmm. I've never seen the whole thing, but it isn't large. I don't think there are more than five people working there. I've only ever dealt with two of them."

"Okay, here's the plan," Vermeulen said. "I'm going to pay them a visit. Nothing suspicious about that. It's my job to audit GA. I'm just going to introduce myself and make an appointment. While I'm in there, call the number on the GreenAnt card. Let it ring until someone answers and hang up. Don't say a thing."

"But that's a mobile phone number. Whoever answers will have my number even if I don't say anything."

The plan in Vermeulen's mind was only a vague outline. He didn't know if Chipende's number on someone's phone would pose a problem later.

"Well, ask for someone, then say it was a wrong number."

"Or we could buy a cheap phone and toss it afterwards. I'm catching enough trouble for my activism already. I don't need my number to end up on some list."

Chipende directed him around the hotel, past a nicely restored two-story building with a filigreed balcony along both floors and a red roof.

"That's the Clube Chinês. Back from the days when Chinese workers finished their contracts and stayed on," Chipende said.

Across from the Chinese Club was a Chinese restaurant, and next to that a shop that carried cheap trinkets, woks, and other Chinese wares. Chipende negotiated for a while and got a phone for around five dollars. *Probably money well spent,* Vermeulen thought as he paid the shopkeeper, who wasn't Chinese.

Back in front of the MCel building, Vermeulen told Chipende to wait about twenty minutes before calling the number on the GreenAnt card. He'd be past the receptionist by then and talking to whomever was in charge.

* * *

THE GROUND FLOOR OF THE MCEL building looked airy, bright, and open. But it was a clever illusion. Nobody could get to the elevators without first checking in. The placement of the planters and seating arrangements funneled all visitors straight to the reception, and from there to the security desk. No surprise visits here.

Vermeulen checked in at the reception, where the young woman in a white blouse and black slacks examined his credentials with a pleasant efficiency. She picked up a receiver and announced his visit. The person at the other end obviously didn't object, because he was told to go to the security check. A team of security men who looked like an African version of Laurel and Hardy waved wands past every surface of his body. Despite the squeals emitted by the wands, they let him pass. He wondered what sound a gun in his pocket would have produced.

Next to the elevators was a directory. MCel, one of Mozambique's mobile phone providers, occupied the bulk of the building. Global Alternatives had a suite on the third floor. There was an assortment of other names with no indication of the nature of the businesses they were conducting. GreenAnt was not in the directory.

Vermeulen rode to the third floor and walked along a light-yellow hallway to a double-glass door that sported the Global Alternatives name and logo. He checked his watch. Twelve minutes since he left Chipende. The ground floor security theater had taken too much time.

A smiling receptionist greeted him. The lilt of her Portuguese accent was faint. Before Vermeulen could explain the reason for his visit, the receptionist said, "Someone will be right with you." Her tone told him that they were expecting him. Which was odd. He hadn't told anyone that he was going to Beira. Only Simango knew, because he'd called her earlier. Either he was imagining things, or Global Alternatives was keeping tabs on him.

The big man who greeted him with a broad grin and a Texas drawl looked positively sloppy compared to the receptionist. Frayed jeans, a washed-out blue T-shirt, and worn leather flip-flops. His hair wasn't so much long as unkempt.

"Hi, Mr. Vermeulen. I'm Billy Ray, the boss of GA in these here parts.

Welcome to our humble offices. How nice you made time in your busy schedule to visit us. I'm sure Isabel has filled you in on the numbers down in Maputo."

"Hello, Mr. Ray ...."

The man looked behind him, then back at Vermeulen.

"Oh, I get it," he said. "There's no Mister Ray. Billy Ray is my first name. We don't do last names around here. Can I call you Val?"

"I'd prefer Valentin."

"Sure thing. What can I do you for, Valentin?"

"Well, I've audited the books in Maputo, but you know, spreadsheets don't tell the whole story. I'd rather like to see what's been done with the UN money."

"Sure thing. I can show you around. Give you some of the particulars." He checked his watch. "Too late for today though. It's a longish drive. Better if we get an early start tomorrow."

"Maybe you can introduce me to your staff?"

"My pleasure. You've already met Graça. She's the backbone of this operation, aren't you, dear? Two of the others are out doing their jobs. Which leaves me and Antonio. Let me check and see where he's at."

Billy Ray didn't ask Vermeulen to follow him, so he stood in the no-man's land between the reception desk and the rest of the office. He craned his neck trying to see the rest of the office, but all he saw were a hallway and four open doors. Vermeulen checked his watch. It was twenty-four minutes since he'd left Chipende. He hadn't heard a phone ring anywhere since entering the office. The owner of the phone wasn't here.

Billy Ray came back with a man a head shorter. The man had olive skin and black hair.

"Antonio here came over from our Brazilian office. We figured, same colonizer ... maybe he can compare notes with the locals. Turns out they barely speak the same language. But he's learning. Say hello to Valentin, big cheese from the UN, here to make sure we don't waste his money."

Vermeulen and Antonio shook hands. The man wore what could be called office casual. Chinos, beige shirt, and a tie. Billy Ray's sloppiness either didn't appeal to the others, or it was his prerogative. Antonio examined Vermeulen with dark eyes. The man's gaze seemed to go right though him.

"Don't worry," Billy Ray said. "He checks out everybody like that. Makes you feel naked, don't it?"

Vermeulen shrugged and said, "No, not really. What do you do at Global Alternatives, Antonio?"

"I do operations management for our clients. I help them streamline processes, decision-making structures, and program administration. Some

NGOs here have barely scratched the surface of what's possible today. I train them to get up to speed with the latest technology available."

"For example?"

"Meetings. A waste of time and resources, especially if people aren't in the same location. Today, tech has made meetings obsolete. We're using what's essentially a private social network. Just like the big ones, except for a single organization. All users post updates on their work, communicate via online video chat. Everything is based on mobile devices. Makes everyone more agile."

"I can see that," Vermeulen said. "But face-to-face meetings allow people to get to know each other, get a feel for how the other person operates."

"I'm sure that's how the UN does it. But the rest of the world doesn't have time for such quaint practices. We'd rather spend money on what helps people than on travel."

"And on technology, I assume. Who makes and sells the software and devices?"

"They're a small startup. You wouldn't know it. They just landed a new round of venture capital. Vincent put a lot of money into them."

"Is that Vincent Portallis?" Vermeulen said.

Billy Ray looked at Antonio, then back at Vermeulen. "Yes, the very same."

"So his foundation buys products that one of his companies makes? Isn't that a conflict of interest?"

"Not at all," Billy Ray said. "He donates to the foundation, and we make the decision to purchase based on the merits of the product. His products are simply the best for our purposes. Besides, it's not his company. His hedge fund is one of the company's angel investors. Once the company goes public, he cashes in and moves on to the next thing."

Vermeulen scratched his chin.

"So it's not really his money, just the money his fund manages?"

Billy Ray nodded eagerly, probably thinking he'd gotten away from the conflict-of-interest charge.

"And can you describe his relationship with GreenAnt Investments the same way?" Vermeulen said.

Before Billy Ray could answer, a phone rang. Both Billy Ray and Antonio patted their pockets. It was Antonio's phone that had interrupted their conversation.

"Excuse me," he said and turned away to take the call. He remained silent for a moment, then looked at his phone, shook his head, and put the phone away again. "Wrong number. You were saying?"

"GreenAnt Investments? What's Portallis's connection to them?" The ringing phone had already provided the answer he was looking for, but Vermeulen was curious how they'd answer this question.

"Not really sure," Billy Ray said. "The man's got a lot of irons in the fire. It's all about leveraging resources."

"Like five million dollars from the UN?"

"Exactly."

CHAPTER FOURTEEN

PONTE DO PÚNGUÈ

———◆———

AFTER LEAVING GLOBAL ALTERNATIVES' OFFICE THE afternoon before, Vermeulen had waited for Chipende, wanting to know if he had called the number on the GreenAnt card. But Chipende wasn't waiting for him and didn't answer his phone. Vermeulen went back to Tessa's hotel. When he told her about the trip scheduled for the next day, she'd asked to come along. "It'll save me the trouble of finding my own driver."

Vermeulen called and asked Billy Ray, who saw no problems. "The more the merrier," he said.

That's how Tessa and Vermeulen ended up on the rear bench of an older model Land Rover with Billy Ray as the chauffeur and Antonio in the passenger seat. Vermeulen still didn't know either of their hosts' last names. It seemed odd to ask for them, but equally odd to have skipped them during the introduction.

The first twenty miles were slow going. The N6 was both highway and main street as far as Inhamizua. There were long trucks headed for Zimbabwe, *chapas* darting in and out of traffic, hawkers selling their wares at the roadside, and a cluster of kids surrounding the car at every stop. The road was in surprisingly good shape. Tessa explained that it was the shortest link to the ocean for landlocked Zimbabwe and therefore well maintained. For a while it ran parallel to the railroad tracks, which served the same purpose.

After Dondo, the vista opened up to a vast plain of orange earth, green vegetation, and scattered trees in the distance. The sky was blue for a change, and the trip could have been a pleasure outing. But Vermeulen knew it wasn't. This was a show-and-tell tour, meant to keep him occupied, direct his attention away from what was really going on. As if he knew what that was. His hope was that Tessa would find time to interview farmers while he diverted the attention of Billy Ray and Antonio.

"Eons of flooding by the Rio Púnguè have made this a very fertile area," Billy Ray said over the tire noise. "Great potential, little action. There are sugar cane plantations up the road, but the rest? Let's just say a lot more is possible. And we're here to unlock those possibilities."

They drove through Mafambisse, which looked like a prosperous town. A new church; several modern gas stations; a two-story school, recently painted; solid houses, some half concealed by lush gardens; and lots of people on the road. After the town, the landscape turned rural again. To the left of the road were large fields intersected by dirt roads. Orange tractors, big as elephants, pulled alien-looking implements. There was nothing but bush land on the right. At regular intervals, they passed pedestrians going in both directions. With no houses or settlements in sight, their origins and destinations remained a mystery.

The road ran past an oxbow of the river, and Vermeulen wondered if that was the same oxbow he'd seen on the maps at Nossa Terra and LaFleur's presentation. From his window, he could see another oxbow in the distance. The land bounded by the river looked fertile, but there were no crops planted. A couple of tall birds with black and white feathers and strange red and black bills waded through the river shallows.

Billy Ray slowed down. "Saddle-billed storks. Biggest birds I've ever seen," he said. "Up ahead is the infamous Ponte do Púnguè. During the war, the rebels blew it up regularly. Zimbabwe stationed some of its best troops here to protect their access to the ocean."

"I heard that RENAMO has taken up arms again," Tessa said. "Have you seen any evidence?"

"Yes, there have been incidents. The RENAMO leadership can't accept the fact that they'll never get a majority of the popular vote and will always be the minority party. Which is frustrating to them, so they are returning to what they know best. The government gives them plenty of reasons. When they're not heavy-handed, they're corrupt."

They reached the bridge and crossed the Punguè. Vermeulen could see the strategic value of the bridge. The river was wide and deep, with marshy banks.

"How does Global Alternatives deal with this?" Tessa said.

"We try to stay away from it. It's their problem, not ours."

"But you have to get government permits for your work. Don't the rebels see you as working with the government?"

"Well, we have contact with both sides and keep communication channels open. So far, we've had no problems."

About a mile after the bridge, Billy Ray slowed down and turned right. There was no road, not even a dirt road. Just two ruts. Billy Ray looked at Vermeulen in the rearview mirror and said, "You can't beat an old Land Rover."

* * *

THE RIO PÚNGUÈ WAS IN NO hurry to reach the ocean. It had carved bow after bow into the flat valley, as if trying to delay the inevitable. Languid wavelets lapped against the banks. Another flock of wading birds picked through the silt. They didn't have the red and black bills. Perfect farmland. Vermeulen could see that. They stopped near an oxbow that enclosed about a square mile of good land. They had driven past two similar-sized tracts. They reminded him again of the map in Nossa Terra's office.

"Is this the project you subcontracted to Nossa Terra?" Vermeulen said, after they'd gotten out of the car.

"Well, that was the plan," Billy Ray said.

"It isn't anymore?"

"I'll let Antonio explain."

Antonio had walked behind a row of green shrubs. They followed him. Next to the greenery, a metal post had been pounded into the soil. Two strands of barbed wire connected it to the next post and the next as far as Vermeulen could see. All the land enclosed by the river had been fenced off.

"Antonio, tell Valentin here why the project with Nossa Terra fell through."

Antonio shrugged. "Where to start? For one, they didn't have the capacity to deliver. Their projects around Maputo were much smaller. They promised us their model would scale up, but apparently it didn't. So they didn't really have anything to show for the money they spent."

"How much did they spend?" Vermeulen said.

"I don't do the books, but Paolo told me it has been a lot. Their local rep, Chico, is more of a rabble-rouser than a development worker. He promised people pie in the sky but didn't really get anything done. We took over. We had to. This land is too valuable to sit idle."

"Are the local farmers still going to farm this land?" Tessa said.

"Local farmers? We're talking large-scale farming here. Of course, some of them'll be employed, but no, this isn't going to be the usual mishmash of cassava, corn, and beans."

"What will you grow here?"

"At first, jatropha."

Vermeulen did a double take. He didn't know what jatropha was. Tessa obviously did.

"What an odd choice," she said. "Why use such good land to grow biofuel rather than food? I thought the appeal of jatropha was that it would grow in marginal soils."

"Yes, jatropha grows almost anywhere, but if you want to get profitable yields, you'd better treat it like any other plant and give it good soil, plenty of water, and fertilizer."

"So they will grow biofuel?" Vermeulen said. "That doesn't sound like the plans Nossa Terra had. What happens to the people who were farming here before?"

"This land was empty." There was an odd expression on Antonio's face. More annoyance than anything else. "There were no titles, no claims. We checked with all the relevant offices and got the necessary land use certificates. There won't be any displacement here."

"That's not what I've heard." Tessa said.

"Then you must have heard wrong."

"There's no need to argue," Billy Ray said. "Land investments can be touchy topics, and I know that there have been some bad apples. But not this. Global Alternatives would never participate in a project that would displace farmers. Portallis himself wouldn't stand for it. Neither would Isabel. When we get back to Beira, I'll show you all the paperwork."

"What about your partner in this project, GreenAnt Investments?" Vermeulen said. "The UN has no record of GreenAnt Investments doing anything in Mozambique. Nothing. This is a large project. I find it rather strange to partner with an unknown company without a track record."

"GreenAnt is new. We all have to start somewhere," Billy Ray said. "The aid field is shifting fast. The old organizational structures have failed. We are pioneering a new approach. Public-private partnerships. Investment funds, foundations, and the UN. It's a new paradigm."

"But who is behind GreenAnt Investments?" Vermeulen asked. "Your partner is a rather obscure enterprise." He looked at Antonio. "Are you working for GreenAnt?"

Antonio shook his head.

* * *

THEY STOPPED AT A BAR/RESTAURANT/GAS STATION across from the train depot in Tica. Unlike the depot, a well-kept structure with arched supports at each of its four corners, the restaurant looked shabby. Billy Ray pulled in to fill up.

Tica was not as neat as Mafambisse and much more spread out. The gas station and the depot seemed to be the center of town. A long-haul truck had pulled off the road and a gang of kids were trying to sell the driver drinks and food.

"Let's go inside. There's a toilet, and we can get something to eat. Afterwards, we'll go and look at another project."

The restaurant could have been any truck stop anywhere in the world. Two shelves next to the cash register held more varieties of potato chips than Vermeulen knew existed. There were peanuts, too. A rack with yellowed road maps and cheap sunglasses. A rattling cooler displayed *refrescos* and domestic beer.

The rest of the counter was part of the restaurant. Against the back wall stood a large griddle, operated by a woman who was wider than tall. Anyone expecting an array of Mozambican cuisine would be disappointed. A picture menu offered hamburgers, chicken burgers, fried chicken, and toasted cheese sandwiches.

Billy Ray and Antonio ordered hamburgers. Tessa went to the toilet, and Vermeulen couldn't make up his mind. What to eat when all choices are poor? He settled on a toasted cheese sandwich with tomatoes and went to use the facilities himself.

The restaurant had seen better days. The tables were wobbly and the chairs creaky. About half of the tables were taken, and the patrons gave the newcomers a quick glance before going back to their meals. Vermeulen sat down with the rest and ate his sandwich. Tessa munched on a bag of peanuts and drank a Coke. Vermeulen was tempted by the beer but decided against it. On a warm day like this, he'd just fall asleep in the car.

"What other project do you want to show us?" Vermeulen said between bites.

"It's back the way we came, on the other side of the bridge," Billy Ray said.

"I'd like to speak with a few of the farmers here," Tessa said.

Billy Ray wiped some grease from his mouth. "I figured you would. It'll take some time to set up, though. I didn't know you were coming until last night. No time. But I'm sure we can arrange something for later. How long are you in Beira?"

"I have a week."

"Hmm. That's tight. You journalists need to spend time on the ground. Not just swoop in and out."

"Believe me, I'd love to spend a month here, but nobody would pay my bills. So a week it is. I'd appreciate any help you can give me."

"Sure. We'll see what we can set up. Maybe there'll be someone at the next stop."

Billy Ray popped the last bite of hamburger into his mouth and pursed his lips.

"Pretty damn close to the worst burger I ever ate," he said. "And I've had some doozies."

They finished their meals, got back into the car, and drove back the way they'd come. As they reached the bridge, Vermeulen's phone rang. It was Chipende.

"Sorry for leaving you yesterday. I got an urgent call from KillBill and had to meet with him. Did someone in the office answer a wrong number call?"

"You didn't call when we agreed."

"No, that's when the kid called. It took a while to sort that out. I think I was about fifteen minutes late. A man answered. Did you see who?"

"Yes, I did. I'll tell you later. What was the emergency?" Vermeulen said.

"Raul called the gang together for another job. This time it's out of town. They drove off in their blue vans. I have no idea where they went. The kid can't call me because they aren't supposed to know he's got a phone."

"And you don't know what the job is?"

"No, but it can't be good. Probably roughing someone up. I'm on my way to Tica to warn the farmers. I have a bad feeling."

"We've just left Tica," Vermeulen said.

"You did? What were you doing there?"

Vermeulen turned and said in a low voice, "Getting a tour of the new project."

"Global Alternatives?"

"Yes."

There was a long pause.

The Land Rover reached the bridge. From the corner of his eye, Vermeulen saw the glint of a vehicle through the bushes lining the approach to the bridge. He couldn't tell its shape or color. The Land Rover started across the bridge. Vermeulen looked ahead through the windshield. Something moved across the road at the other end of the bridge. As they got closer, Billy Ray slowed more. A vehicle blocked the bridge. Vermeulen looked back. Behind them another vehicle rolled across the road.

"I found your blue vans," Vermeulen said to Chipende and ended the call.

Chapter Fifteen

Gunny Sack

———◆———

VERMEULEN KNEW ALL ABOUT AMBUSHES. THEY were like litmus tests, confirming that he was on the right track. A dangerous confirmation, to be sure, especially when there was no way out. Like this bridge. Barely wide enough for a K-turn, and blocked at each end by a blue van.

"Don't worry, it's just an extortion scheme," Billy Ray said. "Some of the local *bandidos* put up a barricade, you give them a little cash, and they let you go."

He couldn't be more wrong.

"This is different. They came from Beira and they aren't looking for cash," Vermeulen said. "They are here for me."

Antonio turned around, staring at him with his black eyes.

"How do you know that?" he said.

"I have my sources."

Billy Ray let the Land Rover roll forward until they reached the van at the far end of the bridge. The youths mobbed the Land Rover. Most of them carried clubs and knives, but several of the older ones pointed handguns at the car.

Billy Ray lowered the window. "How much do you want?" he said with a big smile.

Vermeulen checked out the gang. They wore ragged clothes. Their clubs were homemade, their knives old. The handguns were cheap Chinese models, as likely to injure the shooter as the target. A man in his late twenties pushed through the gang toward the Land Rover. He pointed a pistol at Billy Ray. It had to be Raul. Chipende's description was spot on. The man was high, his pupils dilated, the whites of his eyes bloodshot. Billy Ray stayed calm. He looked at the muzzle of the pistol as it were a display model in a shop.

"*Dez mil meticais*," Raul said, slurring the words.

"Ten thousand?" Billy Ray said. "Too much. *Cinco mil.*"

"*Dez mil. E eles.*" Raul pointed at Vermeulen and Tessa.

That didn't come as a surprise to Vermeulen. But it didn't make it any less dangerous. Especially being caught in a car, suspended between fight and flight. His adrenals pumped epinephrine into his system. He gripped the door handle. His knuckles shone white through the skin.

Keeping the door shut wasn't an option. One of the kids shattered the window with a tire iron. An avalanche of glass glittering like fake gems showered Vermeulen. Fight it was. The kid slashed at Vermeulen's arm. Vermeulen was ready. His hand shot out, grabbed the iron, and used it to smash the kid's arm against the door frame. The kid howled. The tool fell into Vermeulen's lap. He grabbed it. Another kid yanked the door open. Vermeulen slashed at the hands trying to pull him out of the car. With his other hand, he released the seatbelt.

A club connected with his arm, sending hot pain up his shoulder. He turned toward the door. A solid kick propelled the kid with the club backward. The next one came. He dispatched it with another kick. The tire iron connected with someone's arm. Another scream. The door frame limited the range of the tire iron. The kids regrouped, trying to hit him with their clubs. He didn't have enough legs to kick them all away. A pipe hit his thigh. The epinephrine in his blood couldn't mask the pain. He screamed, dropped the tire iron. The kids took it as encouragement and pressed in on him. They dragged him by his legs out of the car. He held on to the door frame, his muscles straining. That left his body unprotected. A blow to his gut was all it took. He let go of the car. Next thing he knew, he was on the ground, curled into a ball, hoping to ward off the inevitable blows. They didn't come because a shot rang out. The gang froze. Antonio stood next to the Land Rover pointing a pistol at the closest thug.

"*Pará-lo agora!*" he said. His tone left no doubt of his intent.

It didn't end the ambush. It only made it worse. Raul, on the other side of the car, opened Tessa's door and held his gun to her head.

Standoff.

Vermeulen scrambled to his feet again. Except for a few bruises, he was okay. Looking at the vacant eyes of Raul, he knew that pointing a gun at one of his gang members was a meaningless threat. Raul would sacrifice any of them.

"Put your gun away," he said to Antonio. "He's high as a kite. He's going to shoot Tessa. We need to de-escalate. Let's find out why they want me."

Antonio wasn't having any of it. In a world of thugs, the gun was the final arbiter. He grabbed the kid and held the gun to his temple. Raul yanked Tessa from the car and reciprocated.

Vermeulen went around the rear of the Land Rover. The kids let him pass. "What do you want, Raul?"

Although Raul didn't understand the question, he did hear his name and that made him hesitate. He stared at Vermeulen. Tessa, drawing on yet another of her linguistic talents, translated the question.

"Money," Raul said. "From UN."

A kidnapping for ransom. Way more lucrative than a highway toll.

"The UN isn't going to pay," Vermeulen said. "They have a standing policy not to negotiate with kidnappers."

Tessa translated again.

Raul only grinned.

"Just imagine if they did?" Vermeulen said. "There's UN personnel around the world. If they paid once, they'd be paying forever. If you let us go, we won't tell the police."

Raul didn't care.

"Listen. I'll come with you. Just let her go. She isn't with the UN. There's nobody who'd pay for her."

Tessa translated again. Raul just shook his head. He shouted something, and two youth came and tied Vermeulen's hands. When they moved on to Tessa, one of them grabbed her breast. She slapped him so hard his head flew sideways. He raised his fists, eyes ablaze, but Raul shouted again, and the hoodlum shrunk back. The others tied her hands and led the two of them to the van. Inside, Vermeulen looked back. Raul must not have insisted on the ten thousand *meticais*. At least Vermeulen didn't see any money change hands. If anything, Raul seemed at ease around Billy Ray and Antonio, like he was going through the motions. Then a foul-smelling gunny sack was pulled over his head and the world disappeared.

* * *

THE DRIVE TOOK FOREVER. SITTING WITH his hands tied behind him was uncomfortable. If he hadn't been seated between Tessa on one side and a gang member on the other, he would have tumbled left and right, because the van was driven erratically. Vermeulen hoped that Raul was not behind the wheel. Getting into a car crash while tied up and blindfolded would be really bad. He twisted just enough to reached Tessa's hands. She noticed and leaned her head against his.

"Thanks for trying to keep me out of it," she said. "Are they really only after ransom?"

"I hope so. But I don't know."

"What if they're just trying to get rid of us?"

"I doubt it," he said, turning his head so his lips were separated from her ear only by the coarse fabric of the sack. "Too many witnesses. You hire professionals for an assassination. Like the men who came after me in Maputo."

"What if they don't get the money?"

"We won't be around to find out."

His fingers felt for the rope that bound her wrists. She must have sensed his intent and shifted so he could reach her hands better. If the drive lasted long enough, they might get each other's ropes untied.

It wasn't a complicated knot. But it was pulled tight and having only one hand to manipulate the loops made loosening it impossible. He kept tugging, switching hands when one cramped up. It wasn't good enough. During all that time, he didn't pay attention to the driving. They'd been on the road for quite some time, and the traffic must have gotten denser, because the van's progress was much slower now. Vermeulen visualized the map Simango had shown him. There were cities to the west of the bridge, but they hadn't crossed the bridge. That meant they had gone back to Beira. Which was good news. Chipende knew the gang and knew that they'd been ambushed.

At last, the van bumped over a potholed street, barely faster than walking speed. It came to a stop. The doors opened. Vermeulen could hear ocean surf not far away. They were back in Beira. He was dragged from the van and marched along a rough path. Progress was slow, and since their captors didn't speak English, he got no warnings about holes or obstacles. He lost his balance when he stumbled over something. His captors were smaller than he, and barely managed to keep him upright. He heard Tessa complain behind him.

They entered a building. Their steps echoed like in a great hall. The floor was hard and crunchy with grit. With the sea breeze gone, he smelled smoke and rotting garbage. He stubbed his toes against an object that turned out to be the riser of a stair step. The staircase was wide enough for him and the two hoodlums who guided him. He inched upward in a wide curve, carefully testing each step. *Almost like a grand staircase in a mansion*, he thought. It brought to mind Chipende's description of the Grande Hotel Da Beira, the vertical slum. Of course. They'd been taken to the gang's headquarters.

* * *

WHEN THE GUNNY SACK WAS FINALLY taken off his head, Vermeulen found himself in what appeared to be an empty VIP suite. Not just devoid of furnishings, the room had been stripped of everything, leaving only the oppressive gray of the concrete walls, floor, and ceiling. There was a gaping rectangular hole where a picture window must have been a long time ago. Through it, Vermeulen could see a beach in the distance. There were no doors, either. Just holes. A piece of cloth covered the one at the hallway. The other opening led to an alcove that used to be the bathroom. A filthy blanket, a tin pot with a hole in it, and plastic bags full of trash lay in the room—the jetsam of previous occupants. Except for the beach view, the room had all the ambiance of a dungeon, albeit a roomy one.

Tessa stood next to him, eyes wide. She said nothing.

Raul leaned against the wall by the door while three of his minions with clubs and knives stood guard.

Raul said something.

"He wants us to sit down," Tessa said.

"I guess we better do that," Vermeulen said.

Nothing is more ignominious than trying to get down on the floor with your hands tied behind your back. They lowered themselves to their knees and then plopped on their butts. Two of the youths came forward and tied their ankles. They patted Vermeulen's pockets, took his wallet and phone, and gave them to Raul. He left. The youth remained as guards.

"Now we wait," Vermeulen said.

"For what?"

"For our rescue."

"And how's that going to happen?"

"Chipende knows we were ambushed. I was on the phone with him when the bridge was blocked. He knows this gang and he has an informant here. It's only a question of time before they get us out."

"From your lips to God's ears."

Vermeulen looked at her. "What? You don't believe me?"

"Of course I do. But I'm worried. These kids are like a box of grenades with the pins pulled. They aren't the kind of people you can argue with. I doubt they even care about the ransom. Have they asked you for a contact at the UN?"

"No."

"See? The ransom is just a pretext."

"They have my phone and wallet."

"But they haven't asked you to unlock it."

She had a point.

"What about your bag?" he said.

She shrugged. "No idea. It might still be in the car. I didn't see them take it."

"Was it just me or did you think Billy Ray and Antonio were rather calm about the whole thing?"

"I don't know, " she said. "Antonio did fire the gun and threatened one of the hoodlums."

"Yes, but … I don't know. Maybe he just wanted to stop the struggle and get the thing over with."

"So, what are you saying? They were in on the ambush?"

"Yes. Remember, someone tried to kill me in Maputo. I got away. Maybe this is the follow-up."

"Then we better get out of here fast. There won't be any negotiations."

CHAPTER SIXTEEN

GARBAGE CHUTE

———◆———

ONE OF THE DISPOSABLE PHONES IN Gould's desk drawer rang. He opened the drawer and flipped it open. No name, just a number.

"Yes," he said.

"The Beira operation was successful. The targets have been acquired." It was Antonio in Beira.

"Targets? There was only one."

"A woman journalist joined the trip at the last minute. She knew the target. Our guy and his crew took both."

Gould didn't answer. He should have known. No plan survives the first encounter with the enemy. A woman. And a journalist. That could be trouble.

"Any chance of tracing the action back to us?" he said.

"No. The ambush was convincing. Our guy made it look like it was a kidnapping for ransom. Happens often enough to be a good cover."

"Who is the woman?"

"A freelancer. Sticking her nose into land deals. I'd say trouble."

"Well connected?"

"She's a freelancer. I don't think so."

"Where are they now?"

"They're at the hotel. It's only a short-term solution," Antonio said. "Frankly, our guy isn't stable. We need to move the targets soon."

"Already ahead of you. Rent a skiff large enough for four with a decent outboard engine and plenty of petrol. Leave it in the mangroves where Avenida Antonio Enes meets the seawall. Go back after twenty-four hours and take the boat back to where you rented it."

An hour later, a different phone in the same drawer rang. Gould answered.

"We've landed and picked up the equipment. Where is the target?" The man had a South African accent said. Gould knew that voice.

"At the hotel."

"Exact location?"

"Not provided."

"That'll increase complications."

"Just do what needs to be done. Nobody will remember afterwards."

"Post-extraction strategy?"

"Swimming accident. There'll be a skiff in the mangroves off Antonio Enes. Return it there when you're done."

* * *

AVÓ ANTIA'S FACE LOOKED LIKE THE Púnguè delta at low tide. She was older than the hotel, older than anyone or anything KillBill knew. She had no family anyone was aware of. So KillBill didn't really know if she was a grandmother, but everyone called her *Avó* anyway. Her stand was just a big cardboard box with three oranges, five tomatoes, and a bunch of greens. Nobody ever bought anything from Avó Antia, because the oranges and tomatoes were always shriveled and the greens limp. That didn't keep her from sitting at the bottom of the stairs in the eternal shadows of the Hotel Da Beira.

"Did you see a white man go up the stairs?" he said.

"Buy an orange," she said, handing him one. "Sweeter than honey."

He gave her a coin but didn't take the orange.

"Many go up, but no white man," she said.

"A man with a sack over his head, then?"

A smile crossed her face, realigning the channels of her face. She held out the orange again. "Buy an orange."

KillBill gave her another coin.

She nodded. "Two people with sacks over their heads came by."

"Two? Obrigada."

He ran up the stairs. How Raul had found an empty room was a mystery to him. The hotel was always packed with people. But Raul had his ways. People were afraid of him.

Raul's prison was hard to miss. A couple of guys from the gang lounged outside a cloth that covered the doorway.

"Raul wants you. New orders or something," he said. "I'll stay here till you come back."

"He told us not to move," the taller of the two said.

KillBill shrugged. "And now he sent for you. You know how he is when he's high. Better do what he wants."

The two shrugged and got up. KillBill sat down in their spot and watched them go downstairs. The moment they disappeared, he pulled the cloth aside and went into the room. The two captives sat propped against the wall, their legs stretched out. KillBill took his knife from his belt to cut the ropes. The man looked at him and shook his head. He pointed to an alcove with his chin.

Another guard in the room. KillBill hadn't thought of that. He went to the alcove and heard the splashing of someone urinating. He stepped into the alcove. The kid was younger than KillBill, not one of the tough ones.

"Zip it up," KillBill said. "Raul wants you. Hurry up. He's angry and won't wait all day."

The kid did as told and ran out of the room.

KillBill cut the ropes tying the man and the woman and motioned them to follow. The fastest way out was the way he'd come. Except that would lead them right past Raul's room. His bodyguards were always there. So were the hangers-on and wannabes. Waiting for him to issue an order that gave them a chance to prove their value and move up in the ranks.

He'd have to take the foreigners the long way around. The man and woman followed him without asking questions, which was good. The man didn't look like a warrior. He'd be no use in a confrontation. The woman had a fire in her eyes that told him she'd be able to handle herself.

They hurried along the corridor to the other grand staircase. Someone shouted behind them. He looked back. The guards he'd sent away and Raul came running after them. He hustled the foreigners down the stairs. Halfway down, he veered left through a doorway that led to the annex. This part of the hotel had smaller rooms, but more of them and therefore more people. Smoke from cooking fires made the air hard to breathe. The approaching evening only added to the claustrophobic feeling. Getting ahead was difficult. Fortunately, Raul and his goons faced the same problem.

KillBill had explored every inch of the hotel. He knew there was a narrow staircase in the middle of the annex. It was used by the employees who had to be invisible back when white people stayed at the hotel. Today it was more like a garbage chute. He pulled the foreigners through the opening. The stink of trash was overwhelming. Raul would expect them to go downstairs. So he hurried upstairs, feeling his way up in the gloom, dodging the garbage bags on the steps, and trusting that the foreigners understood his plan. After two turns of the staircase, he stopped, pressed himself against the wall, and told the foreigners to be quiet. They followed his example.

A moment later, KillBill heard Raul swearing at the guards. Sure enough, they ran downstairs. KillBill waited until he could no longer hear them. Then he led the foreigners upstairs.

They reached the roof of the annex, a flat expanse the size of three tennis courts. The sun was getting closer to the horizon. The salty breeze from the sea cleared away the rotting smell. KillBill ran across the concrete until he reached a bridge that brought them to the roof of the hotel proper. At each end stood a gazebo-like structure where the grand staircases ended. He headed for the one that didn't lead past Raul's room.

As they passed the spot where KillBill practiced sword fighting, Maria popped up from behind a corner.

"Hi, KillBill. Whatcha doing? Who are they?"

"They are my captives."

"If they're your captives, how come they are not tied up?"

"Because we are in a hurry. I'm looking for Raul. D'you know where he is?"

"Want me to look?"

"Sure. Run downstairs, look around, and come back and tell me if he's there."

She hopscotched to the south gazebo, just as KillBill had hoped. If she found Raul, she'd bring him to the roof, while KillBill took the foreigners down the other staircase. When Maria had disappeared, he headed for the other gazebo.

Sometimes, visitors came to check out the place, to look at the poor people living in the trashy former hotel. They all had sad and concerned expressions. They all had suggestions how to make things better. But KillBill knew that, deep down, they all thought the poor people had made a mess of the place. That it'd be better if the white people came back to lie by the pool and have KillBill bring them drinks with ice.

"Just act like you are reporters or from an NGO," he said.

The woman translated for them. They walked down the stairs as if KillBill was giving them a tour. They looked around, nodded, looked concerned.

* * *

THEY'D MADE IT TO THE GROUND floor when Vermeulen saw Raul cross the former reception area. He pulled Tessa behind the stone banister. The kid hadn't noticed and walked on. Raul saw him and shouted something. The kid stopped, looked back as if he thought Raul were talking to somebody else, then did a pretty good *oh, you mean me* act. It seemed odd that Raul wasn't accompanied by his clique. He was the kind of guy who'd need acolytes around him all the time. There were some boys hanging out, but none he recognized from the ambush.

Vermeulen watched Raul and KillBill argue through the space between the two stone balusters. Raul was taller and bigger than KillBill. He grabbed the kid by the arm and hauled his right arm back to punch him in the face.

"Hey, Raul!" Vermeulen said, rising from behind the banister.

Raul's arm hung in the air while he searched for the origin of the voice. When he saw Vermeulen in the shadows, he let go of KillBill and ambled across the lobby. Which made Vermeulen realize that, standing between the staircase and the wall, he had no escape route. The grin on Raul's face showed that the assessment was correct.

Raul pulled a pistol from his waistband and pointed it at him. Vermeulen raised his hands. Seeing Tessa behind the stairs, Raul's grin widened. Vermeulen and Tessa moved toward him.

"*Vamos!*" he said, waving the gun at them. It was the same cheap Chinese pistol Raul had held during the ambush. The safety was off, but the hammer wasn't cocked. Either Raul hadn't racked the slide and the gun wouldn't fire, or he'd fired a round earlier and the next one was already in the breech.

"*Vamos! Agora,*" Raul said, louder now.

Vermeulen hadn't heard any shots since the ambush. Chances were Raul was too stoned to get his gun ready for action. Not a sure bet, more like seventy-thirty. Raul also didn't look like the kind of guy who took care of his gun. With all the dust and grit in the hotel, the pistol's firing mechanism would be crusted with grime. So it was more like eighty-twenty. Still a risk, but better than being tied up again.

"Forget it, Raul. You may be able to bully these kids, but not me. We're going to walk out of this dump and you can't do anything about it."

Raul stared at him. He didn't understand and wasn't used to disobedience. He jabbed the pistol in his direction.

"What are you doing?" Tessa said. "That guy is stoned. He'll shoot you without compunction."

"He'd like to, but he can't."

Vermeulen took a step forward. Raul pulled the trigger. Nothing happened. He looked at the pistol. Big mistake. Vermeulen grabbed the pistol and twisted it from his hands with a hard jerk. At the same time, he stepped on the arch of Raul's foot with his full weight. The crunching of bones was lost in Raul's scream. He grabbed his foot and hopped on one leg. Vermeulen gave him a tap against the chest and Raul crashed to the concrete. Vermeulen was on him in a flash, pinning him to the ground. He racked the slide and pressed the pistol against Raul's temple. Raul squirmed under him but couldn't budge Vermeulen's weight. His eyes were wide, the pupils dilated. Sweat pearled on his forehead.

"Tell the kid to pull Raul's pants off."

Tessa translated. Vermeulen raised himself just enough to let the KillBill yank off Raul's trousers. KillBill searched the pockets, found some cash, Raul's phone, and Vermeulen's phone and wallet. Raul lay defeated, unable to comprehend what had just happened to him. Vermeulen turned him on his belly. His knee pressed against the small of Raul's back, he tied Raul's hands with one pant leg and his ankles with the other. He pocketed the phones and his wallet, leaving the cash for KillBill, who stared at him with both fear and admiration.

"Let's get out of here," Vermeulen said.

They walked outside. The once-grand driveway curved from the street to the porte-cochère and back again. Several shacks had been built where servants once had waited for guests. A baobab tree surrounded by a low wall stood at the center of the oval formed by the drive.

The shacks forced a black SUV to stop far short of the entrance. Three men, Africans wearing black outfits, got out. They carried automatic guns. Even in the dusk, they looked familiar.

Chapter Seventeen

Grit

———◆———

THE RECOGNITION WAS MUTUAL. THE GUNS came up. A hail of bullets followed. Vermeulen, Tessa, and KillBill dashed behind one of the fat columns that held up the porte-cochère. Ricochets whined into the dark sky.

"Those are the guys who came after me in Maputo," Vermeulen said.

"I would have preferred Raul, after all," Tessa said.

KillBill said nothing. He was peering around the column. Nudging Vermeulen, he pointed to the baobab. Vermeulen wanted to go back into the hotel. With all the people inside, it would be easy to disappear.

KillBill said something to Tessa, who turned to Vermeulen and said, "He doesn't want to go back inside. The gang will have freed Raul by now. They'll be on the lookout. We'd be caught between them and the killers."

"But there are so many places to disappear inside, and he knows them all."

"He's worried about the automatic weapons. It'd be a massacre in there."

"So what does he suggest? We can't stay here. They'll split up and get us."

She spoke to KillBill again. He pointed at the tree.

"See that Baobab? We have to get behind that wall. From there, we can reach the street and find a *chapa* to get us to town."

Vermeulen nodded.

The black SUV was to their left. Where the killers were lurking was anyone's guess. Their best hope was the cover provided by one of the shacks. KillBill took the lead. He dashed across the potholed driveway to the wall. No shot, no movements. Tessa followed. He'd seen her dodge bullets in Darfur and she hadn't lost her moves. By the time she made it across, KillBill had taken cover behind the wall. Still no shots. Tessa flew over the wall and dropped down the other side. A single shot rang out. Vermeulen saw the muzzle flash next to the shack. It was his turn to run. Halfway across the driveway, a burst of automatic weapons' fire hit the broken blacktop. He dove to the ground. The rounds were about ten feet short. Bits of dirt and tar rained on him. He crawled toward the wall, knowing it'd ruin his pants and jacket, which made him even angrier. Where was he going to get new clothes? He rolled over the wall. Another burst of gunfire hurled stone splinters into the air. In daylight, he'd be dead already.

Tessa and KillBill were waiting for him. The baobab's canopy was at least ten yards in diameter, and its trunk could shelter two people abreast. Vermeulen stared over the wall into the darkness, willing himself to see the black-clad assassins. It was no use.

KillBill, who had crawled to the other side of the tree, pointed across. It'd be the way to the street and to town. Unless the gangsters wanted to cut them off. The enclosure was defensible, but not for long. If Raul and his gang came to the aid of the assassins, they'd be surrounded. It was dark enough. Better to make a run for the street.

There was a crunching noise. A step. Then another one. The killers knew where they were. Vermeulen rested against the wall and listened. The others were quiet. Another sound. Someone carefully choosing his steps not far from where Vermeulen lay. He eased himself up, peered over the wall. Nothing. Just darkness. Cooking fires flickered in a few windows of the massive hotel.

A shadow darkened the glimmer of one of them. Just for a moment.

Vermeulen stared.

It happened again.

A spot, darker than the night. Fifteen, twenty feet away. Maybe. Making that crunching noise again. Easing toward him. Vermeulen raised the pistol over the wall and aimed at the mere hint of something. An impossible shot even with a decent weapon.

He pulled the trigger. The action wasn't smooth. Metal grinding against grit grinding against metal, the lever inside straining to move the hammer. He could hear the spring stretch. The trigger stuck. He squeezed harder. It didn't budge. A terrible gun, indeed. Then the grit gave way without warning. The hammer smashed against the firing pin. The pin hit the primer. The charge exploded with a deafening boom. His hand jerked up as superheated gas hurled the bullet out of the barrel. An awful shot.

A fraction of a second later, a howl told him that, against all odds, the bullet had found a target. He didn't know if it was the intended one.

"Let's go. Now!" he said.

They put the tree between themselves and the killers, vaulted over the wall, and ran through the bushes to the street.

There was no taxi waiting for them.

* * *

THE HIGH BEAMS OF THE BLACK SUV flooded the hotel grounds. Its engine roared to life. The tires spun on the dirt before gaining traction. Then it shot into the street.

Vermeulen, Tessa, and KillBill had made it across the street and ducked behind a shrub, waiting for the SUV to pass. The rundown former hotel notwithstanding, the neighborhood was upscale. Large homes surrounded by tall walls topped with razor wire. No alleys, no place to hide.

The street was only a block long. The SUV would be back very soon. They needed time, a diversion, anything.

The third house had a wall like the others. But it also had a solid steel gate. Vermeulen went to it. A combination padlock secured the latch. Human nature being what it was, most owners of combination padlocks didn't bother to change all four digits when they closed the shackle. They just turned one. He turned the first dial one click up and tried the lock. Nothing. Two clicks down. Same result. He switched to the last dial and tried the same trick. The lock stayed closed.

The SUV should have come back by now. He could hear the engine but didn't see any lights. They must've gone around the block.

He tried the second dial. Same routine, one up, two down. Nothing.

The sound of the car came closer. If the killers had any sense, they'd park the car at the end of the street, turn on their high beams, and start searching the trees and bushes. Anyone trying to run would be visible. One would stay with the car, the others beating the bushes.

He messed with the third dial. One up, no result.

The car came around the corner and stopped. The light shone down the street. A door slammed. The cone of light didn't quite reach the gate, but the space between the tree and the gate was well lit.

Vermeulen turned the dial two down. Click. The lock opened. The shadow of one of the killers was visible in the bright cones of light coming from the SUV. He eased the door open, hoping that its owner had oiled the hinges. There was no squeal, but the door wouldn't budge after opening a little over a foot. It'd be a tight squeeze. He whistled quietly. KillBill came first, low and silent. He slipped into the backyard. Tessa was taller and not as flexible. But she was fast. Still, a shot rang when she reached the gate. The bullet hammered against the gate like a rivet gun. She squeezed through.

Another shot hit the wall. Then another. A brick fragment hit Vermeulen's head. More annoying than painful.

He pressed himself into the opening and got stuck. Too much sitting behind the desk. He was halfway through when he heard steps in the grass.

He sucked in his gut and pushed as hard as he could. The metal frame grated against his back hard enough to take some skin with it.

He'd kept the padlock. But to use it, he needed to close the gate completely. Someone on the other side pulled hard at it. KillBill came to help. Together, they pulled the gate closed. Vermeulen slipped the shackle through the holes of the latch. A frustrated bullet banged against the gate and bounced off.

The racket in the garden had alerted the occupants of the house. The garden lit up with the harsh glare of security lights. On the patio, a black man appeared carrying a pump-action shotgun. Vermeulen heard the unmistakable crunch of the gun's action. He stopped and raised his hands. Tessa and KillBill did the same. No use challenging an irate homeowner.

The man on the patio yelled something. Tessa translated. Before she even finished, the man repeated himself in English, "What the fuck are you doing in my yard?"

"We were attacked by criminals and had to get away."

"How did you even get inside? Don't tell me the damn gardener left the gate open."

"No, but you better tell him to move more than one dial when he closes the lock."

"That idiot. Listen, I don't know you and I don't want you in my yard. So get out of here." The man waved his gun at them.

"We can't go back out. The gangsters are still there."

"That means they know you came into my yard. I have no interest in dealing with them. So get lost."

Vermeulen wasn't going back outside. The ratty gun was no match for the weapons of the gangsters. Besides, the best way to win a fight was to avoid getting into one.

"We don't want to be a nuisance," he said. "But can we make a call first and have someone pick us up?"

"No. That'd take forever. In the meantime, those gangsters show up at my door. Leave. Now."

"Listen," Vermeulen said, "if we just sneak out the back again, they will still show up at your front door. They need to know we left."

The floodlights flicked off. Vermeulen heard a generator start. The lights came back on. The owner stepped off the patio and came toward them, the shotgun still cradled in the crook of his arm.

"They'll know, because I'll tell them," he said. "Now scram. Get out of here."

Vermeulen shrugged and turned back to KillBill and Tessa. They didn't offer any alternative solution. Back at the gate, he pulled the pistol from his jacket pocket and opened the lock again. The owner pointed the shotgun at them. Vermeulen told Tessa and KillBill to stand next to the gate. The pistol in his right hand, Vermeulen stepped next to them and pushed the gate open. No shot, no movement. Just silence. He peered out. The slice of ground illuminated by the floodlights on the patio was empty. He eased outside. Tessa and KillBill followed. Still no sound. Behind them, the man pulled the gate shut with a bang. They were back in the night, at the mercy of the killers.

"You got ten seconds to get away," the man said from behind the wall.

Or what? There wasn't anything the man could do now. But Vermeulen didn't wait to find out. He hustled the others along the wall toward the end of the block. Ten seconds later, the boom of a shotgun blast shattered the quiet. A second one followed. Then another. It sounded like someone getting rid of vermin. Or uninvited guests.

The SUV wasn't in sight. No light, except for what came from the windows of houses. They entered the cross street and hurried along in the shadows. At the end of that block, Vermeulen thought he heard a car engine. They waited, huddled behind a tree. The car, if that's what it was, didn't seem to come closer. After a while, KillBill rose again and led the way. He knew the neighborhood inside out and would be the best guide through the maze of streets.

They'd walked about two blocks on the Rua Sancho de Toar when a pair of headlights flashed on. Blinded by the sudden glare, Vermeulen dropped to the ground.

"Down!" he said. "Don't be a target."

The car engine started and revved in place. He could feel the sight of a gun settling on his body, imagine the finger squeezing the trigger. The bang, when it came, wasn't a gunshot. It was a door slamming shut. Someone ran across the street to the car. The tires spun in the dirt and the car shot past them, music now blaring from its windows.

* * *

A TAXI HAD DROPPED THEM AT THE Praça Gago Countinho where they'd met Chipende, who offered a bed for KillBill once he understood that the kid couldn't go back to the Hotel da Beira. From there, Vermeulen and Tessa walked to her hotel. The city center streets were lit, and the usual denizens of the night hung around bars and restaurants. The lilting notes of *marabenta* music sounded through the open windows of a bar. Vermeulen wanted to stay and just enjoy the melodies and drink a beer. They'd be safer there than any place they'd been that day. But Tessa wanted a bath, so they passed up the music and continued to the Beira Inn.

Vermeulen stopped at the corner and peered into the Rua Luis Inacio. Their hotel was all lit up, making the rest of the street feel dark. He checked the parked cars. No SUV on this end of the street.

"Let's go around the block and check the other side," he said.

Tessa groaned. "Really? They don't know where we're staying. I'm tired and need hot water."

"They know a lot more than we think. We've gotten this far; no need to take risks now."

They crossed to the next street and walked under a large, unlit marquee advertising the *Nacional* cinema. Disappearing into a movie, even one in a foreign language, was right up there with spending the evening listening to music. But the theater looked like it hadn't featured a movie in quite a while.

VERMEULEN WAS STILL THINKING ABOUT THE bar. Spending the night there listening to music sounded really good. And it'd be a move the killers wouldn't anticipate.

"I can just feel the bath," Tessa said. "Let's hurry."

"That's what they expect us to do after a harrowing day. We should find a different place to stay."

"All our stuff is at the Beira Inn."

"I know."

"Let's check first. Then we can decide."

At the end of the block, they crossed back to the Rua Luis Inacio, choosing the sidewalk on the opposite side of the hotel. The street was as quiet as before. A taxi stopped at the hotel and let out a guest. Vermeulen checked for parked cars. Nothing resembling a black SUV. They ducked into a doorway that turned out to be the Hindu Association of Beira. A little help from Ganesha, the remover of obstacles, would be more than welcome.

The hotel entrance and lobby were all lit up. Entering through the front was not an option. They'd be a perfect target.

"Is there another entrance?" he said.

"Yeah, through the car park," Tessa said, pointing to a walled-in area across from the Hindu Association. "I have the code for that door."

They walked across the street, arm in arm like a strolling couple, and slipped behind the wall. The area was lit, and a smattering of cars stood there. Again, no black SUV. Tessa punched the code and opened the door.

A hallway led to the reception desk and the lobby with the elevators. The staircase was closer and safer. They reached a mezzanine. Vermeulen checked the lobby area, and sure enough, a black-clad African was sitting there, keeping an eye on the door. They hurried upstairs to Tessa's room. Inside, they locked the door, put the chain on, and turned on the lights.

"We better pack our things and find another hotel," Vermeulen said.

"You want us to lug our bags down to the street and wait for a cab? They'll notice that for sure. What about the bill? You want to walk up to the reception and pay that? As long as we keep the lights off, they won't know we're here."

CHAPTER EIGHTEEN

NO ALTERNATIVE

———◆———

ISABEL LAFLEUR STOOD BY THE WINDOW watching the first rays of the morning sun reflect off the waves in Maputo Bay. It was a quarter to six. Way too early. Even the imported coffee didn't change that fact. She had no choice. Vincent Portallis was in San Francisco, and that meant she had to haul herself out of bed for the weekly call.

Last night Gould had reported the bad news. She'd barely managed to keep her cool. The string of failures was getting too long. So far, she'd trusted Gould to handle the hands-on stuff. He had the temperament to deal with the lowlifes and scumbags one needed for that kind of work. It was better for her to keep those operations at arm's length. She had plans. Which meant unsavory dealings were okay as long as she wasn't actually linked to them. If anything ever blew back, it was all on Gould. She'd look shocked, then she'd wring her hands and take full responsibility for not having been more vigilant in her oversight of the bad apple in her organization.

In the meantime, she needed that damn investigator off her back. By now he knew the five million dollars had disappeared before the funds ever reached Nossa Terra. He knew that Global Alternatives had partnered with GreenAnt Investments to develop a whole lot more land in Sofala than Nossa Terra had been led to believe. And he knew there was an effort to eliminate him. The killers had his picture and there were only a few places from where that picture could have come. It didn't take much imagination to put these pieces together. The only saving grace was that it was all based on conjecture.

Ordinarily, she enjoyed talking with Portallis. Maybe it was only her imagination, but she felt a special connection to her boss, a connection she hoped to capitalize on once her tour in Maputo was over. That's why she'd shied away from bringing the Vermeulen problem to his attention. She didn't want Portallis to think she couldn't handle her job. Now it was time to cut her losses. Her phone rang. She answered.

"Please hold for Mr. Portallis," a female voice announced. It was the same voice every week. LaFleur imagined a woman in her late fifties in a sensible pantsuit with a sensible haircut who anticipated Portallis's every whim. Had she come along on the trip to San Francisco? Probably not. That meant she was working at midnight in New York. Poor thing. If there was one thing LaFleur knew, it was that she wouldn't end up in that kind of position.

"Good morning, Isabel. I hope you are well?" Portallis said.

"I am, Mr. Portallis. Thank you for asking. How's San Francisco? Are you enjoying the California climate?"

"Actually, it's colder here than in New York. We had an odd warm spell there. But it's good to be on the left coast for a change. Life here seems more relaxed, even though I've had no time to experience that myself. So, where are we with the land project?"

"Right on track. GreenAnt Investments and I signed the Memorandum of Understanding with the provincial ministry. The land use titles are approved at the provincial level. Our liaison at the ministry told me that the okay from the national government should come in a matter of days. They are desperate for foreign investment."

"Good, good," Portallis said. "Glad to hear we're on schedule. I trust that disentangling ourselves from the old partner ... what was their name again ...?"

"Nossa Terra."

"Right. That went without problems? Nothing to come back at us?"

This was the moment she'd dreaded. "Nothing major. Just a small problem."

"Yes?" Portallis sounded perturbed.

"We're being audited by the UN since we're taking some of their money for the project."

"But everything was in order, right?"

"Yes, except there's the money Nossa Terra can't account for."

"So? That should be their problem."

"Exactly, sir. Both Paolo and I impressed that on the investigator. But of course, the Nossa Terra folks told this Mr. Vermeulen that they never received the money. We have all the paperwork and showed it to him, but he seems to believe them. He even went up to Beira and bothered Billy Ray. Frankly, he's becoming a nuisance. If there's something you can do on your end, it'd let us focus on what we're here for."

"Of course. How do you spell his name?"

LaFleur gave him the information and the office Vermeulen worked for.

"Consider it done," Portallis said. "I'll call the Secretary-General's office right away. Well, I have to go. Goodbye."

LaFleur smiled as she replaced the receiver. "Well played, Isabel," she said to the window. Building trust with Portallis had paid off. She'd found just the right tone. Now all she had to do was lead Vermeulen on the wrong track until he was recalled. She sat down at her computer, started her Tor browser, and connected to an anonymous email service. She created a new email address and sent a message to Vermeulen. It only contained one sentence. *Ask Mauritius Bank and Trust what they did with the five million.*

She deleted the new account again and closed the Tor browser. There was no way anyone could trace any of this back to her computer. Not only had she sent Vermeulen a diversion, she'd also ensured that he'd come back to Maputo. All Gould had to do was monitor the passenger lists and send his hit squad to intercept Vermeulen, should he leave the airport. Some extra insurance.

She finished her coffee. The sun had risen, and it looked like it was going to be a gorgeous day.

* * *

THE SUN WOKE VERMEULEN EARLY THAT morning. During the night, every noise had set him on edge. He needed coffee and a good idea. The coffee was easy. There was a machine in the room, and the maid had added more filter packs. The gurgling of the coffeemaker took his mind off having to come up with an idea.

Tessa yawned and stretched in bed. "I fell asleep in the tub and woke up when the water got cold. I looked like a raisin. How was your night?"

He handed her a cup of coffee.

"We can't stay here," he said.

"At least let me enjoy the first few sips."

"Fair enough. I'll check my email."

"You could come back to bed."

"Believe me, there's nothing else I'd like to do more, but we can't. It doesn't take a lot of mental arithmetic to figure out we snuck in last night. We need to sneak out before they break down the door."

He tapped the email icon on his phone and swiped through the junk mail and messages until one without a subject line stopped him. It came from an anonymous account. He'd gotten a few messages like that in the past, usually from people who feared retribution for revealing confidential information. He tapped on the message. It was only one line, long enough to catch his interest.

"Listen to this," he said. "I just got a message telling me to check Mauritius Bank and Trust about the five million dollars."

"Who sent it?"

"Anonymous."

"Hmm. You going to?"

Vermeulen leaned back in the chair and drank more coffee. He'd been waiting for something to break loose.

"I don't know. The bank was always suspect. Someone there could have diverted the money."

"Five million dollars?" she said. "That's a lot of diversion."

"I know it sounds weird. But international wire transfers are weird. They basically rely on trust. There is no global legal framework. SWIFT is just a messaging system intended to make transactions traceable. The actual transfer is a private matter among the sender, the correspondent bank, and the recipient. A lot can happen along the way."

"Like what?"

"For example, correspondent banks like Mauritius Bank and Trust charge fees for their service, which are taken from the total amount transferred. Those fees aren't regulated or known beforehand."

"So they could have subtracted a five-million-dollar fee?" Tessa said. "That sounds crazy."

She flung back the sheets and swung her legs over the side of the bed.

"I know," he said. "Nobody would ever do business with that bank again."

He poured himself more coffee, looking at Tessa putting on a T-shirt. He put down the cup, went over and hugged her. She gave him a kiss, then nuzzled against his chest. He let go. There was too much on his mind for more tenderness.

"Are you going back to Maputo?" she said.

"What could I do there? I have no authority, and they have no obligation to tell me anything. The only person who could do anything about it is Aisa Simango. She could file a complaint against the bank and force them to explain what happened to the money. That'd take a long time."

"Maybe the message is a diversion?"

The thought had occurred to Vermeulen. The attacks, the kidnapping—it just didn't feel like something Mauritius Bank and Trust would do to cover up fraud. A bank had other means to hide that.

"If that's the case, it means someone wants me to come back to Maputo," he said. "A good reason not to go there. I'd better stay."

"I was hoping you'd say that."

"We still have to leave here," he said.

She sighed. "Where to?"

"Somewhere more private. I'll call Chipende. Maybe he knows a quiet guesthouse. But first, I'll take a shower."

"Oh, I also have to get my briefcase back from Billy Ray," Tessa said.

* * *

CHIPENDE MET THEM AT A HOLE-IN-THE-WALL grocery store cum coffee shop on a side street. It seemed impossible that the proprietor had managed to squeeze two tables and four chairs between the shelves filled with bags of rice and sardine tins, and a display case with greens and chunks of dried fish. It didn't help that Tessa and Vermeulen had brought their luggage. They'd managed to leave the hotel via the side door and hustle into a taxi she'd called.

"I have a place for you," Chipende said. "It's a few stars down from the Beira Inn, but it's clean and nobody'll find you there. There's one downside. You'll need a car. It's on the way to the airport and I expect you don't want to have to rely on *chapas.*"

"For now, *chapas* will have to do. We can rent a car at the airport if we need to," Vermeulen said.

"The bigger issue is getting my briefcase back from Billy Ray," Tessa said. "I left it in their Land Rover after Raul and his gang kidnapped us yesterday."

"It'd be best if you just go there and ask for it," Chipende said. "They aren't after you and won't do anything to you in broad daylight. They still have to pretend they don't know Raul. If you'd like, I'll come along. You," he looked at Vermeulen, "better stay here. There are armed men looking for you."

The two left the shop. Vermeulen ordered another coffee and checked email messages on his phone. There was one from Aisa Simango. She told him that her confrontation with Isabel LaFleur at the symposium was having its first effects. Two funders sent auditors without so much as a message announcing their intentions. Not that they had anything to worry about, but it confirmed her fear. Nossa Terra's and her reputation had been damaged. Aisa sounded defeated. She did ask for news about the Sofala Project. She hadn't heard from Chipende since Vermeulen's arrival in Beira. Vermeulen didn't think it was his place to respond. He decided to wait.

The shop owner brought him a pastry, which turned out to be savory rather than sweet. It tasted good. He asked for another. Who knew when there'd be another opportunity to eat?

Who knew anything?

The last day had been as chaotic as any he'd encountered in his work. No, it was worse. He'd been in more dangerous situations before, but in each case, he'd known what to do next. This was the first time he didn't. He wasn't even sure who the bad guys were. Sure, there were plenty of sleazy characters to choose from. But who'd done what and when? He had no evidence. Only suspicions and conjecture. Even Bengtsson in Nairobi, who'd learned to give him the benefit of the doubt, would laugh him out of the room.

The anonymous email message didn't help. If true, he'd been pursuing the wrong suspects. If not, someone was trying to lead him on. Who? No idea. His gut told him it was Isabel LaFleur. His gut had been wrong before.

The only person he hadn't spoken with was the man in the provincial directorate of agriculture, Lionel Sukuma. Vermeulen had found a tentative link between Sukuma and Raul, but it was just a phone number. Meeting with Sukuma had to be his next step. The only alternative would be to give up. Which was no alternative at all.

CHAPTER NINETEEN

AIR CONDITIONER

———— ◆ ————

TESSA CAME BACK AN HOUR LATER. Neither Billy Ray nor Antonio had been in the office. The receptionist simply handed her the briefcase. A quick check told her that nothing was missing. But Tessa was sure that everything in it had been examined.

"I don't know about my phone or laptop—they're password protected—but smart people can get around that. There's no evidence of someone breaking in, but there wouldn't be if they know what they're doing. I only hope all my contacts and messages are still safe."

"Let's get to the new place," Vermeulen said. "I want to drop off these bags."

Tessa nodded and told him that she'd arranged with Chipende to speak to the farmers who'd been prevented from going to their farms. "I have to get my article finished."

Tessa called a cab. A *chapa* would have been cheaper, but two people, one of them European, dragging their luggage along the road, would attract attention.

The new place, Hotel Estrela, just off the airport road, was a one-story building with a shabby exterior, but the inside was well swept and the man behind the registration desk was friendly. They got a double room. Chipende was right—it would take a while for someone to find them here.

"Chico will take me back to Tica to interview the farmers there," Tessa said. "I'll be gone all day. What are you going to do?"

"Talk to the one person in Beira I still haven't met yet, Lionel Sukuma. I got his address from the ministry's web."

"He might not want to speak with you," Tessa said.

"That's why I won't make an appointment. I'll just show up."

There was a knock on the door, which Vermeulen opened. It was Chipende.

"Do you know if Sukuma is out a lot?" Vermeulen asked him. "I want to talk to him without making an appointment so he won't have time to prepare, or worse, call Raul or the hit squad."

"A surprise visit? I like it. Probably the only way to approach him. He's pretty lazy. You won't see him in the field. But he does go out to get his coffee. You know what he looks like?"

"No."

"Medium height. Nothing distinguishing about him. I wish I had a picture to show you. Always wears a suit and a white shirt. His office is on the second floor at the corner facing the street and the old exhibition halls. With your UN credentials, you should have no problem getting into the building."

"Okay," Vermeulen said. "I think I'll go to the airport first and rent a car. Easier to get away when I need to."

He kissed Tessa goodbye, locked the room, and went to the street where he waited for a *chapa* to take him to the airport.

* * *

THE PROVINCIAL GOVERNMENT BUILDING WAS A nondescript modern high-rise, fifteen stories tall. Air-conditioning units sticking out of the windows in an irregular pattern indicated where the offices of the important bureaucrats were. He concluded the one at the corner window on the second floor belonged to Sukuma.

Entry was a little more complicated than Chipende had predicted. The guard with the submachine gun didn't pay any attention to him. The man at the reception desk posed a bigger obstacle, mostly because of the language barrier. Vermeulen presented his UN ID and said that he wanted to see Mr. Sukuma. The man at the desk shook his head. Vermeulen didn't understand what he was saying. All he could make out was Sukuma's name. So he gave the man a big smile, said "*Obrigado*," walked to the elevator, and pushed the button with the up arrow. The man kept speaking as he left him behind. He turned and waved in a friendly way. The elevator dinged, and the door opened. Vermeulen got in and pushed the close door button. Inside was a helpful listing of offices next to the floor numbers. He pushed the button next to the word that looked most like agriculture.

The elevator door opened again, and he half expected to see another armed guard waiting for him. There was no one. It took him a moment to get oriented. Heading to the right, he found a series of doors that indicated they belonged to the directorate of agriculture. The last one belonged to Lionel Sukuma. It had no door handle. Clearly Sukuma was an important man. He had a secretary to control access.

Vermeulen opened the adjacent door and entered into a reception area. The woman behind the desk looked like she'd just come from a beauty pageant— light skin, tight dress, bright red lips, purple eye shadow, and an elaborate coiffure. She was busy maintaining her red fingernails, which were long enough to make typing complicated. A computer stood on her desk. There were filing cabinets and wilting plants. The window had no air conditioner. A second door led to Sukuma's office. The woman looked at him with the annoyance of someone who'd been interrupted doing something important.

"I'm here to see Mr. Sukuma," Vermeulen said.

The woman put her nail file down and cocked her head.

"*Você tem um encontro?*"

He didn't know what she'd said. Maybe he needed an appointment. He ignored her and went straight for the door.

"*Ei!*" the woman shouted.

Before Vermeulen could get his hand on the door handle, she'd shot up from her desk and yanked him back by the shoulder. He could feel her fingernails through the fabric of his jacket.

"*Pode't ir para lá.*"

"I'm going to speak with Mr. Sukuma right now."

He opened the door and saw the man Chipende had described. Medium height, white shirt, gray suit, and utterly unremarkable. Sukuma rose from his chair when he saw the commotion at the door.

"*Desculpa,*" the woman said. "*Ele só andava em.*"

"I have to speak with you," Vermeulen said.

"You need an appointment," Sukuma said.

"I'm Valentin Vermeulen from the OIOS of the United Nations. I don't have time for an appointment. Besides, it doesn't look like you're busy. It won't take long."

"*Esta bem,*" Sukuma said to the secretary, who shook her head and closed the door. "Have a seat. Why do you need to speak with me?"

The office was much nicer than the secretary's. No institutional furniture and no filing cabinets. A mahogany desk and matching chairs dominated the space. There was a photograph of Mozambique's President Filipe Nyusi on the wall. Blinds kept the sun out and the air conditioner was humming in the window.

"I'm auditing Global Alternatives' projects in Mozambique and there are a number of discrepancies. Since your department works closely with the foundation, I thought you could help me."

"I'll do my best."

Vermeulen explained the missing money and the sudden change in Global Alternatives' partners.

"Yes, I'm aware of that," Sukuma said. "Nossa Terra turned out to be unreliable. What you are telling me about the missing money just confirms that. Honestly, my experience with them has been terrible. They are good at protesting but not at building sustainable development."

The man sounded like he'd practiced those lines carefully.

"Tell me about GreenAnt Investments," Vermeulen said. "What's your office's relationship with that company?"

"There is none. They are partners with Global Alternatives. Have you spoken with Billy Ray? He'd know more."

"Have you ever spoken with anyone at GreenAnt?"

Vermeulen noticed the momentary hesitation.

"Er, no. I have not. Again, Billy Ray would be the person to contact."

"That sounds a bit strange to me. You've approved a major development project, but you haven't spoken with the project partner."

Sukuma looked ill at ease.

"As I said, my dealings are with Global Alternatives. They are responsible for their partnerships."

"Who are the principals at GreenAnt? Can you give me their names?"

More hesitation. Beads of sweat appeared on his forehead.

"I don't have the names."

Sukuma was lying. The names had to be in the paperwork necessary to approve the land use permits.

"Why are you lying to me?" Vermeulen said. "Who are you covering for? Yourself? But let me ask you something else. What is your relationship with a hoodlum named Raul?"

"I don't know anyone named Raul."

"And yet you have his telephone number."

"I do not."

Vermeulen should have left it there. He didn't want to cause trouble for Chipende or KillBill. But he said it anyway.

"You had the phone number in your wallet."

The statement electrified Sukuma.

"Did you send that kid to steal my wallet?"

"I don't know who stole your wallet. But the wallet was found afterwards, and it had Raul's number in it."

"I'm calling the police. I don't care what you say. You know the pickpocket."

Vermeulen had heard all he needed to know.

"Don't waste your time. My job is to make sure that United Nations money isn't stolen. You are obviously involved in this scam. I'll inform my superiors and they'll contact the government in Maputo. If you confess now, I'll put is a good word for you."

It was worth a try, but Sukuma wasn't having any of it. He had already lifted the receiver of his phone. It was time to go.

* * *

VERMEULEN GOT BACK TO THE HOTEL Estrela without incident. He was certain Sukuma hadn't actually called the police. More likely he'd called Billy Ray or Antonio. Vermeulen had parked the rented Corolla a safe distance from the government building and was certain that nobody had followed him to the hotel.

The hotel didn't have a kitchen, but the proprietor had a deal with a small restaurant nearby. Vermeulen ordered a late lunch and coffee and settled on a small, shady veranda in the back of the hotel. The food came soon—something with potatoes and meat—and he had a solitary meal.

The biggest question mark was GreenAnt Investments. It was as if the company didn't exist. Its name was there, but nobody knew about it or was willing to say that they did. It was time to tackle that problem from a different angle. He dialed his daughter's number. In her position as head of the Africa section of a major European shipping and logistics firm, Gaby had access to information not available to mere mortals or UN investigators.

"Hi, Dad, are you still in Maputo?" she said.

"No, I'm up in Beira. How are you?"

"I'm fine, just got back from a late lunch. Long meeting this morning."

"I'm having a late lunch, too. I don't want to make your week any busier, but I'm hoping you can help me. I'm trying to find out who's behind a company called GreenAnt Investments. They popped up during my investigation and nobody can tell me anything. It could be one of those letterbox firms incorporated on some Caribbean island."

"If that's the case, you shouldn't hope for much. Usually, the registering agent is just a law firm. The whole idea is to hide the real ownership. But I'll check. What's the name again?"

"GreenAnt—one word—Investments."

"Will do. Everything else going well? How's Tessa?"

Ever since meeting Tessa a couple of years ago in Düsseldorf, his daughter and his lover had become good friends. At first he'd thought it odd, but now he was glad.

"Not as well as I'd hoped. There's something fishy going on. But I can't figure it out. Tessa is well. She's out interviewing farmers about land grabs."

"Sounds like the Tessa I know. I'm sure you'll get to the bottom of it. Just make sure you don't burn all your bridges in the process."

"Oh, don't exaggerate," he said. His daughter knew him too well.

"You know I'm not. I'll call you as soon as I find something."

"Thanks, darling. Talk to you soon."

All he could do now was wait for Tessa to return. And the best way to pass that time was a nap. Who knew what was headed toward him?

* * *

THE RINGING PHONE YANKED VERMEULEN FROM a deep sleep. He didn't nap often, in part because he tended to sleep hard, which left him feeling loopy when he woke up. By the time he located his phone, the call had rolled over to voicemail. Arne Bengtsson's name appeared on the display. With a pang of guilt, he realized that he'd never called Bengtsson back about his decision to go to Beira instead of Nairobi. Which was probably the reason for Bengtsson's call.

He tapped the call-back button and waited for the call to connect.

"Arne, it's me. Sorry I never called back, but I went to Beira instead." He added, "Tessa was there," by way of explanation.

"So I heard," Bengtsson said. "I wish you had come to Nairobi instead."

"Don't you care about my love life? You're nice company, but it was no contest."

"I'm not talking about comparing Tessa with me. I'm talking about you getting into trouble yet again. Goddamn it, Valentin. Can't you ever just do a job and not break all the china in the shop?"

"Why? What happened?"

"The secretary-general happened."

"Huh?"

"The SG's office called the under-secretary-general at OIOS, who promptly called me about one of my investigators going rogue in Mozambique and impugning the valuable work of one of the world's finest foundations—Global Alternatives. What the hell have you been doing there?"

"I'm convinced they stole five million dollars from the UN. That's what I'm doing here."

"You got any proof?"

"I'm working on that."

"It's too late for that."

Bengtsson explained in excruciating detail how Vincent Portallis, multibillionaire extraordinaire and chairman of Global Alternatives, had called the secretary-general in the middle of the night to complain about an investigator by the name of Valentin Vermeulen of the OIOS interfering with his world-changing humanitarian work. "Don't ask me how he got the SG's number. I guess the rich are different."

Vermeulen said nothing. Isabel LaFleur must have made the call. Which meant she had an in with Portallis, who in turn was the kind of man from whom even the secretary-general would take a call in the middle of the night. And that meant only one thing. Whatever was going on here was way bigger than five million dollars.

"You are in such deep trouble even I can't see the bottom of it," Bengtsson said. "For one, you are to leave Mozambique immediately and report back to New York. In the meantime, you are suspended with pay, which is another way of saying that you cannot under any circumstances conduct more investigations. You are to book the next flight to New York and sit on your thumbs until you get there. Are we clear?"

Vermeulen remained silent. The display of sheer power set into motion halfway around the world was awful in the literal sense of the word. It wasn't the first time OIOS had tried to put him on a leash. It happened routinely when he did a thorough job and followed the leads, even if they implicated someone higher up. And each time, he asked himself why he kept beating his head against the wall of complacency. *Don't rock the boat; don't make the organization look bad.* That was more important than helping those who the UN was supposed to be championing—those at the margins, like Nossa Terra. Usually, the call came because he'd interfered with the plans of one of the powerful member states. This time was different. Worse, really. It's one thing for a member state to complain. After all, it's their organization. It was an entirely different matter when private interests bullied the UN.

"Are we clear, Valentin?"

The hell we are. Not while I still have this job. Not while Portallis ruins Nossa Terra.

Vermeulen took a deep breath and said, "Yes, we are. I'll be going to New York. I won't be doing any more investigating. I'll be good."

Chapter Twenty

Backfire

———◆———

The wait for Tessa's return was excruciating. Patience just wasn't in Vermeulen's DNA. He used Tessa's laptop to check on flights from Maputo to JFK and booked the least direct flight, which left Maputo in two days. It was the cheapest option. That should make the beancounters at OIOS happy. Then he got a ticket to Maputo for the next day. He'd have the afternoon and evening to meet with Simango.

When Tessa finally returned, he told her about Bengtsson's call. They sat on the veranda for a long time without saying anything. Eventually, the hotel owner came out and asked if they wanted something to drink. They both chose *Laurentina Premium*. A cold beer seemed appropriate for the heat Vermeulen was feeling.

The weird thing was the sense of déjà vu. The last time he'd upset the UN hierarchy, Tessa had urged him to go back to New York and set the record straight. This time, she did the opposite.

"Don't go. You have no solid evidence to support your suspicions. Portallis holds all the cards. I don't have to tell you how much the UN has gotten into bed with corporations and foundations. You'd be running into a buzz saw and would lose your job."

"I'll lose my job for sure if I stay here."

"Maybe there's some wiggle room. How close are you to solving the case?" Tessa said.

"Not close at all. I have a lot of pieces, but nothing adds up."

"What do you still need?"

"I need to know who's behind GreenAnt Investments. That company is the key. I already called Gaby and asked her to check it out. She didn't give me much hope."

"What do you suspect?"

"I'm not sure," Vermeulen said and took a swig from the bottle. "But where does a company that has no record, no trail whatsoever, get its capital to partner with a large foundation like Global Alternatives? At the same time, five million dollars of UN funds are missing. What if the missing money somehow found its way to GreenAnt investments?"

They sat in silence again.

"That would mean Global Alternatives is in on it, right?" Tessa said after a while.

Vermeulen nodded. "I don't know if it's just the local branch—LaFleur and Gould—or if it goes all the way to the top. If Portallis is involved, I might as well stop now. There's no way I could bring him down. I'm hoping it's just LaFleur and Gould. Those two I can nail."

"Let's find dinner someplace," Tessa said. "Better not to make weighty decisions on an empty stomach."

* * *

THEY ENDED UP IN A TINY restaurant off the N6 heading out of town. Tessa had seen it on her way back from Tica, and Vermeulen was happy to avoid the city center of Beira. The N6 was busy as usual, cars and long trucks vying for space and *chapas* darting in and out of traffic in their eternal search for passengers. Vendors occupied what little open space there was at the closest intersection, and their hollering added to the cacophony of the early evening.

Tessa and Vermeulen sat on a wooden deck, facing the street. A few planters with mangy shrubs separated them from the bustle. A skinny girl, maybe twelve, was awed enough by the rich-looking guests that she tried to wipe the rough wooden table with a suspiciously brown-tinged rag. Tessa smiled and thanked her. The girl beamed. A woman came and asked what they wanted to eat. At least that's what Vermeulen assumed. Tessa handled the conversation.

"They have meat or fish," Tessa said. "What would you like?"

"I'll go with the fish."

"I think it's a wise choice. I'll do the same. Beer?"

Vermeulen nodded.

The woman left, and the girl reappeared with two bottles of *Laurentina Clara*. Vermeulen took a big swig and sighed. The warm air, the bustle around them, and the cool beer were exactly what Vermeulen loved about his job—a pleasant spot to relax and enjoy the ambiance of a place. Except Bengtsson's call had changed all that.

"I'm going to New York. I booked a flight already," he said. "I'm leaving tomorrow. I'll spend a day in Maputo, then leave for JFK, flying via Jo'burg and Abu Dhabi. It'll take two days with a long layover in Abu Dhabi, but that's good. I'll have time to sort out what I'm going to do once I get there."

"So all this talk about staying was just … what? Stringing me along?"

He heard the edge in her voice.

"Sorry, I just had to sort out what might be possible here. If we had come up with a plan, I'd have cancelled the reservation. But I don't know how to get the evidence I need. That means I have to go and face my boss."

The woman came back carrying two plates, each piled high with rice, a chunk of fish, and stewed greens. She was about to put them on the table when there was a loud bang, like a car backfiring. Given the traffic and the number of ramshackle cars on the road, the sound was ordinary. The planter next to their table exploding was not. Clods of dirt laced with bits of shrubbery rained on everybody. The woman dropped the plates and huddled on the ground. Tessa was right behind her. Vermeulen took a quick glance at the road and saw the black SUV not too far away. He huddled behind the other planter.

"Are you okay?" he said to Tessa.

Her answer was drowned out by another explosion when a bullet hit one of the dinner plates, sending stewed tomatoes flying everywhere.

"God damn it!" Vermeulen said. "How the fuck do they even know where we are?"

"Our rental car?" Tessa said, wiping a piece of tomato from her face. "It has a GPS in it."

"We'd better get out of here. Ask her how we can get away. I'll give her fifty bucks for the damage."

Tessa explained their situation to the woman. When Vermeulen handed her a fifty-dollar bill, her eyes lit up. She pointed to the back, and they crawled across the deck into the shack that served as a kitchen. Inside, there were two gas burners hooked up to propane tanks. They were lucky the bullets hadn't hit the tanks. The woman lifted a hinged window at the rear, and the two climbed outside.

They found themselves in a tiny backyard, surrounded by a wooden fence. The woman lifted one of the planks and Tessa peered outside. Everything seemed calm. There hadn't been any more shots. That could mean the hit men had driven away. Or they were coming closer on foot, looking to eliminate their prey at close range. Their record from a distance had been terrible.

"Where are we parked?" he said.

"Do you think it's wise to go to the car? That's how they located us."

"I'm not sure that's the case. How would they know how to locate our car?"

"Don't be dense," Tessa said. "Once we disappeared from the city center, they knew we'd find a hotel farther away. Europeans usually don't ride in a *chapa,* so they figured you'd hire a car. All they had to do was go to the airport and bribe the right person."

"Good point. So how do we get back to the hotel?"

"By *chapa,* how else? It's non-traceable transport. At the hotel, you can phone the car rental place and tell them that the car malfunctioned and where they can pick it up."

Which was what they did. The *chapa* tour took over an hour with the transfers and the misunderstandings. Back at the hotel, they fell on the bed.

"I guess that was a clear sign I should leave tomorrow," Vermeulen said. "I won't be able to do anything around here. I think you'll be safe. You're just a journalist."

"*Just* a journalist? What's that supposed to mean?"

"Sorry. That came out the wrong way. What I meant is, they don't have a beef with you. You should be safe after I leave. Journalism is a noble pursuit."

Tessa punched him in the arm. He knew better than to complain.

* * *

VERMEULEN WAS PACKING HIS CLOTHES THAT evening when his phone rang. It was Gaby.

"Are you working late?" he said. Since Düsseldorf and Beira were in the same time zone, Gaby should've been home a couple of hours already.

"Don't worry, I'm at home. I have some information on GreenAnt and I figured you'd like to hear it."

"Not sure it matters anymore. I got recalled to New York headquarters."

"What? Why?"

"Somebody way above my pay grade called the secretary-general to complain about me. He called the under-secretary-general of OIOS, who called Bengtsson in Nairobi, who called me."

"What have you done now?"

"What I always do. Investigate fraud. Except this time Global Alternatives is involved."

He could hear Gaby suck in her breath.

"*The* Global Alternatives? Vincent Portallis's Global Alternatives?" she said.

"The very same."

"Oh, Dad. When will you learn to pick the right battles?"

"This is the right battle. The evidence points to the local office of Global Alternatives having diverted five million dollars. It's just not yet conclusive. So the local folks called in Portallis before I could make it stick."

"Is GreenAnt connected to this?"

"It sure is. Not that it matters now, but what have you found out?"

There was a pause.

"Okay," Gaby said. "At first I thought I was right. GreenAnt is registered in Panama. Your ordinary tax avoidance scam. A post office box address in Panama City and the registrant is a law firm from Panama. That was a dead end. But there are other ways. Do the letters 'KYC' mean anything to you?"

"KYC?"

"Know your customer. A set of rules for businesses, especially banks, to comply with money laundering and anti-terrorist financing rules passed by the U.S. and a bunch of other countries."

"Oh, right." He did know about these guidelines. They specified that before selling something or transferring funds to an account, the seller/sender must know the true owner of the business partner, not just the law firm that signed the incorporation papers.

"Well, my company hasn't done any business with GreenAnt," Gaby said. "We have no records. But as you can imagine, there's an informal network of people in positions like mine who know each other. A grapevine for information on shady companies. Nobody wants to ship something to an unknown customer only to be indicted later for supporting a terrorist cell. I asked about GreenAnt."

"And …? Come on, Gaby, tell me."

"Yes. Just now one of my contacts called. He told me that according to his records, the actual owner is one Lionel Sukuma. Does that name mean anything to you?"

"You better believe it. I confronted this man earlier today. Can I use this information?"

"Of course, but remember, this is completely unofficial. I thought it'd help you fit together the other information you have. If my information is your only evidence, it's useless, unless the law firm that registered GreenAnt confirms it, which they aren't likely to do. Secrecy is how they make their money."

Vermeulen wiped his face. The last-minute breakthrough he'd hoped for turned out to be a dud. Enough to confirm that he was right, but not enough to keep the wolves at bay. The buzz saw in New York City was waiting for him.

CHAPTER TWENTY-ONE

CARDBOARD BOXES

———◆———

THE GRAY CLOUDS WERE BACK OVER Maputo when the commuter jet of Mozambique's national airline began its descent. Vermeulen sat in row 7 and looked at the drab landscape. Through a break in the clouds, a slice of ground glowed in vibrant colors. What a difference a ray of sunlight made. A moment later, after the clouds reasserted themselves, the land below turned dull again. Not much different from his situation. Clouds as far as he could see. For a moment the case had been lit up by Gaby's information, only to be hidden by the clouds again.

Sukuma was behind GreenAnt Investments. No surprise there. A public official enriching himself by using his public position for private benefit. Happened every day the world over. The methods varied, but the outcomes were the same. Still, it seemed too sophisticated a scheme for a mid-level provincial bureaucrat. A front company, incorporated by a law firm in Panama City? That was a lot of leg work for five million dollars. Tax scam setups usually didn't pay for themselves until the amounts reached double- or triple-digit millions. Either Sukuma wasn't alone, or he had a lot more at stake than a piece of land in Sofala province. Or, and that was a depressing thought, there were so many law firms competing for the tax-evasion and money-laundering clientele that their rates had come down to rock bottom. Gray clouds indeed.

He'd stayed at the hotel in Beira as long as he could. A van going to the airport stopped when he flagged it down. Tessa didn't come along. Once past security, he was fine. There were no familiar faces in the waiting area. Of course, he hadn't actually seen the faces of the black-clad assassins.

The plane touched down and the reverse thrusters slowed it to taxiing speed. Small jets didn't get a jetway, so the plane taxied to a designated spot. The flight attendant opened the door. Five minutes later, Vermeulen walked down the steps and across the tarmac to the arrivals area. Nobody was waiting for him.

Maputo's airport didn't have a hotel, which was probably for the best. It'd be the first place they'd look for him. He didn't want to go to a hotel in the city center either. It was too predictable. He was certain they were tracking his movements, if only to make sure that the intervention by Portallis had produced the desired outcome. Since he still didn't know who'd hired the hit squad, it was better to stay off the radar as much as possible. That left the guesthouse where he'd stayed before.

He waited in the shadows of the ground transportation section until the passengers who'd been on his plane had found their respective means to get to town. He kept looking for a black Land Rover. There was none in sight. He tagged along a couple of stragglers who headed for the taxi stand, got in the next free cab, and gave the driver the address of pension Chicari.

* * *

"*Bom dia, Senhor Vermeulen*." The proprietor of the pension Chicari was delighted to see him again. "*Desculpe*, but I must give you a different room."

"No problem at all. It'll only be for a night."

Vermeulen dropped his bags and washed up in the tiny alcove that served as the bathroom. He still hadn't contacted Simango about his short stopover. The last twenty-four hours had been too crazy. She wouldn't mind his showing up unannounced. It'd be different than his first visit. In the message she'd left for him, she'd sounded depressed about the prospects of Nossa Terra. Not that he could do anything about that. Maybe she'd found out more about GreenAnt. There had to be some paperwork with the Mozambican government, although he doubted Simango would have access to that.

The offices of Nossa Terra were only a mile away. He decided to walk. The market at the intersection of Julius Nyerere and Vladimir Lenine was as busy as ever. The aroma of roasted meat reminded him that he hadn't eaten anything since breakfast. He stopped and bought a skewer with spicy chicken pieces. Street food was always hot, quick, unpretentious, and never disappointing.

As he chewed his chicken, he looked around the stalls. Same as before. Cheap shoes, racks of used clothing, candy, cigarettes, vegetables, housewares. He dropped the cardboard tray on top of an overflowing trashcan and headed south on Vladimir Lenine. About a block away from the office, he saw Simango get into a *chapa*. He waved, shouted, and ran toward her. Too late. She didn't see him, and the van drove off.

Damn. He should have called.

The office was quiet. Only Zara Nyussi sat at her desk. None of the other employees were there.

"You just missed Aisa," she said.

"I know, I saw her get into the van. Too bad. I only have a few hours and wanted to check in with her. How come it's so quiet here?"

Nyussi looked at her screen and tapped on the keyboard. After a minute, she stopped again.

"We're closing up."

"You *what*?"

"Nossa Terra is closing shop after twenty-five years. I still can't believe it."

"What happened?"

"Two donors pulled out. They came to check up on us. Everything was fine, but they still ended the contract."

"But why close up?" he said.

"Because, between them, they accounted for over half of our funding. Add to that the failure of the Global Alternatives project and we don't have the money to pay staff."

He looked around the office. One desk was already bare. A few cardboard boxes with picture frames, potted plants, and other personal detritus sat on another desk.

"What about you?" he said.

"I'm just cleaning up, taking down the website, deleting our digital presence."

"And after that?"

"Find a job elsewhere. Fortunately, I have transferable skills. Others aren't in such good shape. Tendai is already out there knocking on doors."

Vermeulen sat down in a chair next to her desk.

"And Simango?"

Nyussi was quiet again, but this time she didn't type. She just stared at her screen.

"Don't worry about Aisa," she said finally. "She's the only one who came out on top."

"I find that hard to believe. She put her heart and soul into this organization."

"That's what I thought, too. But she's already got a new job."

"Where?"

"Global Alternatives."

Vermeulen jumped from his chair. "What? That's impossible."

Nyussi grimaced.

"She hasn't actually told me, but it's not impossible."

"So how do you know?"

"There were two calls from Isabel LaFleur. I answered one. That made me suspicious. I went into her email last night and there it was. A very generous contract offer. Guess where she went just now? To their office to sign it."

"You hacked her email?"

"I didn't really hack it. I'm the admin for our hosting and email service, so I have all the passwords. I needed to know. Shouldn't have trusted her."

Vermeulen started pacing.

Unbelievable.

It wasn't an expression of surprise. It was literally his assessment. Simango couldn't have done this. Take a job with the very people who took down her organization? It just didn't make sense. Not after all she'd said about Global Alternatives. Either she'd been duplicitous from the very beginning or Global Alternatives had something on her. Something that would make her change her mind.

"She's not the only one who has kids to worry about," Nyussi said. "Tendai has three. Why didn't she put in a word for him with Global Alternatives?

Vermeulen shrugged. He'd forgotten about her children. Maybe that was all there was to it. Take care of the family even if that means betraying your principles. No, it was still unbelievable. He'd known her for only a few days, but she couldn't have done that.

"Have you spoken with her about this?" he said.

"And admit that I read her emails? No way. I'm waiting for her to tell me. See if she comes clean. If not, well, that alone speaks volumes, doesn't it?"

"Could it be that Global Alternatives is blackmailing her?"

Nyussi's eyebrows arched. "Blackmail?"

"I know I've only just met her," he said, "but I'm a pretty good judge of character, and Aisa Simango doesn't strike me as someone who'd switch sides so easily. There has to be something else going on."

Nyussi looked down and smoothed the front of her blouse.

"Maybe you're right. I'm still too angry to even consider that possibility."

"When you looked at her emails, was there anything that looked suspicious?" he said.

"Besides the job offer from Global Alternatives? No, but I didn't look at everything. Once I saw the message with the job offer, I had all I needed. Do you want me to check again?"

Vermeulen hesitated. Snooping on Simango didn't seem right. Even if her actions were totally out of character.

"I guess not," he said. "It doesn't feel right. We'll just have to wait until she tells us. Or you. I'm going to New York City tomorrow."

"What about the five million dollars? Have you completed your investigation?"

"No, that money is still missing. I was called back."

"Why? What did you do?"

Vermeulen didn't answer right away. The reasons seemed confidential, but the whole affair had gotten so strange he didn't care who knew.

"I bothered Global Alternatives too much. Its billionaire CEO called the secretary-general. The gist of that call was passed on to my boss, who ordered me to come back."

"It sounds like they're getting rid of anyone who gets in their way," Nyussi said.

That made Vermeulen think of Helton Paito.

"Did you ever find out more about Helton? Is there an investigation into his death?"

Nyussi shrugged. "The police were here. They asked Aisa a few questions and left again. We still know nothing."

"Have you tried to check Helton's email account?"

"No. Why?"

"Maybe he was Global Alternatives' first victim," he said.

"Maybe. But the police took his computer."

"He did have a smartphone, right? So his email would still be on the server."

Nyussi didn't say anything and started typing away on her keyboard.

Vermeulen dialed Simango's number and stepped outside. If she answered her phone, he wanted to have a private conversation. He listened to the ringtone until the call rolled over to voicemail. He left a message, telling her that he'd be in Maputo for the evening and the early morning before continuing to New York City.

Back inside the Nossa Terra office, Nyussi waved him to her desk.

"I think I have something," she said.

She turned her monitor so he could see the screen better.

"A day before Helton disappeared, he sent three messages, one each to our bank, Mauritius Bank and Trust, and Global Alternatives," she said. "The one to our bank was asking if there had been any account activity at all that could be related to the missing five-million dollars. He got a rather quick response saying only that there had been a deposit and a chargeback, but nothing involving that much money."

She moved her mouse pointer to the next message. "He did get a response from Mauritius Bank and Trust, but it basically reiterated what our bank manager told him, that there had been a deposit and a chargeback."

The message to Global Alternatives was more direct. Paito had asked them if the deposit and chargeback they made could explain why it appeared that

Nossa Terra had received the funds even if it never got into their accounts. There was no reply to that message.

"That doesn't really tell us anything new," Vermeulen said, "except that everyone Simango and I spoke to a day later already knew about the problem. I don't think that's important. Is there anything else in his emails?"

"No. Nothing else sent, nothing received."

"Did you check his deleted messages?"

Nyussi rolled her eyes.

"Sorry," he said. "I know I'm grasping at straws. All I can see are the vague outlines of a serious fraud, but I can't put the pieces together. I'm pretty sure that Global Alternatives engineered the whole thing to skim off UN funds for their private investment. But I don't know how they did it, and I don't know how high in the hierarchy it goes. I was hoping for new clues."

"Those might well be on Helton's phone. Which we don't have."

* * *

BACK IN HIS ROOM, VERMEULEN TOOK stock. He'd hoped that somehow he might find the one bit of evidence that would settle the case, that would allow him to come home and prove that he was right all along. It hadn't happened. If anything, things had gotten worse. His one ally had gone over to the other side. The rest were out of work. It happened too fast. Either Simango had planned this all along and was just waiting for the right time to pull the trigger, or she'd acted in haste, without thinking, which didn't sound like her at all. There was the possibility of blackmail, but unlikely. As far as the missing money was concerned, he'd seen enough to know that there was no case against her. Maybe Global Alternatives wanted her inside the tent pissing out rather than vice versa.

CHAPTER TWENTY-TWO

STALLS

———— ◆ ————

V ERMEULEN'S PHONE RANG. IT WASN'T SIMANGO returning his call. It was Gaby.

"What's up, darling?" he said.

"That company you asked me to check out, GreenAnt Investments? I kept digging. I went to the Offshore Leaks database and found more information. In addition to Lionel Sukuma, I found two more names, Antonio Freire and—you won't believe this—Calvin Kline."

"The fashion guy? What's he got to do with rural investments?"

"No Calvin Kline, K-l-i-n-e. He's VP for finance at Portallis's hedge fund."

"How come nobody knows this?" he said.

"Because Offshore Leaks is just a data dump on a website. Lots of names in there and lots of legitimate operations too. Unless you're looking for a name, nobody will tell you. But there's more. Once I found this, I checked the Luxembourg tax leaks website and found that GreenAnt is definitely connected with Portallis. Calvin Kline negotiated a preferential tax treatment for the firm. Why would they do that if they weren't connected?"

"What do you make of all that?" Vermeulen said.

There was a pause.

"I'm not sure. You're the one fingers-deep in the stew. Just based on what I saw, it could all be aboveboard. Offshoring can be legitimate. Negotiating special tax exemptions isn't illegal, at least not in Luxembourg. The only thing odd is that they have this deal with Luxembourg and an office in Panama. That seems like overkill, but again, it depends. Maybe the Luxembourg deal applies only to Europe. Anyway, I gotta run. I hope this helps."

She ended the call before he could thank her.

Should I stay or should I go?

He hadn't thought about that song for a long time. There was a time when he had the Clash always close by. A soundtrack for his crazy life. Eventually that petered out, more from exhaustion than conscious choice. But the song was apt. Its refrain—something about staying meaning trouble and going being double—hit home. Although The Clash sang about the mundane conflicts of love lives, it perfectly captured his options. Defy the UN and lose your job, or follow orders and … what?

As much as he resented being called back on the orders of some multibillionaire, he couldn't think of a good reason for staying in Mozambique. He'd found bits and pieces of fraud, but no obvious evidence. Most importantly, he hadn't found the missing money, which was his job. The rest didn't matter. Everything Global Alternatives had done—terminate the contract with Nossa Terra, enter into an agreement with GreenAnt, change the terms of the Sofala Project—was legal. It might raise eyebrows in some quarters, but those were usually ignored anyway. Without an explanation of how the five million dollars had disappeared, he had nothing.

Maybe it *was* time to go home.

* * *

IN THE BAR OF HIS *PENSÕE*, he bought a beer and a cigarette. He'd held off smoking long enough. His predicament was a good enough reason to indulge. He sat, smoking and brooding. What else could he do? Go back to Antwerp, see if he could work at the crown prosecutor's office? If they even looked at his résumé. It had been a decade since he left. Everyone he knew there had either retired, gotten a job in the private sector, or would be his boss. Not enticing options.

He took a deep swallow of beer. Honestly, he couldn't think of any job he was qualified for that came close to his job at OIOS. Despite all his bellyaching about the encrusted bureaucracy, working there let him do what he wanted to do without the kind of micromanaging that would drive him up the wall. It was a good job. And he was good at it, god damn it.

He dragged at his cigarette and coughed. A good sign. His body was no longer used to smoke. Better keep it that way. He stubbed the unsmoked half of the cigarette into the ashtray and finished the beer.

So. At least one decision.

Keep his job.

Okay.

What did that mean?

He needed another beer, but the proprietor was nowhere in sight. The bar was empty. Which was odd. He checked his watch. Five p.m. Sundowner time if ever there was one. He got up. Without another beer, he might as well go back to his room. Or better yet, take a walk. Browse the market stalls at Avenida Vladimir Lenine. Pass the time and think. Although he'd done enough thinking. There was only one way to keep his job. Find the missing money. Everything else would fall into place.

Halfway to the traffic circle where the market stalls were, his phone rang. The display announced *Unknown caller*. He answered anyway. It was Chipende.

"What's going on down there?" he said. "All I get is an email from Zara Nyussi telling me that Nossa Terra is closing shop and that I'm out of a job."

"I'm afraid that's correct. I went to the office to speak with Aisa. She wasn't there, but Nyussi told me that the organization went out of business because two major funders pulled out. No money to pay the staff."

"Where's Aisa in all this? Why didn't she call me?"

"I haven't seen her. She didn't tell me anything either. According to Nyussi, she took a job with Global Alternatives."

"What?" Vermeulen could hear the incredulity in Chipende's voice.

"I know," Vermeulen said. "It seems impossible, but that's what Nyussi said."

"There's no way she'd take a job with those idiots. No way."

"I'd like to believe that too, but I haven't heard from her even though I've left several messages on her phone."

"Something is up and it's not pretty. I should come down there and sort it out."

"What would you do?" Vermeulen said.

"I don't really know. Whatever is going on is bad and I feel stranded up here, unable to do anything."

"How soon could you be here?"

"The bus takes seventeen hours. If I get a seat on the next one, I could be there tomorrow around this time."

"That'd be great. I need help."

"But your friend told me you were going back to New York."

"I've just changed my plans," Vermeulen said.

* * *

ON THE WAY TO NOSSA TERRA, Vermeulen dialed Tessa's number. She didn't answer, and he left a message, telling her that he'd decided not to go home. Then he called the airline about his flight. The agent told him she could rebook him a day later. After that, no seats were available for the next week or so. He thought of checking another airline, but that meant forfeiting the money for the ticket. That'd make the bean counters at OIOS angry. Vermeulen took the day.

He went back to Nossa Terra because he had an idea and needed a computer. Nyussi was still there, winding down the operation. Apparently removing one's digital presence required more effort than just deleting a website. When he entered the office, she looked up, none too pleased about his visit.

"I'm just about to wrap this up and I don't want to be here any longer than necessary. Bad vibes," she said.

"I need a computer and your help. I don't think Simango went over to the other side. I think she was lured into a trap. We need to find her."

"And how are you going to do that?"

"Her mobile phone is still active. When I call her, it rings a while, then switches to voicemail. If the phone were off, it'd go to voicemail right away. Can you tell me what kind of phone she had?"

"Some Chinese brand. I don't really know."

"Not an iPhone?"

Nyussi snorted. "Who do you think we are? None of us could afford one, not even Helton."

"That's what I was hoping. She's got an Android phone. Which of these was her computer?"

Nyussi pointed to a desk.

"Can you get me logged in?"

"Sure," Nyussi said. "We all know each other's logins in case we need to access documents."

She got up, started the computer, and after a delay, typed in Simango's credentials.

"What do you want to do now?"

"I'm going to find her phone."

Vermeulen opened the browser on Simango's computer, connected to the Google website, and typed *find my phone*. Google responded with a prompt to sign in.

"This is where I need your help," he said. "I need her Google login and password."

"What makes you think I have that?"

"You are the tech person here. I'm sure you helped everyone set up their devices."

"Yes, but not her Google account. That was her private email."

"Yes, but most people aren't terribly creative when it comes to passwords. So just tell me her password for her office email. I know you've got that."

Nyussi reached for the keyboard and entered the necessary information.

The website took a few seconds, then displayed a map of Maputo with a blue circle centered on the Jardim Tunduru Botanical Gardens. A label indicated that the location was accurate to three hundred feet.

"I'll find it," Vermeulen said. "I have a bad feeling. You want to help?"

* * *

THE *CHAPA* RIDE TOOK ALMOST A half hour. At least it was a straight shot, no transfers required. They got to the gardens and realized that a radius of three hundred feet was a big area. They went to the spot at the center of the circle they had seen on the map, just west of the tennis courts. Around them were different kinds of deciduous trees, none of which Vermeulen knew, and a few beds that looked like they had been prepared for new plantings.

He looked for trashcans. There were two nearby. He checked the closest. Full of garbage, fruit peels, chicken bones, assorted wrappers. He dialed Simango's number, waited for the call to connect. No ring came from the receptacle. Nyussi had gone to the other can. She shook her head. Nothing there either. There were no other obvious places to dispose of a mobile phone.

He stopped. If whoever lured Simango into a trap had taken her phone, they'd have disabled it, taken out the battery, or destroyed it. The fact that it still rang and showed up on Google meant that Simango had had a plan. He stood up straight and looked around. There, farther west, was the Casa de Ferro. Beyond that was the Banco Terra, where they had inquired about the transfer. He turned in the opposite direction. Past the gardens stood several tall office buildings. A block over, he could see the top of the building that housed the offices of Global Alternatives.

It was obvious. Simango had taken a *chapa* to her appointment at Global Alternatives. She was under no illusions about the job offer. There was a chance it could end badly. As she crossed the botanical gardens, she left her phone somewhere. If all turned out well, she'd come back for it. If her worst fears came true, the phone could be found with all information intact.

He examined the trees around him. The phone had to be hidden, but also accessible for a woman on the short side. That eliminated the crooks of branches sticking out from the trunks. All of them were too high, even for Vermeulen. He checked for holes made by nesting birds. There were none large enough to hold a phone. That left roots. And there was only one possible tree, an ancient behemoth that emerged from the ground with a tangle of roots thicker than a weightlifter's thigh.

Vermeulen dialed Simango's number again and slowly walked the circumference of the giant root system. There was no ring. He stopped and listened. Nothing. He walked farther, stopped after five steps, listened again. There was something. An angry insect trapped inside the tree. He took two more steps. The buzzing got louder. There it was. A slit between two roots. He reached into the slit and pulled out Simango's phone.

CHAPTER TWENTY-THREE

GOLD NIB

———◆———

Nyussi plugged the phone in as soon as they made it back to the office. "Let's let it charge awhile. The battery was almost dead, and we don't want it to die right when we find out what's on it," she said.

"You're pretty optimistic that we'll find something."

"I don't know about you, but we all live on our phones. The computers in the office were basically for writing proposals and accounting. So yes, if Aisa had any information, it would be on her phone. Why else would she hide it?"

Vermeulen couldn't quite imagine what Simango could have found out that she hadn't shared with him. Her messages hadn't offered any clues.

Nyussi checked the email messages, which were identical to the ones she'd seen on the computer. The two new ones were irrelevant. Next came the call history. Over the past three days, Simango had indeed received two calls from Global Alternatives. The first one before she'd called Vermeulen in Beira. The last calls were to her kids' school and a number that neither Nyussi nor Vermeulen recognized.

"Let me see the message from Global Alternatives again," Vermeulen said.

Nyussi opened the message. Vermeulen scanned it.

"Did you see that line about her kids? That could be a threat. I wonder if she arranged for her kids to go to a safe place," he said. "She must have been expecting the worst. Why did she even accept the invitation?"

Nyussi shrugged. "I don't know. Maybe the job offer was enticing enough."

"I don't think she was serious about taking a job at Global Alternatives," Vermeulen said. "She was the heart and soul of Nossa Terra. She'd do anything to save the organization."

"You'd think, but I have seen people turn around for a whole lot less."

Nyussi checked the calendar app. No appointments for the past three days. The meeting at Global Alternatives was missing, too. Simango's notes were next. Again, nothing of importance stuck out. The last note had been entered the day before the symposium where she and Vermeulen had listened to Isabel LaFleur outline the plan for the Sofala Project.

"I'm starting to think there's nothing on this thing," Nyussi said.

"Where else could we look?"

"Games, Music, and Photos."

"I doubt she played games on her phone."

"You'd be surprised. Some game involving pieces of candy was her favorite. But you're right. Let's check photos."

Simango was a haphazard photographer. Many of the photographs showed her children mugging for the camera. The last series showed street scenes. They were taken just two days ago. He saw nothing remarkable about them. People milling about on a square next to a modern building.

"Do you know where that is?" Vermeulen said.

"Wait." Nyussi zoomed in. "That's outside the Lusomundo Cinema, near the Maputo Shopping Centre."

"She wouldn't take pictures of a cinema. So there's something else. Can you enlarge them?"

Nyussi fished for a cable from her desk and connected the phone to her computer. A few mouse clicks later, a gallery of thumbprints appeared on her monitor. She double-clicked the first of the pictures outside the cinema. The image filled the screen. There was a façade covered with tiles in primary colors. A glassed-in atrium jutted from the façade into an open-air courtyard filled with café tables and chairs. Most of the tables were empty.

"It's late morning," Nyussi said. "The sun is casting a shadow over the entrance."

"It can't be the cinema. It has to be the people sitting at the tables," Vermeulen said.

Nyussi zoomed in on the first of the occupied tables. Just three teenagers sipping on soft drinks.

"They should be in school," Nyussi said. She panned to the next table. More teenagers. More panning.

"Hold it," Vermeulen said. "There. That's Paolo Gould. Next to him is Isabel LaFleur. Who's sitting with them?"

"I don't know. I didn't even know that the other two were the Global Alternative bosses."

"Can you enlarge it more?"

Nyussi clicked the mouse, but the image pixelated.

"Try the next one," Vermeulen said.

The image didn't offer any more clarity. There were two more photos. For the last one, Simango had repositioned herself, and the face of the third person was clearer now. He was of Indian extraction. Vermeulen had met him once before. It was Mr. Pai from Mauritius Bank and Trust.

* * *

THEY'D SEARCHED HER BAG. THEY HADN'T believed her when she told them she'd lost her phone. Gould had patted her down. Didn't try to hide his lewd grin while he was doing it. They'd locked her in this closet three hours ago.

None of it came as a surprise to Asia Simango. The moment she'd read the email inviting her to discuss future employment, she knew they were after her.

This is an exciting opportunity for you. Your children will thank you.

Yes, those two sentences sounded innocent enough. Just an example of how nice Global Alternatives was. Except that no prospective employer mentioned your children before you even set foot in their door. It would be something to discuss when agreeing on terms. No, it was a threat, posed in the most innocent manner, should those emails ever be seen by anyone else.

First thing was making sure her children were safe. She'd called the school. Yes, Alima and João were in their classes. Then she'd called their minder, a middle-aged widow, whom she paid good money. In return, the widow made sure the kids got food whenever she had to work late or go out of town. Yes, she'd pick up the children from school right away.

By the time Aisa entered the office, she knew her children were safe at the widow's house. It was all she needed.

The meeting was predictable. The job wasn't real. Global Alternatives had no intention of hiring her. But an employment contract lay on the table in the conference room. The contract included a non-compete clause, preventing her from working in any development-related field in Mozambique. Next to it lay the real reasons for the job offer, a non-disclosure agreement prohibiting her from discussing anything related to Global Alternatives anywhere in the world, even after her employment ended. A gag order that would begin the moment she signed the agreement.

The last item on the table was a check for sixty thousand *meticais*. A thousand dollars for her soul. The supply of souls had to be high if hers fetched so little. Or it was a sign of the disdain they felt for her. She didn't even warrant a decent bribe. Not that the amount would have made a difference.

She didn't sign.

LaFleur and Gould looked at each other.

"I had hoped we would handle this in a civilized manner," LaFleur said.

Civilized? Simango shook her head. Nothing had changed in a century.

Europeans were still *civilizing* the savages. This time with legal documents instead of guns.

"But now I need to remind you that your children will be grateful if you sign," LaFleur said.

"My children will be grateful to know that their mother could not be bought."

"I doubt that very much," Gould said.

They took Simango to the janitor's closet and locked her in.

* * *

"I'D HAVE THOUGHT HER KIDS WOULD be enough of an incentive," LaFleur said. "It made her come here. Why didn't she take the next step and sign? Maybe I should have offered her more money."

She stood by the window of the conference room and looked out at the gray ocean in the distance. Gould sat at the table.

"It wouldn't have made a difference," he said. "I'm worried about her phone."

A break in the cloud let through a slice of light that bathed the office in a soft gold.

"She should've had it on her," he said. "No way she comes to an appointment without her phone."

"Why does that worry you?"

"Because it means she left it somewhere. She didn't lose it."

"We'll just go for her kids. The phone won't make a difference."

"I don't think her kids are in play anymore."

LaFleur raised her eyebrows. "Come on. We know their school. We know where they live. It's not rocket science."

Gould got up and started pacing.

"Unless they aren't there anymore. Then it's harder than rocket science." Gould held up a hand. "Listen, Simango came here knowing full well she wouldn't take this job."

"Then why did she come at all?"

"Because she needed time."

His phone rang. He looked at the screen, answered, and listened.

"You've checked all known places?" he said and listened again. "Okay, come back to the office."

He turned to LaFleur.

"Just as I thought. The kids were picked up early. They aren't at home, on the way, or any other place we know of. Simango knew what we were up to and took our leverage away. If we had her phone, we could see who she called. That's why she didn't bring it."

LaFleur looked out of the window again. She said nothing. Gould knew better than to interrupt.

Five minutes later, LaFleur turned around.

"I'm not going to let some pseudo-revolutionary throwback stand in my way. You ever listen to that Nossa Terra struggle rhetoric? As if the last thirty years had never happened."

Gould stood looking out the window, knowing she'd reel off her usual litany. He'd heard it often enough. How the only way Africa could ever feed itself was through intensive agriculture using high-tech tools and GMOs. How anyone disputing this was living in a dream world, or the past. How they'd be responsible, condemning the entire continent to malnutrition and starvation.

He tuned out, because she was wrong. He'd been in development long enough to know that the continent only tolerated outsiders, even if it led them to believe that whatever new ideas they brought would be embraced—this time for sure, really, cross our collective hearts. Of course, nothing of the kind would happen. There was something ancient about this continent that white people with their puerile belief in progress couldn't fathom. It wasn't so much a rejection of modernity. If anything, Africa was *amodern*. Life wasn't about getting from here to a better place. Life just was. Seasons, cycles, call it what you want. No European idea could crack that. He'd once broached these thoughts with LaFleur. She'd called him a racist.

"I say we do what needs to be done," LaFleur said at the end of her rant.

"Don't let's be rash," he said. "Two bodies from the same organization washing up at Maputo Beach will rouse suspicion even here. Paito's case is still open. And Vermeulen is still around."

"Not much longer. He's leaving tomorrow. We can hold her until then. After that, nobody will care. When they find her, we'll even issue a press release, mourning her death and telling everyone she'd decided to come work for us. That'll shut up anyone holding a candle for her."

* * *

SIMANGO HOPED THAT VERMEULEN WOULD FIND her phone. She'd stuck it into the old baobab on the chance that he'd be clever enough to search for it. Nobody else would be looking for her. Most of the staff was already gone, and Zara seemed rather cold when she left for her meeting. If she didn't know about Global Alternatives, she probably suspected. She'd always sided with Helton, and she could have read her emails. It came down to Vermeulen trusting her enough to realize she'd do the right thing.

It was time to reassess her strategy. Refusing to sign the contract with the odious clauses was her first step. It got her inside the office. The next step would be offering to sign after all. They wouldn't give her the job. No, they were trying to shut her up. But it might give her more time to find the evidence she needed. Once their criminal actions were made public, she'd speak out. Contracts with criminals weren't enforceable, were they?

The wire transfer was the key. Why else would LaFleur and Gould have met with the manager from Mauritius Bank and Trust? It was sheer luck that she'd come upon them. She'd been on her way home from the Maputo Shopping Centre and cut through the courtyard when she spotted them. If Vermeulen found her phone, he'd find the picture. It should confirm what he already suspected.

Simango banged against the door. It took a few minutes before Gould opened it.

"What do you want?" he said.

"I have changed my mind. I will sign the contract and take the signing bonus."

Gould said nothing. She could see his mind at work, parsing the information, sorting the options, and mostly figuring out what her angle might be.

"Wait," he said and locked the door.

Five minutes later, the door opened again and both LaFleur and Gould stood outside.

"I'm delighted to hear that you've changed your mind," LaFleur said and stretched out her hand.

Simango took it. It was cool and smooth. A well-manicured hand. They shook just a moment too long.

"What made you change your mind?" Gould said.

"I just asked myself how I could best make a difference. Of course, Nossa Terra would have been my first choice, but that is over. What do you Americans say? If you cannot beat them, join them. This way I can still use my expertise to help poor farmers."

"I'd hoped you'd come to see it that way," LaFleur said with a brilliant smile. Her teeth looked as smooth as her hands.

They led Simango back to the conference room. The contract and the check were still on the table. LaFleur handed her a pen. It was solid metal, its golden nib etched with a floral pattern. She had never held a writing instrument like it in her life. The pen glided over the paper like a feather. Her signature looked more impressive than it ever had. She felt a pang of sadness when she handed it back to LaFleur. It was a beautiful thing.

"Welcome aboard," LaFleur said. "Let me show you your office."

They walked across the hallway to a door. Inside stood a desk, a chair, and a file cabinet. No window. The desk was empty. No phone, no computer. It had all the ambiance of a prison cell, except even prison cells had windows.

"Make yourself at home. There are paper and pencils in the drawer. You can begin by drawing up a plan on how to persuade the farmers to take a job with GreenAnt."

LaFleur and Gould left the room and the door slammed shut.

She tried the handle. It didn't budge.

Chapter Twenty-Four

Good People

———◆———

T HE PHONE WOKE VERMEULEN THE NEXT morning. He rolled over and reached for it. The sudden motion sent a wave of bile up his gullet. He retched. Right. There had been beer. A lot of beer. Understandable, given the mess he was in. As if on cue, a nasty headache pushed itself into the foreground. *Damn.*

Nyussi and he had decided to meet again to figure out what to do next. They were sure that Simango had gone to Global Alternatives. They weren't sure how to find out what happened to her. Getting inside was the goal. They just hadn't figured out how to do that. Maybe she'd had an idea overnight.

The phone almost evaded his grasp, but he managed to tap the reply button.

"What?" he said in a voice like a hoarse howler monkey's.

"And good morning to you, too," Tessa said. "It sounds like I interrupted a lovely hangover. My apologies. Should I try later?"

"No, I should be up anyway. What time is it?"

"Ten thirty."

Damn. He'd overslept. How long had he stayed at the bar the night before?

"What's up?" he said.

"I'm at the airport. Tell me where you're staying so I can minister to you."

The happy sound he wanted to utter emerged as a raspy snort. He gave her the information. "No need to minister to me; I'll be up and ready when you get here."

"Maybe just ready. No need to be up."

The advantage of being late was missing the bathroom rush. The shower down the hall was empty, and he took his time, letting the hot water ease his aches. He put on his last fresh shirt and underwear. Both sets of trousers needed cleaning. He chose the ones he hadn't worn the day before and went for coffee. A half hour later, Tessa walked into the bar. She dropped her bag and gave him a cautious hug. He squeezed her in return.

"Oh my," she said. "Somebody has made a dramatic recovery. Maybe we should go back to your room."

"Better not; there's a lot of stuff happening. Have you had breakfast?"

"A little on the plane, but I could eat more."

"Let's walk and talk. There are some great food stalls on the way."

They put her bags into his room and made their way to the Nossa Terra office while Vermeulen filled her in on what happened yesterday. Tessa ate a skewer of roasted vegetables while they walked.

Nyussi was waiting for them at the office.

"We need to get inside Global Alternatives," Vermeulen said. "Hopefully Simango is still there. I doubt they had a safe house set up."

"What if she went home?" Tessa said.

"They wouldn't let her go," Vermeulen said.

"Why not? If she signed on, they'd have no reason to detain her."

"They don't trust her," Nyussi said. "They wouldn't let her out of their sight."

"I know you can't call her," Tessa said. "But someone should go by her house."

"Okay," Nyussi said. "I'll go. What will you do?"

"We'll figure out a way to get inside Global Alternatives," Vermeulen said.

"That's easy," Tessa said. "I'm a journalist. I'll ask for an interview. Let me call and set it up."

* * *

AT TWO IN THE AFTERNOON, TESSA walked into the high rise at Rua Timor Leste and presented her credentials at the security desk. A guard was called to announce her arrival and show her to the elevator.

On the fifth floor, she entered through the frosted-glass doors with the gold Global Alternatives logo. There was no receptionist. Paolo Gould came out of his office and stuck out his hand.

"Welcome to Global Alternatives," he said.

Tessa shook his hand.

"I'm grateful you managed to squeeze me in on such short notice. After seeing your operations in Sofala, I wanted to speak to the leadership. Billy Ray was nice enough but a bit fuzzy on the particulars."

"Yup, that's Billy Ray all right. We'd be happy to fill you in. By the way, we were sorry to hear about the kidnapping. It must have been a harrowing experience."

"It was indeed. Fortunately, it all ended well. I've been in worse situations. It comes with the territory."

"Glad to know you took it in stride. Please follow me to our conference room. I'll get Ms. LaFleur."

Once alone, Tessa texted Vermeulen that there was no receptionist and that the entrance was unlocked. She stepped outside the conference room to check out the layout of the office. Across from the conference room was the reception area with a desk and chair. Off to the right was a door with a vent that indicated a janitor's closet. The reception area led to a short corridor with four doors. The one at the end opened and Gould stepped out, followed by a woman. The woman approached Tessa with brisk steps and stuck out her hand.

"Good afternoon, Ms. Bishonga. I'm Isabel LaFleur. Delighted to make your acquaintance. And impressed that you stick to your job even after such a traumatic experience. A woman after my own heart. The rebel and bandit activity in Sofala is causing more and more headaches for us, too. Let's sit and talk."

They settled around one end of the conference table. LaFleur put a batch of papers in front of her and looked at Tessa, eyebrows raised.

"You run on a skeleton staff here," Tessa said. "Unlike many development organizations I've come across."

"Well, we do have a receptionist and a couple of support staff. They are out today. So it's just us. But we try to run a lean operation. Development is too important to spend a lot of money on overhead. That's how Global Alternatives is different. We focus on results, not plush offices like some of our competitors."

"Such as?" Tessa said.

"Oh, let's not get into name calling. They are doing their work; we are doing ours. We're just better and more efficient."

Tessa took a portable recorder from her bag.

"Do you mind if I record this interview? It's better for all of us."

"Of course. Let me start by telling you the basic philosophy of Global Alternatives. I know you probably read some of that on our website, but that was written by marketing consultants in the U.S. It's in places like Sofala province that the rubber meets the road and where our philosophy makes a difference."

LaFleur fell into a well-rehearsed spiel throwing out the usual development lingo like *efficiency, stakeholders, efficacy, long-term solutions*, and of course, *sustainability*. Tessa had heard it all before. The only new addition was the focus on technological solutions. Even that wasn't new. Technology had been development's magical solution for the past thirty years. It was depressing to hear yet another white person telling her what was wrong with her continent and that she knew just how to fix it. The one thing nobody had ever done for the better part of a century was sit down and listen.

* * *

THE SECURITY DESK AT THE GROUND floor was an obstacle. No way Vermeulen could get past that without announcing his presence. But every building has more than one access point. The trash had to be taken out someplace, and tenants weren't going to carry their furnishings through the front door. He skulked around the rear of the high rise, taking cover behind a large garbage container. It reeked of the complex stench only trash in hot climates produces. Breathing through his mouth, he surveyed the area. It was the kind of space where dogs went to die—concrete, dirt, neglect. The tenants on the lower floors had better get discounts on their rents. Besides the container, there was a wooden shed without discernible purpose, a pile of sand, and as he had hoped, a low loading dock for delivery vans. The roll-up gate was down.

He hopped onto the dock and checked the gate. There was no handle. An arm's length to the left of the gate was a recess that contained a metal box with a red button and lock. He pushed the button. Nothing happened. Bending down, he slipped his fingers under the rubber gasket that sealed the gap between the gate and the concrete and pulled up with all his strength. It had the same effect as pushing the red button, except that his back hurt when he let go. He looked around. Nobody had witnessed this embarrassing effort. Then he noticed a security camera above and to the right pointing straight at him. *Damn.*

Vermeulen jumped from the dock and inspected the shed. The wooden door was rotten enough that it wouldn't have offered much resistance even if there had been a lock. He pulled it open. Inside were two brooms, a shovel, a chair without a backrest, a cot, and a small shelf that held a candle, matches, and two well-used paperbacks. A magazine page with a picture of a black man in military uniform was pinned to one of the walls. Vermeulen picked up the books. One was *The Struggle for Mozambique* by Eduardo Mondlane. The other was by Kwame Nkrumah, its title in Portuguese. Whoever lived here was at least bilingual.

There was nothing that could have gotten him inside the building. He left the shack and closed the door. From the corner of his eye, he saw a figure ducking behind the Dumpster. He looked in the opposite direction and waited a moment before spinning around. A dark and very wrinkled face stared at him.

Vermeulen smiled, waved, and said, "*Bom dia.*" The face didn't disappear. "Can you help me?"

A short man in old clothing emerged from behind the Dumpster. He didn't come any closer.

"What do you want?" the man said.

"I need to get inside."

"You're white. Use the front door."

"That's not an option."

"Not my problem. *Suca!*"

"I really must get inside. Two friends of mine are confronting some bad people on the fifth floor."

"What else is new? All the good people are dead."

"My friends are good people," Vermeulen said.

"Right, more Europeans telling us how to run things."

Vermeulen took a deep breath.

"Where'd you learn English?" Vermeulen said.

"*Majarimani.*"

Vermeulen's face must have signaled his lack of understanding.

"German Democratic Republic. Where'd you learn yours?"

"Belgium. How'd you end up in this shack?"

"Privatization."

"What did you do for a living?"

"*Ouve-lá, pah,*" the man said, his face showing his weariness. "The only reason the building management tolerates my shack is because I keep the riffraff away. So get out of here."

"No, you listen to me," Vermeulen said. "These friends of mine are African. They've spent their lives helping people. You can either sit here and whine about your life or you can do something useful and show me how to get inside."

The man spat on the ground but didn't walk away. "I was a utility technician, *está a ver?* They sent me abroad for training. I came back and I had a good job in Nampula. Then, a few years ago, my unit was let go. A foreign contractor was hired. I ended up here. Who is holding your friends?"

"A foreign foundation, Global Alternatives. They stole five million dollars and are trying to buy land up north to grow biofuel. The kind of Europeans who're telling you what to do."

"I know them. Flashy cars and haughty. Follow me."

The man led Vermeulen around the corner of the building. There was a one-by-two yard opening covered by a grate. The grate was anchored with a chain to the concrete below.

The man lifted a short side of the grate and directed Vermeulen to do the same with the other one.

"We can't lift it—there's a chain," Vermeulen said.

"Tell me something I don't know." The man rolled his eyes. "We're only lifting it high enough to clear the ground. There's enough slack in the chain for that. Then we'll turn it and you'll have your entrance. I use this to get inside when it's raining too much. It leads to the boiler room. From there you can take the staircase."

CHAPTER TWENTY-FIVE

STICKY TAPE

———◆———

VERMEULEN RACED UP TO THE FIFTH floor and entered the corridor. The Global Alternatives office was around the corner. He opened the frosted-glass door, stepped inside, and closed the door quietly. Nobody at the reception. The office seemed abandoned.

The door to the conference room stood open. It was empty, too. About to turn away, he saw something on a chair. It was a pen. Not just any pen, a Montblanc. The hair at the back of his neck stood up. It was Tessa's favorite writing tool.

He stashed it in his pocket and raced through the rest of the office. Signs of a hasty departure were everywhere. A cup of cappuccino and a half-eaten biscotti in LaFleur's office, a cigarette not properly extinguished in Gould's office, and several pieces of paper in a third office that had Aisa Simango's name at the top and looked like a contract. The waste basket contained a small, discarded box. The word *Sedativo* on the label was all he needed.

The last office was full of tech equipment. A monitor displayed a video image of the loading dock and the area behind it. A black Land Rover stood there. Two black-clad men—the same goons who'd been on his tail all along—pushed Tessa and Simango into the back of the SUV. There was no sound, but he could see Tessa shouting.

They had Tessa.

Vermeulen raced back to the elevator. The lighted numbers over the door indicated that the car was on the ground floor. He pressed the down button repeatedly. Nothing happened. Too late. He'd wasted time taking the staircase.

He ran back into the office with the video link to the loading dock. The SUV was still there. He saved a screenshot of the video before it turned and drove away. The image was a little grainy. He enlarged it and saw the oval decal with the letters ZA. The Land Rover was registered in South Africa. The license plate ended with the letters GP—the code for the Gauteng province, which was basically Johannesburg. He printed the image just in case. Maybe the police could help. But how? He didn't even know where the next police station was. And what was he to tell them?

"I thought you'd be on a plane back to New York."

LaFleur's voice startled him. If she was surprised to see him, she didn't let on.

"Where are you taking them?" he said. "Tessa is a journalist. She has nothing to do with your crooked scheme."

"She's involved, just like Simango. I'm tired of all this interference. I have a project to complete."

"Then why not leave them? They couldn't possibly stop you."

"You know how it is with little dogs. They can't really do any damage, but their incessant yapping really gets on your nerves."

"What?" Vermeulen said. "You're calling them yapping dogs?"

"Oh shut up, will you? Those of us who worry about actually getting things done are really tired of all the noise made by those who wallow in the past. Your only saving grace was your UN connection. Last I heard, that isn't going so well. So shut the fuck up, board your goddamn plane, and let me get on with my job."

"Or what?" The heat of his anger made his brow damp with sweat. "I won't leave until I know they're safe. I'll call the police and invite them here. I have some information that ought to interest them."

"You just don't give up, do you?"

She turned and shouted "Jonas!" The man he'd dodged at the café came into the room, his pistol pointed straight at Vermeulen.

"Lock him in the janitor's room for now. We'll deal with him when your colleagues get back," LaFleur said. She turned and left the room.

Jonas motioned with the pistol toward the door.

"Let's go," he said.

Vermeulen needed time and a plan. Making time was easy—just walk slowly. Making a plan was harder.

"Come on, move it," the Jonas said.

Vermeulen didn't obey. The guy wasn't going to shoot him. Not for walking slowly. But he was antsy and might make a mistake. Jonas stepped behind him so he could prod him with the pistol. First mistake. Overconfident, like most people holding guns. They look at the weapon in their hand and think they hold the ace, that the targets are scared for their lives. They think that the gun in their hand will automatically end all resistance.

"Move it," he said again and poked the pistol in the small of Vermeulen's back.

Jonas was right-handed. Which meant all Vermeulen had to do was spin left to slap the hand with the gun away from his body. It was a risky move. But the guy was dumb enough to stand close. By the time his brain had processed that the situation had changed, the gun would be pointing elsewhere.

Vermeulen took a short step forward to put weight on his right foot. The man behind him poked him harder with the gun. Vermeulen visualized the height of the pistol, spun around as if a tightly coiled spring had broken loose, and slapped the arm holding the gun. Except the arm wasn't there. Jonas must have sensed that something was coming. He'd stepped back. Not meeting any resistance, Vermeulen spun farther to the right. Which was his lucky break because Jonas pulled the trigger. The bullet ripped his sleeve. Vemeulen felt the heat blister his skin. A computer monitor disintegrated into tiny pieces.

Jonas' hand looked limp. Firing the gun singlehandedly, without anticipation, must have given his wrist a nasty jerk. Vermeulen lunged at the man's knees. They crashed to the floor. The pistol fell on the carpet. Vermeulen grabbed it and jumped back up. Unlike Jonas, he stepped back. With enough distance, a bullet always beat a fist.

The sudden change of fortune must not have registered with Jonas, because he rushed Vermeulen. A bad choice. Vermeulen aimed at the man's thigh and pulled the trigger. Another shot boomed in the small room. The gangster fell to the floor, screaming and holding his leg.

"Shut up," Vermeulen said. "You'll live, which is more than I can say for your victims."

LaFleur's head appeared in the doorway. She saw her goon on the floor and wanted to run, but froze at the sight of the pistol pointed at her.

"Here's what we're going to do," he said and ripped the cord from the phone and the wall. "You'll tie his wrists behind his back. Make it good and tight."

"No way. You can't make me."

"Don't be so sure. Look at him. A hole in the thigh isn't deadly, but it hurts like hell."

"You wouldn't. I'm the head of Global Alternatives in Mozambique."

"You're a crook, worse than this guy. So don't tempt me. I have nothing to lose."

He must have looked sufficiently crazed, because LaFleur went about tying Jonas' wrists. She did a surprisingly meticulous job. Next, he took her to the janitor's closet. There were no ropes, but the emergency tool of janitors worldwide—sticky tape. He took a roll and cajoled LaFleur back to the office. There, he told her to wrap the tape around the man's ankles. LaFleur complied without a word.

"Now take a seat in this chair," he said.

She sat down.

"Tell me where your goons took the two women?"

She shook her head and said, "Never."

"Suit yourself."

Sticking the gun in his belt, Vermeulen grabbed the roll of tape from her, ripped a long strip off, and slapped it around her right wrist and the armrest. Another strip reinforced the first one. He repeated the process with the other wrist. Her ankles were a bit more difficult, because she tried to kick him. He simply wrapped a length of tape around her ankles and the chair legs, and she was out of commission.

Maybe the old man downstairs had overheard the hit men talk about their destination. He was about to run downstairs, but stopped. Having the run of the office was his chance to get his hands on documents that would reveal the whereabouts of the missing funds. If he were more computer-savvy, he could do it himself, but he didn't have time for that. He called Zara Nyussi.

"Can you come to the Global Alternatives offices right away? Take a metered cab if you need to. But make it as fast as possible."

"No need for a taxi. I'm at Banco Terra dealing with our accounts. I'll be there in ten minutes."

Ten minutes was too long, but Vermeulen had no choice. He used the time to search the offices. There was paperwork in both LaFleur's and Gould's office, but he had no idea if it was related to the five million dollars. The telephone on the reception desk rang. Vermeulen answered, "Global Alternatives, how can I help you?"

Someone at the security station on the ground floor told him that a Ms. Nyussi was there to see them.

"Sure, send her up."

When the elevator on the corridor finally dinged, Vermeulen was already pacing outside the door.

"Good that you could come so fast. We are in a dicey situation. Both Simango and a friend of mine have been abducted and I'm going after them. LaFleur and one of her hit men are tied up. Keep an eye on them. I thought you could find out what happened to the missing money using their computers."

"What about passwords?"

"Sorry, I can't help you there. Ask LaFleur, but don't expect her to cooperate. I found her phone on her desk. Maybe it has clues."

He took the elevator to the second floor and then the stairs down to the basement, past the boiler and the metal grate. The old man was waiting for him.

"You're too late," he said.

"I know. It couldn't be avoided. They had a gun on me. It took a while to get my hands on it. Do you know where they went?"

"They went to the port."

"Which section?"

"They didn't say. But the one who went back up gave the driver the coordinates."

"And you remember them?"

The old man nodded. He recited them as Vermeulen typed them into the map app on his phone. The image of a warehouse by the quay appeared on the screen.

"You wouldn't happen to have an old car stashed away here?"

The old man smiled. "Sorry, I can't help you there."

The noise of vehicle made him look around the corner of the building.

"Maybe I can, after all," he said. "Looks like the black Land Rover just drove up. That's good news."

Vermeulen wasn't listening to him. He was frantically dialing Nyussi's number. When she answered, he said, "Get out of there now. The hit men are back. Drop everything and leave. Take the stairs to the floor below, then the elevator, and walk away. Now."

He ended the call and frowned. "How is that good news?"

"Think about it," the old man said. "They came back fast. That wasn't enough time to kill two people and dispose of their bodies. They stashed them at that warehouse. This is your chance to save them."

Of course, the man was right. And there was a car waiting for him.

CHAPTER TWENTY-SIX

MOLESKIN

———— ◆ ————

UNFORTUNATELY, THE LAND ROVER WASN'T JUST standing there, waiting for Vermeulen to hop into the driver's seat. One of the hit men was leaning against the front fender, smoking and looking bored. The corner of the building where Vermeulen stood was about a hundred yards from the SUV. No chance of sneaking up on the guard.

"How many left when they took the hostages away?" Vermeulen said.

"Three. Two black, one white."

"Too bad we didn't see how many came back. We'll have to neutralize this one. I need you to create a diversion."

The old man saluted and said, "Yes, sir."

But he didn't move. This wasn't the moment to play games. Vermeulen opened his mouth to say so. He closed it again. The old man had already helped him immensely. He'd just taken that for granted.

"I'm sorry," he said. "I've been a real ass. My name is Valentin Vermeulen. What's yours?"

He stretched out his hand.

"George," the man said. "Pleased to meet you."

"I'm very grateful for your help, and I'd really appreciate one more effort."

"Sure thing," George said. "Always happy to oblige a courteous request."

He walked around the corner and adopted the shuffling gait of homeless men.

"*Tem um cigarro, meu?*" he slurred when he was about fifty yards away.

The hit man turned toward him, shrugged, and turned away.

"*Um cigarro, por favor.*" This time a lot louder.

The gangster looked up again.

"Get lost, old man. I haven't got a cigar."

So the gangsters didn't speak Portuguese. Given their Jo'burg plates, that made sense. But why would Global Alternatives hire foreign thugs? Not that it mattered. Hit men were trouble, no matter what language they spoke.

George made it all the way to the car. He was still going on about a *cigarro*—a cigarette. His voice had gotten louder and whinier. He knew how to get on someone's nerves.

"Fuck off, old man."

"Fuck off *você também*," George said. Then he began to sing "Fuck off, fuck off, fuck off" to the tune of some children's song. George's performance was perfectly obnoxious. Enough to drive a sane person up the wall. He shuffled next to the man and got him to turn his back to where Vermeulen waited. The thug didn't have the patience of most people. He pulled out his gun and pressed it against George's temple. George gave him a beatific smile, as if a gun to his head were the solution to all his problems. Even a guy dumb enough to guard the car had to realize that threatening George wasn't going to make him go away.

"I only got cigarettes," the thug said.

"Si, um cigarro."

The guy reached into his pocket and pulled out a pack. That's when Vermeulen pressed the muzzle of his gun against his neck. At least the gangster knew the protocol. He froze. George twisted the pistol from the man's hand. Then Vermeulen spun him around and slammed him against the car.

"Kindly check the car for a rope or anything else to tie him up," he said.

George did so and came back with a coil of sturdy rope. Vermeulen pulled the gangster forward and George yanked his hands behind the back and tied them together. Clearly the man had learned more than an electrician's trade. The figure-eight cuffs he tied weren't going to give way. Vermeulen pushed the man on the ground where George repeated the maneuver with the ankles. Vermeulen went through the man's pockets and found the car keys. George pulled a small pistol from an ankle holster. They dragged the thug against the wall of George's shack.

"They'll find him soon enough," Vermeulen said.

"Yes, and they'll give him another gun and he'll be making mischief again."

"I don't want to take him along."

"Don't worry."

George knelt down, grabbed the tied hands, and with two swift moves, broke the man's index fingers. The thug screamed.

"At least he won't be shooting at us right away," George said. "*Deixe's ir agora, pah!*"

"I didn't know you'd joined the team."

"I haven't, but you need help and you seem to be a good enough guy to deserve it. *Deixe's vá.*"

* * *

THE GPS OF THE LAND ROVER got them to the port in fifteen minutes. They drove past a vast pile of scrap metal that was being loaded on a freighter. Their destination, a warehouse, stood a quarter mile farther. They drove past the warehouse and parked in the shadows of huge grain silos. In the distance, a massive freighter was being loaded with chutes that dumped something very dusty into its holds.

"Cement," George said. "Our export of last resort. Whenever we need hard currency, we ship cement abroad."

Vermeulen wasn't really concerned with the country's trade balance. He was figuring out his next steps. Between the two of them, they had two Berettas and the small semiautomatic from the guard's ankle holster. The Berettas had twenty-eight 9mm cartridges in their magazines, the small pistol ten. Quite a bit of weaponry, but without knowing the layout of the warehouse, he couldn't possibly know if it was enough. Not that Vermeulen wanted to go in with guns blazing. There could be many people inside. A single stray 9mm bullet could wreak havoc far beyond its intended target.

The warehouse dated back to colonial times. Its concrete walls were soot-stained from the days when steamers still docked here. Pockmarks that could have been caused by bullets or shrapnel had never been fixed. Two windows in steel frames looked rusted shut.

They walked over to the quay. The concrete was brittle, and the massive stone blocks at its edge had been chipped by the hulls of innumerable ships. Steel bollards stood like chess pawns waiting for the next move. The rails for the gantry cranes were thick with weeds. Despite its ramshackle appearance, the warehouse wasn't abandoned. A small coastal freighter about a hundred feet long was tied up next to it. A mess of boxes, barrels, and more crates stood on the quay, waiting for loading. Two workers connected the hook of the ship's crane to a net wrapped around four barrels. Two more watched the load rise into the air. The quay-side doors of the warehouse—rusty metal contraptions hanging on steel tracks like barn doors—stood open.

"This can't be right," Vermeulen said. "They wouldn't bring hostages to a working warehouse."

"Why not?" George said. "Looks like this ship is going up the coast to Inhambane, Beira, Quelimane, Nacala, and back again. What better way to get rid of people?"

"But all these people would be witnesses."

George shook his head.

"Why not?" Vermeulen said.

"All you need to do is to pay off the captain and a mate. The rest won't even notice. And even if they did, they wouldn't ask questions."

"But where are they holding the women?"

"Go and find out. You are the European. Make up something official, talk loud, walk around as if you owned the place. That still works, even three and a half decades after independence. Pisses me off no end."

Ordinarily, Vermeulen had no compunction pulling out the UN card and exaggerating his powers when he was up against pretentious officials. This was different, more like pulling out the race card, as it were. But it was Tessa's life on the line.

"Go for that guy," George said, pointing to a man standing in the shade of the open warehouse door. "He looks in charge."

All he had to do was to come up with some vaguely convincing reason why he should inspect the warehouse. He walked up to the man in the shade, stopped two feet away from him, and held out his UN ID.

"Good afternoon. I'm Valentin Vermeulen with the UN Office on Drugs and Crime," he said with more force than he'd thought he'd be able to muster. "I received a tip that drugs are being smuggled from this warehouse and I need to inspect it."

He didn't care if the man understood or not—he walked right past him into the warehouse. It took a moment for his eyes to adjust to the dim space. By then the man had caught up to him, saying something in Portuguese.

"Where is your boss?" Vermeulen said. "I need someone who speaks English."

"I the boss, sir."

"Then you better offer me every courtesy while I inspect this warehouse for illegal drugs."

The man looked flustered. George sidled up to him and translated. The man's eyes grew wider.

"No drugs," he said.

"Well. I'm not just going to take your word for it. I'm going to have to look myself."

He didn't really know where to start looking. There were a few pallets with sacks of something. He took the penknife from his pocket and stabbed it into one of the sacks. Brownish granules ran out. He caught some in his hand and sniffed them. Definitely fertilizer. There was a row of barrels without any labels. No idea what was inside, but he wasn't going to open these. The women would have to be kept in a room. But there was no small office in a corner, no loft or catwalk to some booth under the ceiling. He crossed the space to the rear wall, then marched to the left side. Along the way, he lifted a bag from a pallet, pretending to be interested. No sign of Tessa. He walked across to the right side. Same result.

He went back to the doors. This couldn't be. The GPS had brought them to this spot. It was the last place they had gone. Had they dropped off their hostages along the way? But why come here? He looked at the freighter tied up to the quay. It bobbed gently with the waves. He stepped back into the sunshine and walked to the bulwark of the ship. It was level with the quay, the deck three feet lower. The deck was a rusty green color. Two of the holds were open, the third one closed. The crane was about to lower a pallet of boxes into the second hold. Deep in the belly of the ship, someone shouted a command. The pallet moved over two feet, swaying in the air. Vermeulen had turned back to the warehouse when he saw something in a crack between the rails. A brown booklet. He bent down to pick it up. It was a Moleskin notebook, and it had Tessa's name on the inside.

CHAPTER TWENTY-SEVEN

THIRTY BULLETS

———————◆———————

"SHE'S ON THE SHIP SOMEWHERE," HE said to George. "This is her notebook."

Vermeulen jumped onto the deck of the freighter. George nodded and followed, using the steps. A lanky man in his fifties and of south Asian extraction came running. He was wearing shabby overalls and a peaked cap that once had been white. Vermeulen introduced himself and repeated the story about the drug tip, waving his UN ID in the man's face.

"I don't care," the man said. "I'm the captain and you can't come on my ship. So get off."

"My UN authorization trumps whatever claims you have. My associate and I will search this ship. If you wish to file a complaint with the UN Secretariat, be my guest. The office is at One, United Nations Plaza in New York City."

"Don't you need a warrant or some piece of paper?"

"Unlike the local police, I have universal jurisdiction, so step aside, please. Any resistance and I will make sure to take it to the international criminal court."

The list of lies was getting a little too long for Vermeulen's comfort. He could see that George was struggling to keep from laughing. But the captain had been shut up. Vermeulen took George aside.

"Do you think they'd be in the cargo holds?" Vermeulen said to George.

"There doesn't seem to be a lot of space. Besides, too many people would see them. The crew quarters seem a better option."

Vermeulen went along the bulwark to the bridge at the aft of the vessel. The ship was never meant to be farther from the coast than the water depth permitted. The entire aft structure was only four stories high, the navigational deck at the top, the crew quarters below that. Vermeulen climbed the companionway to the crew quarters. George clambered up behind him. The rest of the crew had already turned away from the diversion and were again focused on loading the cargo. The captain stood near the stairs and talked into a mobile phone.

When they reached the first level of the crew deck, Vermeulen opened the door. The air inside was hot and stale. A narrow corridor led the width of the deck to the other side. The white paint was peeling in places. Rusty streaks were everywhere. There were two doors, and near the center of the ship, companionways up and down.

"I guess we'll have to check each door," Vermeulen said and opened the first one.

The cabin contained a bed, a sink, and a desk with chair and wardrobe, all in the smallest possible space. A book lay on the table. The bed was made. No other signs of occupancy. The thought of spending more than an hour inside this coffin was enough to make Vermeulen shudder. The two went past the companionways to the other door. The room was identical to the first one.

"Not much crew here," Vermeulen said. "They're probably on leave, drinking away their pay."

"Or spending time with their families," George said.

Vermeulen looked at him, waiting for the next part. Nothing came. No criticism.

"Of course," Vermeulen said. "Let's go upstairs."

The next level consisted of a mess and galley, with access to four quarters. The galley was clean except for a pot of cold coffee and a cup, which stood on the table in the center of the room. Despite the vessel's down-and-out appearance, the captain at least tried to keep the parts of the vessel he had control over in shipshape.

Vermeulen opened the first door to the right. It was much larger than the cabins he'd seen on the floor below. The bed was full size, and there was an en-suite bathroom, a sitting area, and a small refrigerator—the captain's quarters, no doubt. The other three cabins were as neat and as small as the others they'd seen so far, and they were empty.

"I'm starting to see why the captain gave up so easily," George said. "At first I thought it was your flawless European performance. But it seems your friends aren't here."

"What about the notebook?"

"All it means is that at one point she was there. But not where she is now. I think the gangsters warned whoever was guarding the women to move them once they discovered the Land Rover was gone."

"We should ask the workers outside. They must have seen them."

"Yeah," George said, "but I doubt they would tell us. Nothing in it for them if they do but a lot of trouble."

"I'm not ready to give up. I'm going to the bridge."

Without waiting for a response, Vermeulen went back to the companionway and climbed upstairs.

Compared to the dim lighting in the crew quarters and mess, the bridge was bright with sunlight, but also much hotter than the rest of the decks. The side doors to the gangways were open, but it did little to relieve the stifling atmosphere. The wheel, the navigational equipment, and a desk with maps and a row of chairs against the rear wall left a lot of space. Vermeulen stepped outside and saw another companionway leading up to the weather deck. He climbed the steps and found himself in the perfect location to scope the rest of the ship. From his vantage point forward, there was only cargo space. Dockworkers were still loading the second hold. He could see at least three men inside the hold moving pallets to the sides. Add to them the crane operator and the quay-side workers, and at least ten men were occupied with the loading process. He had to agree with George: too many witnesses. If the women were on the ship, they were aft.

He walked to the back of the weather deck. A massive exhaust stack rose right behind it. The stink of burned hydrocarbons made him sneeze. And that was just from the generator running. At full steam and with the wrong wind direction, this had to be the worst place on the ship. He took four steps down to the funnel deck, eased past the exhaust stack, and looked down on the stern area. There was a small semicircle of deck between the bridge and the stern. He hadn't seen any access door, but it didn't matter; there was nothing there that could hide two persons. That left the engine room below deck.

As he turned to go back, he saw the lifeboat hang from its davits. There was only one, enough for a crew of six. The lifeboat was covered by a tarp that was tied to its gunwales. The front section of the tarp was loose, the ties hanging down. Had the crew been sloppy? That didn't seem likely, given the neatness everywhere else.

"I think I know where they are," he said to George. Running down the companionways and taking two steps at a time, he flung open the door onto the main deck and faced the captain pointing an Uzi at him.

"You had your chance to get off my ship," the captain said. "Now it's too late."

When Vermeulen saw two black-clad men jump aboard, he knew what the captain meant. The man had let him rummage around the ship because he'd called in reinforcements. Which was good because he didn't rely on his crew and bad because the assassins were more dangerous. Vermeulen raised his hands.

"Where's your friend?" the captain said.

Vermeulen resisted the temptation to turn around. He'd assumed George was right behind him. He must've seen the threat and stayed behind the door. Which, like the entire superstructure on the aft deck, was made of thick steel. He inched backward. The captain made an impatient gesture with the Uzi. Vermeulen was certain that George was following all this through the thick porthole in the door. He leaned against the bulwark, his hands still up. That gave George the space to open the door wide enough to let him inside.

"Don't bother," the captain said. "My gun fires six hundred rounds per minute. The magazine holds thirty cartridges. I'll empty the whole magazine in three seconds. Pretty lousy odds."

"I see," Vermeulen said slowly, taking a small step back. He now stood barely past the arc the door would make when opened. George had better be paying attention, because the next move depended on his instant reaction. "I also see that you've forgotten to set the safety lever to auto fire."

He had no way of seeing that, but the captain bought it and looked down. Just as he'd hoped, the door swung open and he dove into the opening. A volley of bullets hammered against the door as George pulled it shut. One of them shattered the porthole, hit the steel wall, and fell to the deck as a misshapen lump of lead.

"Quick, upstairs," Vermeulen said.

"And have them follow us? All we have to do is keep this door shut and we're safe."

"And how are we going to do that? Remember, there's an access door on the other side of the ship. There're only three of them, but if just one of them gets in there, we'd be fighting on two fronts. We better get off this bridge before they box us in."

George considered this. "We still should block this door to keep them occupied." He pointed at the steel handle that operated the bolt. "Hold this down until I come back."

Vermeulen remained in a crouch and held on to the lever. A moment later, he felt it move up. Someone working the outside handle. He pushed it down again. The handle moved against his hand. Whoever was outside pulled very hard. Vermeulen crouched with his side against the door and pressed with both arms to keep the handle down.

A shot exploded above him, the confined space magnifying the sound a thousand times. A bullet hit the steel deck with the sound of a rivet gun. It howled into the passage. Vermeulen looked up and saw a hand holding a pistol above him, the arm half outside the broken porthole. The shooter couldn't see him. The first shot had gone wide. The muzzle inched toward him. He sat down, his back against the wall, and put his feet against the door handle. He aimed his pistol and fired. A scream outside. The gun clattered to the deck. The bullet hit the ceiling and smashed against the deck a mere inch from his thigh. At least one of the squad was out of commission.

George came back with a length of wood he'd broken off a chair. Vermeulen inched forward and George jammed the wood between the door frame and the handle.

"What happened?" he said.

"Someone shot at me through the porthole. Unless he's ambidextrous, he won't be picking up a gun again."

They ran up the companionway, crossed the passage to the other side of the ship, and ran down again. They opened the door an inch.

Nobody there.

They opened the door a bit more.

Still nobody.

Vermeulen inched out and peered around the corner, across the cargo hold to the other side.

The captain stood back, still holding his Uzi. One of the black-clad killers stood next to him, wrapping something around the hand of the second one.

"Let's take them out," George said.

"Not from here. They're at least forty feet away. I don't like those odds. We need to get closer. I'll get behind them. You go back to the other side. When you hear my voice, open the door, and then we've boxed them in."

He crouched and crawled along the aft cargo hold until he reached a cross passage. After waiting until George had disappeared into the bridge again, he crawled across to the quay side of the ship. A quick peek around the corner of the cargo hold confirmed that the goons were still occupied with their first aid. But the captain was alert, scanning the bridge and the deck in front of it. The distance was still too great for a certain shot. Of course, the captain had the same disadvantage, but his Uzi more than evened the odds by its immense rate of fire. Thirty bullets in three seconds. One of them was bound to find its target. But he had no choice.

He took a deep breath and crawled around the corner and toward the captain. The men were arguing. Vermeulen could make out a few words. Something about not having enough people to get the job done. *Good.* As long as they were angry, they weren't paying attention.

Vermeulen kept crawling forward. When he was twenty feet away, the captain must have heard something. He spun around. Vermeulen flattened himself to the deck. The hail of bullets from the Uzi missed him by a foot or two. He fired once, made a minute adjustment, and fired again. His first bullet missed and hit the bridge structure. The second hit the captain in the shoulder. But the captain had already squeezed the trigger a second time.

A bullet seared Vermeulen's scalp as if someone had parted his hair with a red-hot poker. A burning heat seeped into his brain, trying to shut off all thought. He fought against it with all his will. Still prone on the deck, he saw the captain through filmy eyes, aimed once more, and fired. The man dropped like a sack, his Uzi flying over the bulwark to the quay.

George finally emerged from the door. He aimed, fired, and repeated the process. The two assassins fell to the deck.

Vermeulen pulled himself up. Wetness seeped down from his scalp. He held on to the bulwark and steadied himself.

Air. He needed air. Something dripped on his nose. He wiped it away. Blood. No time for blood.

He stepped over the captain and the goons. They were dead. He willed himself aft to the boat deck, scrambled up to the lifeboat, and tore away the tarp. Inside lay Tessa and Simango. Tied up and tape over their mouths. Vermeulen ripped off the Tessa's tape with a rapid pull. She gulped for air and said, "What took you so long?"

He tried to smile but passed out instead.

CHAPTER TWENTY-EIGHT

DISAPPOINTMENT

———————◆———————

At thirty-two thousand feet, Vermeulen's head pulsed even more than on the ground, as if air pressures had been the only thing that kept the blood inside. For the umpteenth time, he gingerly touched the scab on his head. The rational part of his brain told him to leave it alone, but his somatic nerves had a life of their own. He looked at his fingertips. No blood. Something to be grateful for.

Tessa had done her best to get him into travel shape. The infirmary on the freighter was pretty well-stocked. She'd cleaned the wound—*just a nick,* she'd said, even though it felt like someone had gouged his skull with a chisel. Her first impulse had been to shave his head so she could properly bandage it, but she'd decided that small hairs in the wound would only make things worse.

"Press this against the wound," she'd said and handed him a compress.

After he had bled through four gauze pads, the flow finally stopped, leaving him with a pulsing ache that got worse every time he moved. By the next morning a scab had formed, adding a maddening itch to the pain.

All of which had left him in a foul mood because he couldn't concentrate on what had to happen next. And a lot had to happen if he was going to get out of this with only a scab on his head. Zara Nyussi hadn't found any information at Global Alternatives because her time there was too short. But she had used it well by installing keystroke logger software, which would get her the information she needed to access the network. At least that's what he hoped.

Later that evening, Chipende arrived from Beira with KillBill, who couldn't go back after crossing Raul and his gang. Chipende's arrival boosted Aisa Simango's spirits. Finally someone from the old crew who was ready to step in and help. She'd been quietly grateful to Vermeulen and George for rescuing her, but she seemed depressed until Chipende showed up. They'd returned to the Nossa Terra office to figure out the next steps.

Truth be told, the scab on his head wasn't what angered Vermeulen. Missing out on what his friends were going to do in Maputo did. They would uncover the fraudulent practices of Global Alternatives while he flew to New York City to be fired, or worse, stack reams of paper in the UN print shop. He had no illusions about confronting Vincent Portallis. He couldn't imagine any scenario in which he would come out on top. Hell, he didn't even know if the man was in New York City, never mind harbor any illusions about getting an appointment with him.

The flight attendant brought him another beer.

"That looks like a nasty scratch," she said. "What happened?"

Without thinking, he said, "A bullet."

She gave him the kind of look that implied calling the captain and labeling him a security threat.

"Sorry," he said. "That was a bad joke. It was caused by a stupid accident."

The last thing he needed was to have the plane diverted.

She smiled again. "Aren't they always?"

The combination of painkillers and beer made him mellow and a little woozy. All things considered, not a bad place to be in. He closed his eyes and hoped for a good nap. He was almost there, his mind mulling his words *stupid accident,* when it occurred to him that nothing had been a damn accident ever since he first stepped into the Global Alternatives office. Everything he'd seen and experienced seemed carefully plotted. Whatever decision he'd thought he'd made on his own now seemed part of a larger plan, in which he'd played only a bit part.

LaFleur and Gould had wanted him to see that five million dollars of UN money were missing. They'd wanted him to investigate Nossa Terra. That way they could spread the word that the UN was investigating that little outfit, ultimately drying up their support from other aid organizations. It was only when Vermeulen didn't stop there and began digging deeper that things went awry. The assassination attempts and the kidnapping seemed improvised rather than carefully planned. Raul didn't even know what to do with his hostages.

* * *

THERE WAS NO CAPPUCCINO WAITING FOR Isabel LaFleur. Gould had called the receptionist and the IT guy the night before and told them to stay home. Otherwise there would be too many questions. She still had a hard time wrapping her mind around everything that had happened in the last twenty-four hours. First, dealing with Simango, then with the journalist who was really Vermeulen's partner. Fortunately, Gould had the right pharmaceuticals to keep both women docile.

It was Vermeulen's showing up when he should have been on a plane that had rattled her nerves. She shouldn't have been surprised. Why else would the journalist have come? She still didn't know how Vermeulen had managed to get past the security desk at the entrance. And the way he dealt with her crew. Getting the gun from the guy and shooting him in the leg. No UN bureaucrat had ever come close to exhibiting such ingenuity. He'd brought someone else to the office, someone who had snooped around. Fortunately, there hadn't been a lot of time, and whoever it was had disappeared again. The worst part was his stealing the Land Rover and freeing the women. Gould found out later that he'd had help. Some hoodlum or other who knew how to handle guns.

The long and short of it was that her crew was out of commission—two dead, one with broken fingers, and one with a bullet in his thigh. As if a bulldozer had run across all her plans. She'd hired the crew on her own, without permission from Portallis. He lived in that rarified stratum where one buys people rather than shooting them. He couldn't understand that, in the real world, someone had to break eggs to make sure that his omelet came out right.

She nibbled on the biscotti while laying out the strategy for her phone call. Keep the focus on Vermeulen, Simango, and the journalist. Something about their concocting a campaign of lies to undermine Global Alternatives. That Vermeulen was planning on dragging Portallis's name through the dirt. Her boss hated media attention he couldn't control. He surely had ways of dealing with Vermeulen once he arrived in New York.

That was her only ray of hope. Vermeulen had indeed left. Gould had called around to make sure. Now all she had to do was make sure that he didn't enjoy his arrival back in the States. Then she'd pick up the pieces and continue. So much was already in place. Barring a major disaster, nothing could derail the plan.

She dialed Portallis's number, hoping she'd get his voicemail since she wasn't scheduled to call him. But it wasn't her lucky day.

"Yes?" Portallis said.

"Sir, this is Isabel. I apologize for calling before our appointed time, but I have some unfortunate news. Our efforts to control the situation here haven't worked. The UN investigator managed to stir up more trouble before he left for New York City. He's also been in touch with a Zambian journalist, a bit of a muckraker who's sure to make our project appear in the worst light possible."

She paused, debating how much of the mess she should reveal.

Portallis was silent.

"I'm certain we can manage the fallout in Maputo and Beira. Not a lot of people are paying attention, and the relevant government officials are on our side. But the journalist and Vermeulen are out of our reach. I was hoping you could bring the resources at your end to bear on any untoward publicity. Again, I apologize for not taking care of my mess properly. We simply weren't prepared for who we ended up dealing with. Let me assure you that we'll learn from this. It won't happen again."

Portallis still hadn't said a word. She didn't know if that meant she should be looking for a new job.

"Ms. LaFleur," he said after a minute that seemed like an hour, "I'm rather surprised by this call."

Another pause. He didn't address her by her first name. Not good at all.

"The last time we talked, you assured me you had everything under control. I stepped in to remove this investigator, and I assumed that would be the end of it."

More silence.

"Frankly, Ms. LaFleur, you disappoint me. I had high hopes for you in my organization. This makes me question my own judgment."

"I understand your disappointment, sir. I'm disappointed in my own performance. I should have anticipated the problems rather than assuming that Vermeulen was just another UN bureaucrat who was more interested in collecting his per diem than doing his job."

"People are like books, Ms. LaFleur. You must read them to know them. I thought you'd learned that. Your performance in this matter has been inexcusably poor."

"I understand, sir. I do hope you'll give me another chance to show you I can do better."

Portallis fell silent again.

"We'll see," he said after a while. "First, contain that mess you've made."

There was no click when he ended the call, just the quiet hiss of a dead connection.

* * *

ACROSS TOWN, IN THE SILENT OFFICES of Nossa Terra, Zara stared at the screen of her computer. A continuous stream of words and symbols filled the black LCD panel. Words, punctuation marks, spaces, and numbers. Next to her keyboard lay a pad of paper on which she had scribbled a number of words.

Aisa looked at those. They weren't really words. Just fragments and random characters or numbers.

"What're those?" she said.

"Possibly passwords. It's hard to discern them in the stream of characters flooding in. LaFleur has been on her computer for the last half hour. Mostly looking at files on the system."

"What are the these passwords for?"

"Not sure," Zara said. "Probably to access documents. She must have protected important documents. Wait ... I think she's going online. Yes, she just typed the URL for Mauritius Bank and Trust. And ... there it is, her login and password."

The stream of characters in the screen stopped.

"She's looking at something," Zara said. "The keystroke logger doesn't register mouse clicks or movements."

There was a new burst of characters. Another URL. This one for the Global Alternatives website. And it looked like another login and password. Zara copied this one as well.

"Is there any way she can find out that we're getting her keystrokes?" Aisa said.

"If they do a security sweep of her machine, yes. Otherwise, the chances are slim."

"And anyone on high alert and already angry?"

"Doubtful. It's just a tiny piece of software deep inside the system," Zara said. "Only an IT person checking the system software would find it."

"Can you control it from here?"

"Yes, but not while she's using the machine."

"Whatever you do, I'd feel a lot better about this if we could eliminate any trace of this intrusion. I'm sure it won't take them long to connect the logger to us once they find it."

CHAPTER TWENTY-NINE

LIFETIME PROFESSION

———◆———

GEORGE AND KILLBILL SAT IN GEORGE'S shack behind the building that housed Global Alternatives.

"Is it safe here?" KillBill said. "I mean you took sides against the people inside. Won't they come after you?"

"The dangerous men are dead or back in Jo'burg. And the *muzungos* won't bother with the likes of us. Yeah, we're safe. Probably safer than you were in that hotel of yours. What happened up in Beira?"

KillBill looked out of the listing door at the Dumpster. He began haltingly, telling George of his life at the edge, falling in with Raul's gang, wanting a sword so he could be a warrior, meeting Chipende and freeing the man and the woman from the hotel.

"You want to be a warrior?" George said. "Forget the damn sword. Only people in movies fight with swords, *né*? A stupid man with a gun will kill a smart man with a sword any day. Besides, it's not the weapon that makes the warrior, it's the mind."

"You mean discipline."

"*Si*, discipline is important, but you also got to know what cause you're fighting for. Take that Raul. From what you told me, he's nothing more than a *mafioso*. Working for him isn't being a warrior."

"Are you a warrior?" KillBill said.

"Look at me. Do I look like a warrior to you?"

KillBill shook his head.

"Right you are," George said. "I used to be a warrior, then I was a technician, now I live in a shack on what little pension I have."

"You fought for independence?"

"I did. Helped drive the Portuguese out of Sofala. Saw that hotel of yours then. It was all shiny and new. Then I stopped being a warrior and became an electrician. Got trained in East Berlin and Moscow. Then I got laid off and everybody forgot about me. You see, warrior isn't a lifetime profession unless you get killed doing it. You been to school?"

KillBill said nothing.

"Didn't think so. You want to be a warrior, go to school. Learn. Our country doesn't need people with swords; it needs people with smarts."

KillBill nodded. "But first we gotta fight the bad guys inside, right?"

George sighed. "Yeah. You hang out in front. I'll stay here."

He reached into his pocket and pulled out a sheet of paper with pictures of LaFleur and Gould. Simango had given it to him at the Nossa Terra office. KillBill looked at it.

"If you see one of them leave," George said. "You come back here right away and tell me."

* * *

"Any luck getting into their computer yet?" Tessa said to Zara. She'd just arrived from the pension where she'd taken over Vermeulen's room.

"I haven't tried yet. Not a good idea to do this while they're still in the office. I've checked the other logins I got from the keystroke logger. One is an account at Mauritius Bank and Trust. But the account isn't for Global Alternatives, it's for GreenAnt Investments. Its balance is about one and a half million dollars. The transaction history goes back only a year, so I don't know how much was deposited initially. There was a deposit of five million in early September. The funny thing is that all of that was withdrawn again."

Since Vermeulen had left on his plane, Tessa had switched to her investigative-reporter mode. She felt a familiar vibration in her body, the clearest indicator that she was on the trail of something big. Persistence and patience were the most needed skills now. She flipped a page in her notebook and wrote down the account information.

"We keep coming across transactions that amount to five million," she said. "That's not a coincidence. I'm pretty sure that the switch happened at Mauritius Bank and Trust. The fact that their manager met with LaFleur and Gould outside the bank has to mean something. But we can't trace it back to the UN funds that are missing."

Nyussi just shrugged and kept tapping at her keyboard.

"What other logins have you identified?" Tessa said.

"I'm working on that now. This one is another bank. But not in Mozambique. This one is in Panama."

Nyussi snorted.

"What?" Tessa said, looking over her shoulder.

"The server doesn't recognize my computer, so it's redirected me to the security questions. I guess we're out of luck here."

"Not necessarily. If she's on Facebook, we might be able to answer them."

Tessa opened her laptop and navigated to the Facebook site. Sure enough, LaFleur had a personal profile. "I bet the answers are here." Unfortunately, LaFleur shared her info only with friends.

"You didn't happen to get her Facebook password?" Tessa said.

"I think I saw it earlier, but didn't think it was important."

Zara searched the stream of words for the Facebook URL and found the login information.

Tessa turned out to be right. The first question was her place of birth, which LaFleur had conveniently listed in her profile. The year she graduated from college was there, too. Her father's first name took a little longer, but Tessa found a post from a man with the first name Peter whom LaFleur called Dad.

The account had no name, just a number. It carried a balance of twenty-eight million dollars.

"Whose account is this?" Tessa said.

"I can't tell. Obviously, LaFleur has access to it. But the balance is too high. It can't be her personal account. Maybe it's a place to park money until it can be moved again."

A quick look at the transaction history confirmed that a deposit of five million dollars was made in September. The date coincided with the withdrawal at Mauritius Bank and Trust. But just a couple of days later, there were also two transfers out that added up to five million.

"Help me out here. I'm trying to wrap my mind around what's going on," Tessa said. "First, Global Alternatives' books show the money being given to Nossa Terra, but you guys never got the money and your bank doesn't show that you ever had it. The money was sent from the U.S. via Mauritius Bank and Trust, right?"

"Yes, that's what Aisa told me. They were the correspondent bank for the transaction."

"Somehow, the money was diverted at Mauritius Bank and Trust."

"And deposited in the GreenAnt account," Nyussi said.

Tessa grimaced. "They must have had a deal with this guy Pai, the manager. Let's assume that. Then GreenAnt transfers the money to a third account whose owner we don't know. From there the funds just disappear. So that's what money laundering looks like."

"What about Nossa Terra?" Nyussi said.

"Collateral damage, as the Americans would say."

"And GreenAnt? The project in Sofala?"

"Who knows? Maybe they really are working on the biofuel project there. They needed your organization as the fig leaf to get the land use permits and dumped you as soon as they had those. Everything I've seen so far points in one direction. Global Alternatives plays by its own rules."

"Do you think this entire thing was ordered from the top?"

"Good question," Tessa said. She scratched her head above the right ear. "I do know that Vincent Portallis likes to leverage other people's money. He puts in a little of his own and then tries to get others to pay the bulk. But this looks like stealing UN funds and then casting suspicion on Nossa Terra."

"What should we do next?"

"Well, we can't go to the police. We got this information illegally. It wouldn't stand up in any court I know of."

"So we're still screwed?"

"Maybe not. I'm a journalist. Journalists have anonymous informants. I can definitely write about this. There's just one little problem. My editor won't run the piece unless I contact Global Alternatives and LaFleur for confirmation or comment. Which will alert them to what we know."

"I better delete the keystroke logger before you go public."

"Yes, but let's wait. I want to see her emails. Have you gotten login information for that yet?"

Nyussi shook her head. "No, she didn't use any webmail, so we'll have to wait until she leaves her office."

* * *

THE LAYOVER IN DOHA WAS JUST as tedious as Vermeulen had imagined it would be. In hindsight, he should have booked a more direct flight. The airport was brand-new, the stores expensive, and the restaurants too fancy. He sat in a fake leather chair and connected to the free Wi-Fi. No new emails. Instead, the wound on his head kept claiming his attention. His assumption that the lower air pressure in the plane contributed to the pulsing sensation was wrong. His scalp throbbed just as much at sea level.

He'd been hoping for the breakthrough revelation that would provide him with the ammunition he needed for a confrontation with Portallis. All he had were anecdotes without proof. He had no independent witnesses, no police reports. The hit squad might as well not have been there. The ambush in Sofala could be put down to rebel activity. The shootout at the quay had probably been cleaned up already. He had little to show for all the effort he and his friends had expended except that Nossa Terra hadn't received the missing money. And that made no difference. Global Alternatives had salted that field thoroughly. No other foundation would work with them. Simango was right to close it down. Give the folks a chance to find work elsewhere.

He called Tessa.

"Where are you?" she said.

"I'm in Doha, waiting for the JFK connection. Did you get anywhere?"

"Maybe. Thanks to Zara's keystroke logger we've gotten access to two bank accounts. One belongs to GreenAnt Investments and the other is a numbered account in—you're not going to believe this—Panama. There are lots of transactions, but they always total up to five million dollars. From what we can make out, GreenAnt got the money and later transferred it to the numbered account. From there, it disappeared. Basically, someone stole it."

Vermeulen looked at the steel and glass ceiling of the transfer lounge. That's what all this was about? All that mayhem, that scheming, just to steal UN funds? What a pedestrian motive. But in his line of work, it always came down to the same motive—greed. Not the breakthrough he'd been hoping for.

"Are you still there?" Tessa said.

"Yes, I am. I know this sounds crazy, but stealing five million dollars sounds too pathetic. I don't know. Somehow I expected more, something bigger."

"You do sound crazy."

"I know. The worst part is that whoever finally orchestrated this will never be held responsible in a court of law. All that information you got is, of course, inadmissible. By the time we had the necessary warrants to examine those accounts, the money would be gone."

It was Tessa's turn to say nothing.

"Well, at least I can tell Mr. Portallis that someone in his organization has embezzled UN money and that his foundation is on the hook for it. That if he doesn't reimburse the UN, he won't get future funding. Although I'm sure that's an empty threat, too."

"Don't sound so down," Tessa said. "LaFleur will lose her job, and I'm sure Portallis will have a hard time explaining what happened to that money. I'll write an article that exposes the lax oversight of a major global development foundation and how local organizations are sidelined. Make them look bad. The long-term impact could be quite positive."

"We can only hope. How long will you stay in Maputo?"

"Maybe a couple more days. Then it's off to Ghana for a piece on the impact of offshore oil production on agriculture and cocoa exports."

"Any chance you'll come to the City soon?"

"As long as you promise to be there."

CHAPTER THIRTY

SYSTEM FILES

—————◆—————

"I THINK SHE'S GONE HOME," NYUSSI said to Tessa. Sunday morning was dawning. A faint line of light could be seen in the eastern sky. They'd been waiting all night for LaFleur to go home. As long as the keystroke logger delivered data, someone was working at LaFleur's computer. Not the time to try to access it remotely. The screen on Nyussi's computer had been quiet for almost half an hour.

"Okay, let's do it," Tessa said.

Nyussi started the Remote Desktop app and connected to LaFleur's computer. Since she had the login and password, the entire process took less than a minute. LaFleur's desktop appeared on Nyussi's screen.

"Here we are. What do you want to check first?" Nyussi said.

"How about her email?

The screen filled with a typical columnar screen—mailboxes, message list, and contents. Nyussi scrolled through the messages in the inbox. Tessa saw nothing peculiar there. Updates from various project partners, news from the New York office, a few personal networking items—in short, the type of emails one might expect in a director's inbox, certainly no smoking gun.

"That was less than exciting," Tessa said. "Not even a tiny thrill of reading someone else's email."

"That's because most people's messages are boring. I know my inbox is dull. Let's check the other mailboxes."

LaFleur was very organized. Her inbox only contained twelve messages. Her mailboxes were structured by projects, general administration, and head-office matters. Nyussi chose the projects folder first. It had subfolders for each venture. There was no folder for Sofala. A random check of the other boxes yielded exactly what one might expect from a person administering development projects. Lots of back and forth about specs, implementation, efficacy measurements, and deliverables. Tessa couldn't keep from yawning.

"This isn't going anywhere," she said. "What else can we try?"

Nyussi scratched her chin. "There are two possibilities. Either she kept a separate email account elsewhere for the incriminating messages, or she used hidden mailboxes on her computer. Let me try something."

She opened the web browser and checked the browser history. A long list of URLs popped up. She checked the past three weeks.

"It doesn't look like she had a webmail account like Hushmail. Unless she hasn't accessed it in a while."

"That seems impossible," Tessa said. "With everything that's been going these past weeks, she must have interacted with someone."

"Unless she and Gould hatched this plan on their own and nobody was in on it. Who knows? Maybe Gould isn't in on it either."

Nyussi closed the browser, opened a different app, and typed in an incomprehensible string of commands and characters.

"I'm uncloaking any hidden mailboxes," she said. "If she has any, they should show up now."

Back to the mail app, she checked the list of mailboxes. There were no new ones. She shrugged, telling Tessa the bad news.

"Maybe she did it all on her phone," Tessa said. "That's how I do most of my work."

Nyussi closed the mail app and started looking at folders on the hard drive.

"There's got to be stuff on here," she said. "I mean, the whole thing is like a conspiracy and those don't happen without planning, without leaving a trace."

Tessa shrugged and said that she'd thought so, but that finding that evidence was the real challenge. She got up from her chair and paced back and forth.

"What if Gould is the one pulling all the strings?" she said. "We're focused on LaFleur because she's the boss."

"And because she's got the money," Nyussi said.

Tessa grimaced and said, "Good point. Let's stick to LaFleur."

* * *

ACROSS TOWN, SIMANGO AND CHIPENDE SAT on a bench at the Xavier Cemetery off Avenida Karl Marx. They were waiting for Mr. Pai. The deputy branch manager of Mauritius Bank and Trust at first adamantly refused to meet with them, telling them to come to his office the next day like all bank customers. When they told him they had incriminating evidence, his telephone demeanor changed. They offered to meet him at his house, which generated more protests. The cemetery was the compromise choice.

Only ten minutes late, a frowning Mr. Pai hurried across the brown grass. He saw Simango and Chipende, stopped in front of them, and said, "What's the meaning of this?"

"We want information," Simango said. "My work and my organization have been tarnished and it appears you played a part in it."

"I did no such thing."

"I think this photograph speaks volumes."

Chipende showed him the photograph from the café next to the Lusomundo Cinema.

"That was just a social gathering," Pai said.

"During work hours? Away from the bank? I don't think so. So tell me what you did for LaFleur and Gould?"

"What if I don't?" Pai puffed himself up.

"Then we'll tell everyone at your bank that you, Mr. Pai, are a criminal and they'd be better off banking elsewhere," Chipende said in a tone that made it clear he wasn't kidding.

The threat deflated Pai.

"Here's what we know," Simango said. "Global Alternatives says they sent us five million dollars. We never received that money. Our bank will confirm that. We also know that in the past few months, deposits amounting to five million were made in the account of GreenAnt Investments. Except that these funds were again withdrawn and we don't know where they went after that. What was your role in that?"

"What role?" Pai said. "I had no role in that."

"Then who does?" Chipende said. "You're the deputy manager. Shouldn't you have access to all accounts?"

Pai said something about protecting client privacy, but Chipende didn't let up. "We want explanations as to why money destined for Nossa Terra disappeared at your bank and ended up in someone else's account."

"I don't know."

"Then who's in charge of SWIFT transactions?" Chipende said. "The management wouldn't give access to the secure terminal to a wet rag like you."

Simango raised her eyebrows. Her colleague knew more about international banking than he'd let on. He even knew that banks had to set up a secure room with the SWIFT terminal and that access was restricted to a few trusted employees.

Chipende's challenge worked. The deputy branch manager sat up straighter and said, "I handle *all* SWIFT transactions." The gravitas with which he made that pronouncement was even more amusing once he realized what he'd said. His right hand shot up and covered his mouth.

"Just as I thought," Chipende said. "So tell us about these transfers."

"I'm not saying anything else," Pai said and rose from his chair.

"If you don't, we'll contact your boss and tell him that you stole our wire transfer."

Simango put her hand on Chipende's arm, telling him to slow down. She turned to Pai. "I know you did what you did because you were told to do it. All we want to know is who was behind it. Who told you to divert the money? If you tell us, I won't mention your involvement when I speak with a prosecutor."

Pai sat down again and swallowed. The mention of a prosecutor had scared him. He wiped his forehead and swallowed again.

"They threatened me," he said.

"Who?" Simango said.

"LaFleur and Gould."

Pai wiped his brow again. In his telling of the story, LaFleur had offered him cash for two transactions that violated foreign exchange regulations. It wasn't a big deal—everybody with connections did it. When LaFleur and Gould came back with the demand to make the five million dollars disappear, he'd rejected it out of hand. Messing with SWIFT was an entirely different category of crime. But the little favor he'd done for LaFleur was all they needed to threaten him.

"I tried to resist," Pai said, "but just one violation of foreign exchange regulations could cost me my job. I couldn't afford that. I have a family."

"What did you do?" Chipende said.

"They initiated a transfer of five million one hundred and twenty thousand dollars. I subtracted five million from the wire payload disguised as the fee. They then initiated a chargeback for the hundred twenty thousand."

"So that's why the five million never showed up in our account. You took it out before it ever reached us," Simango said.

Pai nodded.

"Did they tell you why they wanted the five million dollars to disappear?"

Pai shook his head.

* * *

THE SUN STOOD WELL ABOVE THE horizon when Tessa turned off the lights in the office of Nossa Terra. Nyussi was still digging through LaFleur's computer remotely. Despite their two hours of searching, new insights eluded them. Inside the *Projects* folder were more folders containing information about the various undertakings Global Alternatives had funded in Mozambique. None of them contained anything connected to Sofala or GreenAnt Investments.

Tessa sat on Simango's chair and looked out the window. The longer they sat there, the more trouble Valentin would be in. She wanted to be the savior, find the crucial piece of information—the one that made everything right again—and get it to him before he met with his boss. It didn't look like that was going to happen. She checked her phone. Still no message. He should have arrived in the States by now. Why didn't he call or at least text?

"I found something," Nyussi said.

Tessa got up and looked over her shoulder.

"LaFleur was smart. She hid a folder deep in the system files."

"Why is that smart?" Tessa said.

"Because there are hundreds and hundreds of system files and folders. Nobody in their right mind would look there. Look at it." She moved the mouse pointer to a window that contained nothing but icons with unpronounceable names.

"How did you find it?"

"I had a hunch she might try that, so I ran her virus detection program, and it flagged one of the system folders as altered. Sure enough, in it was another folder, one that didn't belong there."

"What's in it?"

Nyussi frowned. "That's the problem. It's password protected. I've tried the ones I gleaned from the keystroke logger, but I couldn't open it."

"So we're still at a dead end," Tessa said.

She leaned against the wall. No scoop, no prize-worthy reportage, no uncovering Global Alternatives' shady dealings. All she had was a story about changing land usage from small-farmer empowerment to large-scale agriculture. It was a big deal, but it wasn't a scoop. And it wouldn't help Valentin.

Nyussi got up from her desk and stretched. Tessa could hear her bones cracking.

"Thanks for all your efforts," Tessa said. "We wouldn't know what we know now without you."

"You're welcome. But I'm not done. There's got to be more I could do. I just need more time. There's something going on that's bigger. I owe it to Aisa and my colleagues to find out why they destroyed Nossa Terra."

CHAPTER THIRTY-ONE

MARROW BALLS

———◆———

ARRIVING IN NEW YORK CITY IN mid-February after spending a couple of weeks in summery Mozambique was enough to depress any traveler. The sky was gray, the clouds low, and according to the captain, the temperature barely above freezing. As usual, Vermeulen wasn't dressed for the weather, but he didn't worry. A quick cab ride to his apartment at Gansevoort Street, a shower, and he'd be in wool trousers, jacket, and a winter coat. That and a decent meal were a must before meeting with his boss and starting the whole process of repairing his reputation. At least the gouge on his head had settled down. He touched it for the thousandth time. The scab was thicker.

After getting his passport back from a churlish Customs and Border Protection agent, he picked up his bag, turned in the customs form to the officer in the nothing-to-declare line, and stepped through the large frosted glass door into a crowd of people waiting for their loved ones.

He knew there was no loved one waiting for him, so he headed straight for the taxi dispatch desk. Two men in dark suits blocked his way. They looked eerily identical. Both had buzz cuts. Their white shirts under the dark suits seemed too starchy for their liking and their ties too tight. Vermeulen could tell that they preferred something looser. Upon further inspection, he saw that the one on the right had a scar, and the one on the left wore an earring.

"Mr. Vermeulen?" Earring said. It wasn't really a question. "Please come with us."

"Do I have a say in that?" Vermeulen said.

"Certainly. But it would be easier for all of us if you just came with us."

He opened his suit coat just enough to reveal a shoulder holster with a pistol.

"You'd be willing to draw your gun right here in the arrivals hall of Terminal Seven?"

"Of course not. We'd have to follow you until you were at a more convenient place. We do know where you live. But please, there is no need for a scene. Just come with us. Our boss would like a word with you."

"And your boss is …?"

"Mr. Portallis," Earring said with an incredulous expression. "Were you expecting someone else?"

"Honestly, I wasn't expecting anybody. I was hoping for a shower and some fresh clothes. Can I at least go to my apartment first?"

"That's not necessary. You'll have time to freshen up before the meeting. Can we go now?"

The three marched to the exit, Earring next to Vermeulen and Scar just a step behind. Halfway across the arrivals hall, Vermeulen thought about running. If he dashed through the crowd, he might be able to lose them, jump into a gypsy cab, and get away.

"Please don't do it, Mr. Vermeulen. It'll save us all a lot of trouble."

Vermeulen was too tired and too stiff to put up a fight. After a fourteen-hour flight, he wasn't in any shape to survive close combat. They exited Terminal Seven and walked to the limo lane. A large black car rolled up. Earring opened the rear door. Vermeulen climbed in and sank into the softest leather he'd ever felt in his life. The car—a Bentley, the 'B' logo sown into the seats—was spacious. Even a big guy like Earring didn't crowd Vermeulen on the backseat. Scar slipped into the front passenger seat. The driver actually wore a cap and suit like the drivers in British TV shows.

The car pulled away from the curb. For a moment, Vermeulen thought the whole world was moving while the car stayed put. After a couple of seconds of disorientation, he felt the acceleration gently press him into the leather. For the first time in his life, the phrase *lap of luxury* made sense.

"How far are we going?" he said.

"You'll see. Enjoy the ride. Would you hand me your phone?"

For a guy who looked like he juggled mini fridges for kicks, Earring had a remarkably calm demeanor.

"Why?"

"Just a precaution. You'll get it back when we're done."

* * *

PORTALLIS'S ESTATE WAS RIGHT ON THE Hudson River, in a little place with the pretentious name Glenclyffe, as if substituting a 'Y' for the 'I' made the name more English. The Bentley glided across gravel the color of freshly fallen snow. The lawns were the verdant green of spring leaves, even though it wasn't spring, and birch trees had been placed strategically to frame the mansion.

In contrast to these surroundings, the house wasn't a British castle. Instead, it was a sprawling clapboard structure that Louis XIV would have called a cottage. At one end was an orangery. At the center stood a tall porte cochère, supported by four columns.

The Bentley stopped so that the back door was lined up precisely with the entrance of the house. The heavy oak door opened, and a man in a butler's suit complete with striped vest stepped out to open the door. It definitely felt like being in a TV show. Earring got out first, and Vermeulen followed. Scar took Vermeulen's bag and briefcase from the trunk.

"Welcome," the butler said. "I trust your drive was pleasant. Would you please come in?"

He turned and went back into the house. Vermeulen traipsed behind him, followed by Scar, who carried his luggage.

Vermeulen's room was pleasing. Despite the gloomy sky outside, it was bright, the walls covered with a discreetly patterned abstract wallpaper. The bed was large with a fluffy comforter—had to be eiderdown. Whoever designed the room had resisted the standard home magazine advice to cover the bed with a hundred pillows. There were only two, right where one needed them for sleeping. Near the large window stood a small table surrounded by two upholstered chairs. A chest-high bookcase held leather-bound volumes. Next to it stood an armoire. Vermeulen made out works by Shakespeare, Dante, and Goethe.

"If you care to freshen up, Mr. Vermeulen," the butler said, "the bath is through this door. I understand you might require fresh clothing after your travels. There are items in your size in the armoire. Mr. Portallis expects you downstairs for dinner in one hour."

The butler and Scar left the room.

Vermeulen stood there like Lot's wife, unable to process the events of the last hour. Outside, the light faded.

He stepped into the bathroom. There was a large claw-foot tub, a glass-enclosed shower, and two sinks. This room was wallpapered with a pattern of green lianas sprouting white blossoms. The floor was tiled with white marble slabs, covered with fluffy white rugs. He turned on the tap. The water came out hot. He went back into the bedroom and sat on the bed.

Portallis wanted to bribe him with this magnificent reception, showing him the carrot before bringing out the stick. That much was clear.

He got back up and tried the window. It opened easily. He tried the door. It wasn't locked either. So this wasn't a prison. It made sense. Dealing with obstreperous people who rejected the opulent surroundings would happen somewhere else. Even if he wanted to run, where would he go? He hadn't seen a car since they left the highway. Before he reached civilization, Earring or Scar would find him.

* * *

AN HOUR LATER, THERE WAS A knock at the door. The butler was back and asked Vermeulen to join Mr. Portallis in the dining room.

Vermeulen was freshly showered, shaved, and dressed. Washing his hair was tricky since he didn't want to get soap into the wound on his head. The clothes in the armoire fit as if they'd been made for him. After spending the last couple of days in well-worn clothing, donning fresh underwear, shirt, and suit was almost enough to put him in a good mood. Which was dangerous.

People like Portallis tried to buy you first. They had all the resources and were used to making offers that most people couldn't afford to refuse. It was when you refused that they became dangerous. But he couldn't worry about that until it happened. Portallis even knew Vermeulen's inseam. In turn, Vermeulen knew virtually nothing about his host except whatever gossip he'd come across, which painted him as choleric, a man who flew off the handle when he didn't get his way.

Outside, the sun had long since set and the house was brightly lit. Every inch was carefully designed with understated elegance. This was not a house that screamed for attention. Instead, it exuded an air of gentility. No need to show off. That wasn't quite what Vermeulen had heard about Portallis.

The butler led him through a hallway to a large dining room. At the center stood a table that could have accommodated at least twenty dinner guests. Mercifully, there was a more intimate table over to the side that had been set for two.

Portallis rose from his chair and came toward Vermeulen, his arm outstretched. He was shorter than Vermeulen, but heavier. His hair was light and wavy. The casual suit—a fine gray tweed—fit him well. His tailor knew how to make the man's bulk disappear. His shirt was cream-colored, and his tie a shimmering blue Vermeulen had last seen in an Yves Klein painting.

"Mr. Vermeulen, thank you for coming. You'll excuse the unorthodox invitation, but we needed to talk as soon as you returned from your mission."

They shook hands.

There was a broad smile on Portallis's pear-shaped face. When young, he must have had prominent jaw bones. Now those lines were softened by age and bulk. His eyes were pale green.

"Good evening," Vermeulen said. No use to even bring up the abduction. He was here. Better to get on with the business at hand.

Portallis pulled out the other chair, inviting Vermeulen to sit. He ignored the head wound. Had he already been informed of the standoff on the freighter in Beira? That would imply a degree of involvement Vermeulen hadn't expected. But it drove home the point that Portallis was running the entire show.

"It must be quite jarring to come back to February in New York after experiencing the late summer in Mozambique," Portallis said.

"It certainly is. In my job, you're never wearing the proper clothing, because the weather at your destination is invariably hotter or colder than where you started out."

"I hope you haven't decided to become a vegetarian. We'll start dinner with a hearty soup. That should warm you up. For the main course, I've decided on filet mignon. I hope that meets your approval."

"Not to worry. Filet mignon sounds great."

Portallis sat across from him and spread the damask napkin on his lap. It was the sign for the butler, who opened the door to a woman who looked like she came straight from downstairs *Downton Abbey*. She served the soup and disappeared silently. The butler followed her out of the room.

Portallis lifted his spoon and said, "Enjoy your soup."

Vermeulen tried a spoonful. The soup was excellent, a fragrant broth with marrow balls, carrots, and leeks. He hadn't eaten that kind of soup since his days in Belgium. As much as he wanted to get on with things, he knew it was no use straining against the golden cage in which he found himself. Portallis would determine the pace of the conversation. All he could do was enjoy the ride. It'd be over soon enough.

"Was your flight bearable?" Portallis said. "Your UN bosses don't let you fly first class, do they?"

"No, they don't. It was like every other flight. Long, boring, with mediocre entertainment, but it ended like all the others and I got here in one piece."

"For which I'm grateful, since we have a lot to talk about. Is the soup okay?"

"It is. Haven't had marrow balls like these in ages."

They finished their soup quietly. Portallis made no mention of the reasons for which Vermeulen had been abducted. The woman came back and removed the soup plates. The butler appeared with a tray holding three terrines. Placing the tray on a side table, he served Vermeulen first, then Portallis, spooning fingerling potatoes, carrots, and turnips in a glaze and finally slices of filet mignon and a dark sauce on their plates.

"I know you are a fan of Belgian beers, but I hope you'll indulge me and try my Bordeaux," Portallis said.

The woman reappeared, carrying a bottle of wine. The butler took it and presented it to Portallis, who nodded. The butler poured and left the bottle on the table. It was a Chateau Margaux. Until now, Vermeulen had never been in the same room with such an expensive bottle of wine.

"I know you are eager to learn why I brought you here," Portallis said. "I would be if I were in your position. But I detest discussing business over a fine meal. It divides one's attention. One ends up neither enjoying the food nor giving the business at hand its proper attention. I hope I can exploit your forbearance a little longer."

There was nothing Vermeulen could say, so he just nodded and sipped the wine. It was very good, but he'd have enjoyed a Chimay Grande Réserve more.

When they finished the meal, the woman came and cleared the table. Portallis got up.

"Please join me in the orangery for coffee and cognac. Time to get to business."

Chapter Thirty-Two

Orangery

———◆———

T HE ORANGERY WAS WARM, SO WARM, in fact, there was a real orange tree in one corner. A couple of lemon trees, a fig tree, ornamental shrubs, and a bevy of orchids completed the subtropical environment. It had an octagonal shape. The glass structure, reaching all the way to the second floor, had a light, airy feel. A glass door at the other end led to the gardens.

Near the orange tree stood a white-metal café table with two matching chairs. The butler had pushed a white, metal tea cart next to the table. It held a platter with a pear frangipane. Two cups and saucers sat on the table. The coffee had already been poured. Vermeulen's coffee was black, just the way he liked it. Next to each saucer stood a snifter of cognac.

Portallis shed his jacket and invited Vermeulen to do the same.

"I like it warm," he said.

As they sat down, the butler came back. He cut the frangipane in wedges and placed a piece on each of the dessert plates.

"So, Mr. Vermeulen," Portallis said after he'd taken a sip of coffee, "tell me why you've been making Ms. LaFleur's life so miserable."

Vermeulen put the fork he'd lifted back down.

"I'd say it's all LaFleur's doing. She accused Nossa Terra of embezzling five million dollars of UN funds, causing funders to drop it as a partner and effectively shuttering the organization. Meanwhile, I ascertained that she shifted the missing funds to another company, GreenAnt Investments, which in turn transferred that money to her personal account. If I were her boss, I'd be concerned that my employee stole UN funds."

Portallis took a sip of coffee and forked a piece of the frangipane into his mouth. The man was nothing but calm, which made Vermeulen wonder if the stories about his verbal eruptions were true.

"Nossa Terra. From the reports, it sounded like a mom and pop outfit trying to get land for landless peasants."

"Yes, it is … uh … was. Now that other funders have jumped ship, the organization had to close its doors."

"I'm pretty sure Isabel had nothing to do with that. The trouble with the small local development shops is that they don't have the capacity to handle large projects. Yet, the UN and rich governments require that we partner with them." He took another bite and put his fork down. "To tell you the truth, these partnerships rarely work out. The local folks can't see past the rim of their world. They are stuck in their ways of doing things. Which is, of course, the reason why we are engaged there in the first place. Their ways of doing things haven't worked."

Vermeulen put down his coffee cup.

"Maybe that's because it never has been *their* way in the first place," he said.

"Oh, please, Mr. Vermeulen. Let's not trot out the old colonialism horse. That's been dead for a long time."

"If that's the case, why did LaFleur tell me that Nossa Terra owed them the five million dollars?"

"That was an unfortunate bookkeeping error. It should be fixed by now."

"What about the transfers to GreenAnt Investments and then to a numbered account? Someone essentially stole that money."

Portallis leaned back in his chair, the calm expression leaving his face. "*If* this information is correct"—Portallis emphasized the *if*—"then surely you must have broken laws left and right to obtain it. Which makes the accusation not only speculative but also useless since it has no legal value."

"That information is correct and I didn't break any laws. An anonymous source gave it to me," Vermeulen said. "I know it won't hold up in court, but I wonder about a boss who doesn't know that someone in his employ has embezzled a large amount of money. I'd thought you'd be a better judge of people."

Vermeulen noted the spark in Portallis's eyes.

"You're in no position to question my judgment, Mr. Vermeulen. You know *nothing* about me. I know about everything that goes on in my operations, including Ms. LaFleur's undertakings and that numbered account."

Portallis took another bite and chewed the frangipane as if it were a steak.

"I also know a lot about you. You're in your mid-forties. You're stuck in a dead-end job at the UN. Promotion is out of the question. Anywhere else, your superiors would have fired you already. It's only thanks to that infernal bureaucracy that you still get a paycheck. The last time you had anything resembling a career trajectory was over a decade ago in Antwerp. You are divorced and your daughter is already more successful than you'll ever be. Am I missing anything?"

This was the Portallis he'd been told about, intemperate and insulting. Vermeulen stifled a smile. He'd taken the bait. "My life story isn't important, but the project in Mozambique is. After all, vast swaths of prime land are at stake. Do you really think that growing a biofuel crop is the best use for that land?"

Portallis had finished masticating his tart and drained his cup of coffee. He seemed calm again.

"We have solid plans for that land. Yes, there will be biofuel, initially. In the medium term, that land is going to revolutionize agriculture, first in Mozambique and then in the rest of Africa."

"And how can that acreage play such a revolutionary role?"

Portallis just waved his hand. "It'll happen, you'll see. That land is ground zero."

"I'm assuming it will include GMOs," Vermeulen said.

Portallis rolled his eyes. "Of course. Anyone who thinks we can solve the future food crisis without GMOs is living in cloud-cuckoo-land."

"But Mozambique doesn't permit the import of GMO seeds. Last I heard, even GMO corn donated as food aid must be ground before it comes to the country, so it can't be used as seed."

"They'll come around because they won't have a choice. In ten years, all this hoopla around GMOs will be long forgotten. You'll see. But let's get back to you. Where do you see yourself in ten years?"

That question hit Vermeulen's sore spot. It was a question he'd asked himself many times, only to push it away again. He knew that the strain of his current job would get worse with age. He couldn't see himself still jetting around the world, eating bad food, and sleeping on lumpy mattresses in his fifties or sixties.

"I see I've touched on something uncomfortable," Portallis said. "Let's face it, you're a washed-up lawyer doing a job that's meant for a young man. Your current prospects look rather grim—"

"Thanks to your intervention."

"That's neither here nor there, but the best you can hope for is continuing what you're doing right now. The worst is being cast back on the street with no ready prospect of gainful employment. I think we can agree on that."

Vermeulen nodded.

"So," Portallis said. "How about you come and work for me?"

Vermeulen sat up. His fork dropped from his hand. Not that he'd been using it.

"Why would you want to hire a washed-up lawyer?" he said.

"I was merely describing how potential employers would see you. My assessment of you is rather more complimentary. You have the seasoned outlook on the world that Ms. LaFleur, for example, lacks. You are aware that you don't have all the answers and are willing to listen. Global Alternatives needs that."

Vermeulen felt hot and constrained. The shirt and tie were suddenly too snug. That was the purpose of his abduction. Wine and dine him before making a job offer.

"You'd be working in New York, of course. A nice office not far from Battery Park and the World Financial Center. And I think I can easily beat whatever the UN is paying you. You'll travel, of course, but only as needed and in business class."

"What exactly would my responsibilities be?"

"Making sure that Global Alternatives doesn't repeat the heavy-handed approach Ms. LaFleur employed. I want you to keep an eye on things for me. Step in when matters threaten to go off the rails. Show the in-country reps how to handle government bureaucracies. First in Africa, but who knows, maybe worldwide eventually. Global Alternatives' projects span the globe."

"That's a rather vague job description."

"And just right for a man like you. You've shown the initiative I expected from Ms. LaFleur. I have no doubt you'll fill out your position just fine."

"Can I think about it?"

"Of course. You'll stay overnight. We'll have breakfast together and you can let me know."

Portallis checked his watch. "I'm afraid I have another engagement, but I have a nice little screening room and a good library of movies. Feel free to make use of it. Francis will be at your service."

The door opened, and the butler came in.

"It's time," he said.

Portallis nodded. "Francis, please make sure that Mr. Vermeulen is well taken care of." He turned to Vermeulen. "Good night. I'll see you at breakfast."

Neither man had touched the cognac.

* * *

DECIDING TO FORGO THE MOVIES, VERMEULEN retired to his room. Francis brought him a bottle of Westmalle Tripel, apologizing that it was the only Belgian beer he could find on short notice.

Thus fortified, he sat in the chair and asked himself if the entire evening had been a dream, or rather, a nightmare. The job offer hadn't come as a surprise. He'd expected that Portallis was going to bribe him. A job with Global Alternatives was the logical option. Especially after Portallis had all but guaranteed that his employment prospects at the UN were in serious doubt.

The answer to the offer was obviously *No*. Vermeulen couldn't imagine any circumstances under which he'd decide to work for a megalomaniac like Portallis. Being forced to spend the night at the man's house was adding insult to injury. He wanted to be in his own bed in his own apartment.

He'd seen Portallis leave in his Bentley, accompanied by Earring. It wasn't clear how many others besides Francis and Scar were in the house. There was the woman who served, probably a cook, and whatever other helpers were in Portallis's employ. Given the time, almost ten, and the fact that the boss was away, they were probably getting ready for bed. Which gave him time to do some exploring.

The hallway was lit by soft nightlights. Vermeulen tried the door next to his room. It opened into another bedroom. Nothing interesting there. The door across yielded a similar result. He walked toward the center of the house. The oak floor didn't creak, for which he was grateful. There was a large open space near the center of the house with a wide staircase to his left leading to the second floor. The entrance hall was to the right. The corridor continued ahead to the orangery and a large living room at the other end of the house.

Would Portallis have his office on the first floor? Probably not. The ground floor was all for public use, including the kitchen and pantry. His private domain would be upstairs.

He peered around the corner of the hallway. Nobody. He hurried upstairs, softly, but taking two stairs at a time. The corridor upstairs mirrored that of the floor below except for the balcony at one end overlooking the orangery. There were doors on both sides. Vermeulen reached for the first doorknob but didn't turn it. The staff probably slept up here as well. He hadn't seen a stairway to a basement, so no downstairs for the servants. If the butler, Scar, and the rest slept up here, their rooms would be farthest from the orangery. Which meant Portallis's personal space had to be in the direction of the balcony.

Vermeulen hurried to the balcony overlooking the orangery. It was dark. He peered over the edge of the railing to make sure no one was still downstairs. It was quiet. The orange tree loomed nearby, the light from the corridor illuminating the closest branches. Leaning over the railing, he saw that the room on the left had a large window facing the trees. It had to be one of Portallis's private spaces.

Vermeulen tried the door. It was locked, which was no surprise. The lock was of the sturdy Yale variety. He had no tools to pick it. He had more success with the next door, which led to a bathroom. Different wallpaper but otherwise much like the bathroom in his room. The next door was locked again.

This was a futile venture. Portallis wouldn't leave his doors open and his documents lying around. Whatever incriminating materials he kept at his house were safely locked away. Except, even villains made mistakes.

He went back to the bathroom, closed the door, and turned the light on. Sure enough, he'd overlooked two connecting doors, one to the room overlooking the orangery and one to the room on the other side. Both were locked. He looked around and found a basket with magazines within reach of the toilet. He rifled through the stack, finding issues of the *New Yorker*, *Inc*, the *Economist*, and *Forbes*. The bathroom reading one would expect from a hedge-fund manager.

Stuck between the issues were two articles copied from plant-science journals. Vermeulen paged through them. The titles of both were enough to make his eyes roll: "DNA Complexity of Maize Fungus Puccinia Sorghi and Uredospores of Puccinia Sorghi" and "Maize Virus Transmission."

The abstracts of the articles made no sense to Vermeulen. Something, something, fungus, something else, maize plants. He sat on the edge of the bathtub and tried to wrap his mind around the technical language. Apparently, *Puccinia Sorghi* was some sort of fungus that attacked corn plants—a rust fungus, to be exact. The authors of the first article apparently had messed with the genes of that fungus and the authors of the second article had demonstrated that, as the fungus spores spread, they could transport a virus as well. Vermeulen paged through the articles and saw that someone— Portallis?—had underlined and circled passages. There were notes scribbled along the margins and exclamation points, but it was the note on the last page of the second article that made Vermeulen's blood run cold.

We can weaponize this thing.

Chapter Thirty-Three

Encrypted Files

---◆---

Tessa had settled at a café with a *café-com-leite* and a sweet roll. She'd taken a *chapa* to the city center and planned on crashing at her hotel, but she was too wired after spending the all-nighter with Nyussi. She'd left her, because Nyussi was determined to access the hidden folder, and there was nothing she could do to help.

She worried that Vermeulen hadn't called. His plane should have landed hours ago. It was just like him not to call. She bit into the roll and realized how hungry she was. She signaled the waiter and ordered an omelet. Some sugary morsel of flour and fat wasn't going to do it this morning.

Her phone rang. She put her cup down and checked the display. It was Gaby. With a smile, she answered.

"Hi, Gaby, what a surprise. How are you? We haven't talked in a while."

"I know. When you're with my dad, I always call him. I bet he doesn't tell you that I asked him to send my love to you."

"Men," Tessa sighed.

"Speaking of my dad, he isn't with you, is he?"

"No, he should be back in New York. I've been waiting for his call."

"That's what I thought. I've been trying to call him but there's no answer. The calls roll over to his voicemail immediately, like his phone is turned off."

"He probably went straight to his apartment to catch up on sleep and turned his phone off," Tessa said.

"But according to the itinerary he emailed me, he arrived yesterday afternoon. I know him. He doesn't sleep sixteen hours. I wonder if something happened."

"Maybe he went straight to the UN this morning to meet with his boss.

He'd have his phone off for that meeting. I'm sure he's fine. Just his usual self. Why did you want to reach him?"

"I found more about GreenAnt Investments," Gaby said. "In my job I have access to all kinds of newsletters with outrageous subscription rates, published for industry insiders. I read things that most people, even reporters, will never see. Since GreenAnt seemed so elusive, I dug into several newsletters and found something interesting. Mind you, this is little more than rumor, but GreenAnt Investments has an interest in biotech. Apparently they invested in two labs that focus on gene technology four, five months ago."

Tessa said nothing.

"Are you still there?" Gaby said.

"Yes, I'm thinking. We know they want to plant jatropha for biofuel. I remember reading that they're working on modifying the jatropha genes to increase the oil content of the fruit and make it more profitable. Maybe that's what they're investing in."

"I looked up the labs, and they seem to focus on food crops. Maize, soy beans, and the like. That doesn't sound like biofuel to me."

"Well, they do make ethanol from maize. I don't know what, if anything, this means. When were these investments made?"

"Last September."

"Oh. We've been following the trail of five million dollars, and the money disappeared in September. I wonder if that's where it ended up. But I still can't figure out the end game here. What else is going on with you?"

"Oh, not much." She proceeded to tell Tessa about her job, the new guy she'd been seeing and was already thinking of dumping, and the great exhibit at the Kunst im Tunnel gallery, Düsseldorf's contemporary underground art venue.

Tessa told her about her piece on land use and the upcoming reportage on off-shore oil drilling in Ghana.

"Once I'm done with that, I'll go to the U.S. See if I can land something more sedentary. Maybe Valentin and I will even settle down together. He seemed much more committed this time. Maybe he is ready."

* * *

GOING HOME WASN'T AN OPTION. EVEN after spending the entire night at the office. Zara made herself a cup of tea and stared out the window while the bag steeped in the hot water. She knew she was going to be in hot water too. Planting that keystroke logger was way beyond anything she'd done before. *Mousy Zara.* That's what Aisa had called her once. It wasn't far off the mark. She just felt more comfortable with computers than people. Only Helton had managed to get closer to her with his affable mien. Even that was more of a camaraderie than a real relationship. And here mousy Zara had broken who knows how many laws by planting illegal software on the computer of a powerful woman and spying on her.

Despite all that, she hadn't found anything crucial. Sure, LaFleur's money transfers showed that she'd hidden the money that was supposed to have come to Nossa Terra. But even that wasn't real evidence. Only the amounts were similar. At best, circumstantial evidence. There had to be more, a real reason to ruin Nossa Terra.

She had copied the suspicious folder to her own computer in the hope of finding a way to crack the password. That would have to come later. For now, she remotely perused LaFleur's hard disk once more. Looking at all document folders with fresh eyes. She'd given herself two hours. Then she'd uninstall the keystroke logger and try to make it appear as if nobody had ever accessed the computer.

Trouble was, she didn't really know what to look for. She'd searched for biofuel and jatropha, but those didn't generate any hits except for two articles saved from a website touting the potential of the plant. That folder also contained a number of documents about genetically modified plants and their future in Africa. One author lamented the opposition of African governments to planting GMOs. Zara didn't have strong feelings one way or the other. As a techie, she was intrigued by technology. Why not change the genome of a plant if it made it grow better? Of course, the plants needed to be tested to make sure they were safe.

The door opened. Chipende and Aisa entered.

"*Que se passa,* Zara. When did you get in?" Aisa said.

"I haven't gone home yet."

"What? Go home and get some rest. Please."

"I wouldn't be able to sleep anyway. This whole thing is eating away at me. What did you find out?"

Chipende filled her in on the conversation with Mr. Pai at Mauritius Bank and Trust. *He sounds dispirited*, Zara thought. Pai's confirmation that he'd redirected the money transfer at the behest of LaFleur hadn't lifted his mood, or Aisa's, for that matter. The damage was done. Even if Pai were prosecuted, it wouldn't get Nossa Terra back on its feet. Maybe eventually. In any case, it would be a long slog. According to Chipende, the only thing that would make a difference was a spectacular revelation of Global Alternatives' fraud to the news media. And for that, they didn't have enough evidence.

"You're right," Aisa said, "the papers would want confirmation, or at least a statement from Global Alternatives."

"What about *Bravo!*?" Zara said. "They seem to publish anything, as long as it's controversial."

Chipende was all excited about the idea, but Aisa shook her head.

"It would be irresponsible. That paper is terrible."

"They've done some great reporting on corruption," Chipende said.

"Yes, but have you looked at the other stuff? It's a misogynistic rag. I don't want our organization associated with that."

"We haven't got an organization anymore," Chipende said.

"Let's sort out what we have," Zara said. "Maybe it's enough for a paper like *Integridade*. They slam corruption all the time."

Chipende ticked off the facts on his fingers. "Global Alternatives sidelined us with false accusations, they partnered with an outfit called GreenAnt Investments, they changed the terms of the project, and they got land-use permits covering over a hundred thousand acres using our name before they dumped us. Rather than empowering farmers, they're displacing farmers in favor of biofuel. Conservatively estimated, that will displace a hundred thousand farmers. I think that's enough."

Aisa massaged her temples.

"It's a lot," she said, "and the paper can verify most of that. We don't even have to mention that LaFleur stole the money."

Chipende didn't wait. Pulling out his phone, he looked up the *Integridade* website, found the paper's number, and called. While the call was connecting, he said with a big grin, "We're going to expose these bastards."

* * *

THE COFFEE WAS LOUSY AND THE biscotti stale. *That's how you know you're in trouble.* Isabel LaFleur sat at a table in the restaurant of the Hotel Elegância, which wasn't elegant at all, and stared at the street outside. Traffic, people, the usual bustle. As if nothing had changed. For her, everything had. Portallis hadn't said anything, but she knew. *Contain the mess you've made.* What he really meant was, *Clean up after yourself and don't let the door hit you on your way out.*

She'd spent the entire night cleaning her computer of any shred of information that could implicate her in the hiring of the South African assassins. What a lousy squad they had turned out to be. Sure, at first they were only supposed to scare Vermeulen away. But after he managed to escape from the café at his hotel, after he moved to a different place, she'd told them to eliminate him. That was her own initiative, without orders from above. Which meant all evidence of the engagement had to disappear. When Vermeulen spoke with Portallis—she had no doubt he would—she needed plausible deniability.

The good news was that she was certain she'd succeeded. All messages, paperwork, and contact information had been deleted, and just to be safe, zeroed out. Not just from her computer but the email server as well. The texts were a different issue, but at least Apple's messaging system was totally encrypted and the company couldn't tell the police anything about their contents. The only way she could be linked to the outfit would be through Gould. And he knew better than to implicate himself.

The money thing was a non-issue. Portallis knew all about it and had okayed it. So, from a legal perspective, she was in the clear. But Portallis's tone on the phone had scared her. He was all calm, but she knew under the surface there was a volcano of anger ready to erupt. The man didn't tolerate failure. And she had failed. Better to just throw in the towel and move on. She had expertise. There'd be other organizations who'd hire her. Probably not with the assistant who made her cappuccino and the imported biscotti, but enough to make a living.

Except she was sick and tired of Mozambique, of Africa. She wanted to be back in New York or—close second choice—Switzerland. Global Alternatives had a lovely headquarters in Geneva. Imagining Lake Geneva with the Alps in the background made her angry. Why should she take the blame for a plan Portallis had conceived? The plan itself was crazy—mad-scientist crazy—but also amazing. Engineer a virus that kills corn and can be spread by common corn rust, wipe out Mozambique's entire corn production, then push on a starving country his own GMO corn, bred to withstand the virus, as the only alternative. The virus would eventually spread to the rest of Africa, and Portallis's GMO seeds would be the only option, all grown on the land she helped obtain for GreenAnt Investments.

She had two options. She could go to the press and reveal the whole scheme. Or she could call Portallis and threaten to reveal the scheme to the press. It should be a threat sufficient to warrant a generous cash remuneration, such as the five million dollars Portallis had parked in the account under her name.

Under her name. That was the rub. Portallis had set it up so she'd take the fall if there were ever an inquiry. She was the one who'd hoodwinked Nossa Terra and used them to obtain the land-use permits. She was the one who'd messed with the money to make it look like Nossa Terra had mismanaged the funds. All Portallis had to do was to eliminate her. The evidence would show her as pulling all the strings. And Portallis would get rid of her. There was no doubt in her mind. Even if she got away now, she'd be looking over her shoulder for the rest of her life.

There was really only one option. Encrypt the entire cache of documents, send it to a place like Wikileaks, store the decryption password on a private server with a little program that would send it to the leaks site unless she reset the program every two weeks, then blackmail Portallis. That would do the trick. The leaks site couldn't do anything with the encrypted files and Portallis had to make sure she stayed alive to keep the files hidden.

She smiled. Okay, maybe not New York or Geneva, but Buenos Aires or Lisbon were nothing to sneeze at. Or the Croatian coast. It was easy to disappear there.

CHAPTER THIRTY-FOUR

ORANGE TREE

———◆———

VERMEULEN HAD JUST STUFFED THE TWO science articles under his shirt when a voice from the door said, "Put your hands where I can see them and turn around."

Vermeulen obeyed. Francis was still dressed in his butler's uniform. If the pistol in his hand was anything to go by, Francis the butler was more like Alfred Pennyworth than Mister Carson. He'd turned on the hall lights.

"Sorry," Vermeulen said. "I didn't mean to cause any trouble. I couldn't sleep and wandered a little. The view of the orangery from the balcony here is really something. I needed to use the facilities and found this door open."

"And the papers under your shirt?" Francis pointed the pistol at Vermeulen's gut.

"Oh, just some interesting reading I thought I'd take to my room."

Francis waved with the gun. "Come with me."

"What is this? Am I a prisoner or a guest?"

"If you have to ask that question, you are more naive than I thought. Let's go."

Ever the butler, Francis stepped back into the hall to give him space. Vermeulen stepped forward, but rather than going outside, he slammed it shut and threw the deadbolt. The feeling of victory lasted only a second. He'd just locked himself in his own jail cell. The butler only had to sit outside until Scar showed up. Together, they'd figure out a way to get to him.

Apparently Francis didn't want to bother Scar. He banged against the door, telling Vermeulen to come out, that he was only making things worse. As if that were possible. Vermeulen examined the two exits to the adjacent rooms. Each had the deadbolt lever that ensured privacy inside the bathroom.

He flipped them, but the doors didn't budge. They were locked from the other side, too. A swift kick would probably break the jamb, but it would also alert Francis that he was about to leave the bathroom. Fortunately, they were simple mortise locks. He searched the cabinets for something he could use as a key.

This being a man's bathroom, there were no hairpins or clips that could be bent into the right shape. He found an aluminum pocket comb in one drawer. It might do the trick. He left the first four teeth in place and tried to break off the next ones. That didn't work so well. The aluminum was of the hardened variety. He placed the comb against the edge of the vanity counter and pressed as hard as he could. Five of the teeth gave way. Once bent in one direction, they could easily be wiggled back and forth until they broke off.

The question was which door to open. The room facing the orangery would likely be an office. Why have a bedroom facing the greenhouse when all you did in it was sleep? But it was also farther from the staircase that led down to the front door. The other door would lead to Portallis's bedroom. Not much to find there, but closer to the way out. Not that it made a difference, because Francis had a gun. Either way, Vermeulen would never make it to the staircase.

He inserted the doctored comb into the keyhole of the door to the office. It took some jiggling to make it fit. He slowly turned it. The teeth caught the bolt mechanism, but it didn't budge. He pulled it back a fraction of an inch. No difference. Pushed it in farther. Still resistance. Just a little bit more. It moved a quarter of an inch. But the comb's teeth slipped again. He angled the comb slightly. This time he could feel the bolt slide back. With his other hand, he turned the knob and the door opened.

Portallis's office was sparsely furnished—a massive wooden desk, an ergonomic chair with many levers, and a small sofa facing the window to the orangery. The window was open, which had turned the air in the office warm and moist. Portallis was either a clean-desk guy or he didn't do much work at home. On the desk stood an iMac computer and a phone. Vermeulen tried the drawers of the desk. Pens, a stapler, a container of paperclips, and a tape dispenser filled the small drawer. The large drawer was locked. He gave it a sharp yank. The wood splintered, and the drawer came open. Inside was a rack with hanging folders. He flipped through them. Plenty of papers but nothing that looked useful. That left the computer.

He tapped a key on the keyboard and the screen came to life, displaying a password window. Vermeulen checked under the keyboard, the mouse, and inside the junk drawer. No paper with a password. He pressed the Return key. The text box wiggled and told him that the password was incorrect. He repeated the process twice more and the screen displayed the password hint.

Street address.

He looked back into the large drawer and found a sheet of Global Alternatives stationery. The address was 21 State Street. The screen came alive and displayed some peaceful mountain scene. The desktop was as clean as the desk. Vermeulen clicked the search icon and typed in *maize fungus*. The screen displayed a list of files. Without reading them, he couldn't determine their importance. He searched for *Sofala* instead. No results. Finally, he typed in *virus*. That search yielded a series of email messages. He clicked on the top hit. The message informed Portallis that the lab trials of a new strain of maize had been successful. Ninety-eight percent of the trial plants had survived the virus.

Vermeulen sat back. *That land is ground zero.* Back in the orangery, he'd wondered about that sentence. Ground zero referred to the spot where a nuclear weapon had detonated. The spot where everything was destroyed. It seemed a faulty analogy for yet another attempt at changing agriculture in Africa. This email combined with the scribbled note in the science article changed his assessment.

A new image of ground zero formed in his mind. Its implications sent chills down his body. If Portallis had indeed *weaponized* a corn virus and bred a strain that was resistant to it, the Sofala Project would indeed be ground zero. The virus would destroy the maize crop there first, then spread to the rest of Mozambique and the continent. His stomach felt like a carnivorous creature had taken up residence there. The thought of a virus destroying the harvest, of the hunger and suffering that would follow, only to have Portallis sell salvation to a desperate country, made him lightheaded. He'd seen a lot of crime in his life, but nothing like this evil scheme.

The sense of dread that had glued him to the chair was quickly replaced by urgency. He needed to get this information out. First, he forwarded the message to himself and Tessa. He did the same with the remaining messages from the lab supervisor. The next step was getting out of the house and back to the City. A key turning in a lock told him it was too late for that. The door to the corridor opened and Francis appeared, pistol in hand.

"Get away from that computer," he said.

"Or what. You're going to shoot me?"

"You'd better believe it. Mr. Portallis left clear instructions."

"You wouldn't dare shoot a future employee."

Francis shook his head in disbelief. "Did you really think he was going to hire you? What planet do you live on? Get over here."

The hollow sensation in his gut gave way to the fierce heat of anger. This comic-book butler wasn't going to stand in his way. He dove behind the desk. Francis fired, then fired again. The bullets smacked into the wood, showering the rug with chips. Fortunately, the desk turned out to be as solid as it looked.

Francis would have to come into the office and circle the desk to use the gun on Vermeulen.

"Come out, Vermeulen," he said. "You can't get away."

Vermeulen didn't answer. He took the wastepaper basket and tossed it into the room. Two more shots rang out. Francis wasn't taking any chances. The downside to the standoff was that the racket from the gun had woken up everybody in the house. It was only a question of time before Scar made an appearance. He had to make his move *now*.

He dove behind the sofa facing the open window to the orangery. Two more shots. The bullets ripped into the stuffing. A cloud of fiberfill wafted into the air. Just the kind of diversion he needed. He leaped through the open window into the darkness. Sailing through the air, he realized that he didn't know exactly how far the orange tree stood from the window or how strong its branches were. The crash into the top told him that he'd jumped far enough, but his rapid descent—branches breaking, beating his face, scraping the scab on his head, and raking his hands—reminded him of the last time he'd fallen from a tree, thirty-five years ago. Back then he'd hit the ground like a sack of flour and couldn't move for what had seemed an hour. This time a lower branch, thick as an arm, bent but held when he grabbed it. He managed to slow his momentum by swinging forward from the branch and landing sideways on the tile. His hip and arm took the brunt of the fall and complained bitterly. Definitely not sticking the dismount.

Francis fired his gun from above, but the shots crashed harmlessly through the leaves. Vermeulen remained motionless, as much to recover from the pain of the fall as to hide from Francis's bullets. There was a sound from the corridor. Vermeulen got on all fours, checking in with his body in the process. Banged up, to be sure, but nothing broken. He crawled to the wall and stood up.

The light in the hallway came on. Someone was running toward the orangery. It had to be Scar. Vermeulen pressed himself against the wall right next to the entrance. The steps slowed down. Scar was smart enough not to barge into an unknown situation. A hand holding a pistol appeared next to Vermeulen. An arm followed. Just before the rest of Scar's body materialized, Vermeulen raised his hands, fingers clenched, and smashed down on the arm with all his strength. Scar screamed. The pistol fell to the ground. Vermeulen swooped down and grabbed it before Scar recovered. Racing past Scar into the corridor, he spun around and pointed the pistol at the henchman.

"Put your hands behind your head," he said.

Scar, still nursing his hurt arm, didn't obey. Vermeulen aimed past his head and fired a shot into the orange tree. That convinced him.

Vermeulen knew his advantage was only temporary. Francis would be downstairs in no time, and he still had his gun. That made an exit through the main entrance difficult without a shootout—the last thing Vermeulen wanted. But he had to get outside and find a car to drive away.

"Okay," he said to Scar, "lower one of your hands. Slowly. Take your car keys from your pocket and drop them to the floor."

"I don't have car keys in my pocket."

Vermeulen fired another shot, this one at the floor next to Scar. The bullet chipped the tile and whined into the shrubs. "I'm not in the mood for your tricks. I see the bulge in your pocket. Get them now."

Scar reached into his pocket and dropped the keys on the ground next to him.

"Now turn around and take three steps forward. Stay there."

The two warning shots must have persuaded Scar that it was better to obey. He turned and took the steps. Vermeulen inched back into the orangery and looked up at the window to check if Francis was still waiting to take a shot at him. It was empty. Vermeulen stepped forward and picked up the keys. Giving Scar a wide berth, he ran to the exit at the other end of the orangery. Almost at the door, he heard steps behind him and turned around. Scar hadn't stayed. He was catching up to Vermeulen. Maybe fear of his employer outweighed his fear of the gun. Vermeulen pointed the gun at him.

"Stop right there," he said. "I have enough bullets left to stop you for good."

Scar slowed down but didn't stop.

"I said, stop!" This time he shouted.

Scar kept coming.

Vermeulen aimed for the legs and fired. The bullet hit Scar's thigh. The man screamed and fell to the ground. Vermeulen yanked the door open and raced into the safety of darkness.

Whoever designed Portallis's mansion had assumed its future owner would have horses and had therefore built a stable. The doors were closed, but a few cars were parked outside. Vermeulen pressed the buttons of the remote. The turn signals of the farthest car flashed. He ran to it, jumped into the driver's seat, and started the car. The engine rumble told him the vehicle had plenty of horsepower. A screen in the center console came alive, displaying the image of a galloping horse. A Mustang. Just the right car for his getaway.

He turned the car around and headed for the road. When he came around the corner of the house, he saw someone standing in the middle of the driveway. It was Francis the butler, and he was aiming his pistol at the car. Vermeulen stepped on the accelerator. The engine growled, and the car shot forward. Vermeulen saw the muzzle flash and heard a loud ping. There was another flash, but by that time the car was about to hit Francis, who jumped aside. The bullet must have missed. Vermeulen saw another flash in the rearview mirror. It was the last. He wheeled the car onto the road and accelerated away.

Fifteen minutes later, he pulled over, since he had no clue where he was. It took a bit of fiddling with the screen to start the car's navigation system. When the map finally appeared, it just showed a dot on a road in a large empty expanse. A few button pushes later, he'd gotten the scale down to where he could see his location in context. He was about three miles from highway 9A, which led to the Sprain Parkway and Manhattan. At this time of night, it was a drive of no more than an hour and a half as long as Francis's bullets hadn't hit a vital part of the car.

CHAPTER THIRTY-FIVE

PEEPHOLE

———◆———

FOR THE PAST COUPLE OF YEARS, Paolo Gould had operated on three key
assumptions. One, he'd always taken it for granted that he'd be the number
two in the operation. The guy who had the chops to handle the money part,
keep the books looking good, and handle the unsavory aspects of the job. Not
the vision guy. That was LaFleur's job. Second, he'd always expected that all
his orders would come from LaFleur. That's how hierarchies worked. Which
meant that, third, whatever dirty work had to be done would be ordered by
LaFleur.

The call he had just ended upset all three. He stared at the phone, uncertain
that the conversation had been real. He'd known early on that his job with
Global Alternatives was about getting results. If that meant ignoring the law,
misleading contractors, or hiring hit squads, so be it. But he'd always assumed
that LaFleur had chosen to do her job that way. That she wanted to exceed the
goals set for her by Portallis to rise to the top of the organization. Getting a
call from Portallis himself telling him to eliminate LaFleur changed all that.

He understood now that LaFleur had only done the bidding of her boss,
which meant that the entire organization was rotten to the core, not just the
Mozambican branch office. It also meant that he was living on borrowed time.
If LaFleur was so easily discarded, what would stop Portallis from ordering a hit
on Gould? He'd be the last link between what LaFleur and he had orchestrated
in Maputo and Portallis. It was time to get out. Close his personal accounts,
grab as much from Global Alternatives as his account access permitted, and
fly to Brazil—to Porto Alegre, where he still had family.

He started his web browser and initiated the necessary money transfers
from his personal accounts to an account in Porto Alegre he'd kept open

for just such an emergency. Next he transferred fifty thousand dollars from
Global Alternatives to Mauritius Bank and Trust—ten thousand to eliminate
LaFleur and the rest to make his getaway. He was tempted to take double
that, but it would raise questions he wanted to avoid. Fifty thousand sounded
like a proper sum for a hit. Portallis didn't know that killers in South Africa
were much cheaper. And he needed to have LaFleur killed. Not just because
Portallis had ordered it, but because she knew about Porto Alegre.

One late night over some Scotch, they'd reminisced about their past
lives. It was one of the rare moments they didn't treat each other as business
associates. She'd talked about running away from what had turned into a
suffocating marriage. He talked about Porto Alegre. Now he had to fix that
mistake.

He pulled one of the disposable phones from his drawer and texted a code
to the number in South Africa. The reply code arrived seconds later. He texted
LaFleur's name and address, adding that the job was to be done right away.
The return text included the confirmation and information for the money
transfer.

Gould initiated the transfer. As always, nothing would point to him. He
called his travel agent to book a ticket to Porto Alegre.

* * *

ISABEL LAFLEUR HAD SECOND THOUGHTS ABOUT her insurance policy. Back
in her apartment with the sun long set, she worried that her plan of leaving
an encrypted file containing all of the Portallis documents with some hacker
website might not work after all. Any encryption she used could be cracked.
She didn't have access to NSA grade software, and any of the websites in
question were staffed by hackers who'd take her encryption as a challenge.

Her only real option was to bring down Portallis before he brought her
down. Which meant being faster than he was. Shift her money, buy the
ticket, reveal the entire plan to the news, hop on the plane, and watch the
disaster unfold. Portallis'd be too busy protecting his own hide to worry about
anything else. By the time he got around to her, she'd have disappeared, new
identity and all. That left the question: where to leak the information. The
local papers were no good. Not a big enough splash. It had to be one of the big
global outlets, the *New York Times*, the *Guardian*, the *Spiegel*, something like
that. Except she didn't know anyone at those papers.

The solution turned out to be obvious, so obvious in fact that she shook
her head over not having thought of it from the get-go. Tessa Bishonga. Of
course. She'd have the connections and the contacts to make a huge splash. Big
enough to keep Portallis focused on his own troubles rather than on LaFleur.

She checked her phone and found Bishonga's number under the recent calls listing. She dialed and waited for the call to connect. The phone rang a long time and rolled over to voicemail. She didn't leave a message and dialed again.

Bishonga sounded sleepy when she finally responded. "Who is this?"

Lafleur stood by her window, looking out at the lights of Maputo.

"This is Isabel LaFleur. I have a proposition for you."

There was a pause at the other end. Finally Bishonga said, "What's changed?"

A smart woman. She knows something is going on.

"A lot," LaFleur said. "The short of it is that I believe my life is in danger. I have crucial information about Global Alternatives' plans, the ones that aren't in the brochure. It's big enough that you'll need some partners to process all the documents."

Another pause. Then a throat clearing. "And why should I believe you? You tried to kill me twice. This could be just another setup."

Watching her reflection in the window, LaFleur raked the fingers of her free hand through her hair. "Everything has changed. Portallis has let me know that he's dissatisfied with my performance. It might not sound like much, but I know I'm in trouble."

"So you blew a land deal," Bishonga said. "That might get you fired, but not killed. I think you're exaggerating a bit about your life being in danger."

"That's because what's not in the brochure is far worse than you can imagine."

She told Bishonga about the maize rust fungus and the engineered virus it would transport, about killing the entire maize crop, first in Mozambique, then on the rest of the continent, and finally about forcing the adoption of Portallis's GMO maize as the solution. When she was done, she could hear nothing but Bishonga breathing over the phone. LaFleur had never considered how monstrous this plan would sound to people not in the know. Bishonga's reaction gave her an insight into how this news would be received around the world. She'd calculated right. The uproar would so engulf Portallis, he'd have no time to worry about LaFleur.

"And you have documentation for all these allegations?" Bishonga said finally.

"Yes, I have it all ready to send."

"Let me make a few calls. It is better that you send it to several people. Any one person having this information will be in the same danger you. Don't go anywhere, don't talk to anyone. Sit tight until I call back."

"I can't afford to sit tight," LaFleur said. "I have to get away, and I need to put my money in a safe place."

"Wait at least an hour. If it's true that Portallis wants to kill you, he'll have people watching you and your accounts. You move your money and he'll know something is up. You want this information in the hands of people who are committed to using it properly before your boss has any idea of what you are doing. So, wait."

"Okay, I'll wait."

The hell I will.

LaFleur flipped open her laptop, started the browser, and navigated to the South African Airways website. There was a flight to Buenos Aires at seven thirty the next morning. Outrageous price, but perfect timing. She packed what she wanted in two suitcases. When she'd first started in Maputo, Gould, ever the conscientious accountant, had informed her that, as a U.S. citizen, she had to declare her income abroad for tax purposes. He also told her to create a separate account in one of the tax havens—she'd chosen the British Virgin Islands—and move most of her income there, away from the prying eyes of the IRS. Conveniently, the bank there gave her a credit card so she could access the money with no one the wiser. She accessed the account Portallis had established in her name to park the five million dollars used to blackball Nossa Terra and transferred the money to her own account.

There was a smile on her face when she finished the transaction. She had things under control. Let Portallis sort out his own mess.

When the phone rang and Bishonga called her back, she was only half listening. Bishonga had lined up some colleagues at respectable news outlets. One of them had already created a digital strongbox for whistleblowers. All she had to do was connect to the site and upload her information. No names required.

She keyed in the URL. The website that appeared—some consortium of investigative journalists—invited her to upload her files. It was all too easy. Drag and drop, watch the progress bar as the uploads happened, close the laptop, pour herself one more glass of wine, and start dreaming about a new start, this time with the funds necessary to make it pleasant.

* * *

LAFLEUR DIDN'T GET A LOT OF sleep on her last night in Maputo. Which was okay. There'd be plenty of time to sleep on the planes. South African Airways' first-class cabin had comfortable beds. She got up at four thirty, ordered a taxi for five thirty, showered at her leisure, dressed in travel clothes, and enjoyed one last cup of cappuccino.

At five twenty, the buzzer at her door rang. That was odd. The cab driver would have texted to announce his arrival. Well, maybe he wanted to help her carry the suitcases. Dragging the two large bags down the stairs would have been a pain.

She went to open the door but hesitated at the last moment. How had the driver gotten past the gate into the building? The residents were usually cautious and didn't leave the gate open. Unless someone had come home late or drunk and forgot to lock it. It had happened in the past. She put her ear against the door. There was no sound.

She looked through the peephole. It was all black. More oddness. The hall was always lit. Why was it dark? Had the bulbs burned out? She strained her eyes trying to see someone outside. Somebody must have pushed the buzzer. All she saw was a round blackness that receded into the distance.

She never heard the shot. The bullet entered her eye, then ripped into her brain, where it spread and eventually lodged near the rear of her skull. She dropped to the ground just as a text appeared on her phone.

Your taxi has arrived.

CHAPTER THIRTY-SIX

EVIDENCE

———◆———

TESSA COULDN'T BELIEVE HER LUCK. THE call from LaFleur could change her life. She'd harbored a fair amount of professional envy for the news outlets and consortia that managed access to the Snowdon Files and the Panama Papers. On one hand, she supported the limited access. Dumping information like that on the whole world could lead to all kinds of trouble. There were names and addresses of real people whose guilt was uncertain and whose lives could be endangered. On the other hand, she resented that, as a freelancer, she'd never get access to that information. The files from LaFleur would change that. She'd be managing access.

She wanted to call Vermeulen, but it would be no use. He hadn't answered any of the messages she'd left. Where was that man, anyway?

As if in answer to that question, her phone rang. The display indicated an unknown caller. She didn't want to talk to an unknown caller. She wanted to know if LaFleur had uploaded her files and when she could get a look at them. But that would take a while, so she answered the call.

"Hi, Tessa," an all-too-familiar voice said.

"Where have you been? Did you get my messages? What's been going on?" She sat down.

"Okay, one at a time. Portallis had me abducted and brought to his estate. No, I didn't get your messages because they took my phone. And you wouldn't believe what's been going on."

"Portallis abducted you?"

"His hired help did. They intercepted me at JFK and told me they were taking me to him no matter what—that I should come without a fight since it would make life easier on everyone. I agreed, what with my head still buzzing from that wound left by the bullet."

"Did he let you go?"

"No. I escaped, stole a car, and bought this phone at a convenience store because they still have mine, plus my luggage, everything. But you won't believe what I found out. I think he's planning to unleash a corn virus in Mozambique that will wipe out the country's entire crop and then offer his own GMO corn as the only plant that's immune to the virus. He called the land in Sofala his ground zero."

"I know. It's the most monstrous plan I've come across."

No one spoke for a long moment.

"How do you know?" Vermeulen said finally.

"I got a call from LaFleur, who told me the same and asked me if I wanted a cache of documents that reveal everything Global Alternatives and GreenAnt Investments had planned. She's jumping ship and going for maximum damage. I haven't seen the documentation yet, but I guess we'll have all we need to derail this scheme."

"Where're those documents?"

"Hopefully in a digital lockbox at a newspaper where a friend of mine works. I was worried that I'd be painting a target on my back accepting these files on my own, so I called three colleagues and we formed an ad hoc consortium to process them."

"That's great. How soon can you get to them? I'm on my way back to the city, heading straight to my office. It's the safest place for me now. I'll clean up, get some sleep. At nine o'clock, I'm going to meet with Suarez. I'm afraid I don't have enough documentation to make a solid case. Do you think you can get something to me in the next nine hours? If I can persuade him that Portallis's scheme is real, I stand a chance of keeping my job."

* * *

VERMEULEN CAME INTO THE CITY ON I-87, took the Third Avenue Bridge across the Harlem River, and merged onto Harlem River Drive south, which turned into the FDR Drive at Willis Avenue. At one in the morning, even the FDR was quiet. He wasn't in a rush and cruised along just below the speed limit. No need to attract attention from a bored cop still looking to make his ticket quota. He took the Midtown Tunnel exit, hung a right at First Avenue, a left at 45th Street, and parked the car in a private underground garage. There was no attendant, which was just as well. Nobody to remember his face when the car was finally found a few days later. He wiped the gun with his shirttails and stuck it into the glove compartment.

At UN headquarters, security was tight as always. He'd managed to make himself look somewhat presentable. The clothes from Portallis's armoire looked a bit scuffed after his crashing exit through the orange tree. At least they weren't ripped. The scratches on his hands and face were a different matter. But the guard was more interested in his phone than Vermeulen's appearance.

As he'd expected, the OIOS office was empty. And much safer than his apartment on Gansevoort Street, because by now Portallis, wherever he was, would have been informed of Vermeulen's escape and his snooping on the computer. He had no doubt that Portallis would send someone to eliminate him. Too much was at stake. He sank into his chair and turned on his computer. As it went through its startup routine, he dialed Tessa's number from his office phone.

She answered almost immediately.

"I've made it to my office in one piece. So I'm safe for now. Any news on the documentation?" he said.

"Yes, she's uploaded the files. I've talked to my colleagues about needing to write an overview article before they have a chance to check all the details. They're okay with that. Even without your deadline, we're under the gun. Countries have different rules regarding leaked information. We need to get this out before a court somewhere issues an injunction. I've sketched the outline already. It's going to be a general layout of the scheme, with enough details to support the main allegation. The rest will come soon after."

"I can't tell you how much I appreciate this. Without it, I'd be twisting in the wind. I better let you get to your writing."

"Will do. How's the scrape on your head? Healing well, I hope."

"Sort of. I had a bit of a struggle trying to escape. It involved jumping from a window into a tree. That didn't help. But I'm not bleeding anymore."

He could almost see her shaking her head.

"Well, get some rest," she said. "I gotta write an article. Love you."

He felt an urgent need to feel her in his arms.

"Me, too," he said, his eyes moist, and ended the call.

There wasn't anything he could do for the rest of the night. He loosened the tension on his chair's backrest, put his feet on the desk, and closed his eyes.

* * *

VERMEULEN WOKE FROM HIS RESTLESS DOZING at seven thirty. In the restroom, he used a fair number of paper towels and soap to clean himself up. The result was not convincing, but would have to do. The scab on his head had turned a dark-brown color and was coming off in places, showing angry red flesh where the hair had been singed off by the bullet. It didn't pulse anymore as it had on the plane, but it was tender enough for him to sense the slightest change in air temperature.

Back in his office, he checked his email again. No news from Tessa. He knew better than to call her. Writing an article on deadline was hard enough without being bothered. In the meantime, he needed breakfast.

Halfway down to the cafeteria, he realized that he didn't have any money and went back upstairs. Brenna, the office assistant, had arrived.

"What happened to you?" she said, wide-eyed. "When did you get in?"

"It's a long story that our boss should probably hear first. I'll fill you in later."

Brenna shook her head. "It's been, what, three months since you last showed up like this. How do you do that?"

"Come on. That time I had only spent a night in jail and didn't have a scab on my head."

"And your clothes didn't look like you'd been digging for truffles. Why didn't you go home and change?"

He laughed. "You won't believe my tree story. But seriously, at the moment, this is the only safe place for me. Can I borrow ten bucks? I need some breakfast before I face Suarez."

She pulled her wallet from her purse and handed him a bill. She fished some more and gave him a small pocket comb. "Try to comb your hair over the scab. It'll make you look less ghoulish."

"I'm too young for a comb-over."

"Suit yourself, but don't blame me when Suarez fires you. Here, take some spot remover to clean up that shirt."

Vermeulen went back to the bathroom and cleaned up his shirt as best he could. Despite his best efforts, his hair didn't obey the comb. There wasn't much he could do.

The food in his stomach felt good, although it came from the cafeteria. Even mediocre coffee was still hot and caffeinated. The clock on his computer switched to eight forty-five. No news from Tessa. He took out the science article with Portallis's notation about weaponizing the fungus, and printed out the emails from the lab. It wasn't much evidence. No judge would grant a search warrant on the basis of such scant information. He'd be lucky if Suarez didn't throw him out.

Eight fifty-five. Still no message. He got up from his chair. Time to face his boss. He stopped at Brenna's desk and returned the comb and spot remover. The door to Suarez's office stood open.

"I washed the comb," he said quietly.

Brenna took it and mouthed, "Good luck."

Suarez sat behind his desk, reading a piece of paper. An open folder lay on his desk. Vermeulen could make out his own name on the tab.

"Good morning, Mr. Suarez," Vermeulen said. "Are you ready for me?"

Suarez looked up. His face showed no expression. If he was astonished by Vermeulen's appearance, he didn't let on. "I don't think anyone can be ready for all the trouble you bring to this office." He shook his head, and the façade he'd maintained fell away. A deep tiredness showed on his face that would have made Sisyphus seem perfectly chipper. He leaned back. "So let's hear it."

Vermeulen started with Portallis's scheme to force his GMO maize into Mozambique and worked his way backward to the fraud committed against Nossa Terra that started his investigation. He took his time, responding with proper detail when Suarez interrupted with a question. He maintained a detached tone of voice, as if recounting someone else's story. When he finished, it was nine thirty. He'd set his phone to buzz for incoming messages. It hadn't buzzed.

"And you have proof for these allegations?"

"Yes, I do, sir."

Vermeulen laid the two science articles and the printouts of the emails on the desk.

"These articles describe how a common maize fungus can carry a virus, and this article describes a specific virus. Portallis's annotation leaves no doubt."

Suarez leaned over and read the note about weaponizing the virus.

"How do you know it's Portallis's annotation?"

"I found the articles at the man's home, in his bathroom."

"Where you were brought against your will?"

"Right."

Vermeulen could tell that Suarez was trying hard to keep from rolling his eyes. It was a crazy tale. In Suarez's position, he wouldn't believe it either.

"Do you have anything else?"

Vermeulen shook his head.

Suarez sat up in his chair and put his arms on his desk.

"I'm afraid this isn't enough. Listen, Valentin, I believe that you've uncovered something devious. But there is no evidence that Portallis is behind it. Or that it goes as far as you claim. You said yourself that this woman, LaFleur, orchestrated everything in Mozambique. To me it looks like a rogue employee pursuing her own agenda."

"But LaFleur wouldn't have the wherewithal to engineer a virus or a maize seed that can survive the virus."

Suarez shook his head.

"I can see LaFleur using her alliance with that Mozambican organization to get the land rights and then getting rid of them by discrediting them over those five million dollars. That's all your evidence supports. Let's just stick to that and forget the GMO conspiracy. Portallis is widely respected. His opinions carry a lot of weight. He'll deny everything. Nobody will believe you, or me for that matter."

Vermeulen opened his mouth to protest, but Suarez waved him off.

"Listen, you've done much better than I expected. You actually proved fraud by Global Alternatives in Maputo. But you won't be able to prove that Portallis, one of the wealthiest men in the world, was behind it. So let's stick to what we can support with evidence."

Vermeulen slumped back in his chair. Yes, he'd done better than expected. Suarez had seen that he had done his job, even given him an underhanded compliment. But it wasn't enough. Portallis had to be stopped.

Nine forty-five.

Suarez rose. "If there's nothing else, I propose you take a few days off. You certainly look like you need them. Let's talk again in a week and we'll see where you should go next."

Vermeulen rose, shook the man's hand, and turned to leave the office. He was just past the door when his phone buzzed. He pulled it from his pocket. There was a text message with a web link. He tapped the link. It showed the front page of the *Observer* in South Africa. The headline read: "Billionaire Set to Unleash Maize Virus in Mozambique."

Chapter Thirty-Seven

Full-Court Press

———◆———

Aisa opened the door to the Nossa Terra office at eight thirty. The morning chill was more pronounced these days. Winter was coming. People on the streets were breathing easier. In place of January's gray rain clouds that chased each other across the sky, April brought white puffs drifting to South Africa and beyond.

As always, she was the first one in the office. The others would wander in around nine. She caught herself waiting for Helton Paito to come through the door after her. He'd always been the second to arrive. A pang of sadness made her stop by the window. She missed his boisterous presence, his can-do attitude. The memory of her mistrust gnawed at her. She took a deep breath and adjusted the picture of her children on the windowsill. It had slid toward the edge again.

She turned on her computer. While it worked its way through the startup routine, she filled the teapot. Back at her desk again, she checked her email. No new messages. Just as well. The phone rang. She answered. It was Chico calling from Beira.

"You are up early," she said.

"Haven't gone to bed yet. But I'm on my way home now. Just wanted to let you know that the original land-use permits are taken care of."

Those permits had been in jeopardy ever since the directorate of agriculture found out that Sukuma had obtained many more permits fraudulently. The bureaucratic response was to cancel all of them. It had taken Chico a lot of shoe leather and patience to persuade the director in Beira that the first ten permits had been legit. Sukuma had been fired, of course, and an investigation for corruption had begun. God only knew what would come of that. She wouldn't be surprised if he walked away.

"They couldn't just reactivate the old applications," he said. "I had to fill out new ones. It took me all night, but they are done. I'll drop them off and then get my sleep."

"That's wonderful news. Thanks for your hard work. How's Tomaz working out?"

Tomaz, as she found out only a couple of weeks ago, was KillBill's real name. Chico had hired him to work as a gofer. Not that he needed one, but the job gave Chico leverage to keep Tomaz in school. Without it, he'd never have convinced the fifteen-year-old to go to elementary school. Even with the job, it was touch and go.

"He's getting used to a more regimented life. He's disciplined in his own way. It takes a little prodding to get him to include school. He'd got little patience for the teachers. But he remembers George's lecture on Mozambique needing smart people. That did more than I could ever hope for."

"Okay, get your rest."

George hadn't just coaxed Tomaz into a different life, he had also become the Nossa Terra handyman. It was only part-time work—they didn't have a lot of money for overhead—but it allowed him to rent a small room close by. He'd printed a few fliers advertising his skills as an electrician and was waiting for the first call.

Aisa loaded the website that the *Observer* had devoted to the Portallis papers. There was no new headline that day. But there had been plenty over the past weeks. The revelations of Portallis's scheme that dribbled out in weekly installments had kept them all rapt like a *telenovela*, the difference being that his plan was terrifyingly real. Deep down, she had a difficult time believing that anyone could hatch such evil plans. But each week she learned yet another devious aspect that made her skin crawl.

The door opened, and Zara came in. The two women gave each other a hug. Over the past weeks, Zara had quietly assumed Helton's place as second in command. To think that Aisa had once called her *mousy*. Nothing could be further from the truth.

"Any new revelations?" Zara said.

"Not today. Just as well. We have real work to do."

That meant implementing their original plan. A Danish and a Portuguese aid organization had partnered with them and provided the startup expenses that allowed Nossa Terra to pay its staff again. She was well aware that all eyes were on her and Nossa Terra. Even though they'd been cleared of any wrongdoing, a pall of fraud still clung to them. She wasn't worried. Their work would speak for itself.

Occasionally Aisa passed the high rise where Global Alternatives' office had been. Lately, there had been a sign outside advertising prime office space. She'd read in the paper that LaFleur had been murdered by unknown assailants. The news brought her no joy. Death was never anything to celebrate.

* * *

IN THE TWO MONTHS AFTER THE publication of the Portallis papers, Vermeulen was at the receiving end of the rollercoaster of publicity that had turned the UN into a regular topic on the nightly news. His suspension was lifted. His nose had been right and Global Alternatives had indeed mismanaged the five million dollars. The UN faced a lot of questions. Given how much money the UN was distributing to non-governmental organizations, donor countries wanted to know if Global Alternatives was just one bad apple in the bushel or the tip of the iceberg. The official answer to the donor countries was that all was well. Any additional incidents of malfeasance, though unlikely to exist, would be dealt with appropriately.

Internally, the scrutiny focused on the Office of Internal Oversight Services. Who was minding the store? Why wasn't Global Alternatives checked earlier and more thoroughly? The under-secretary-general for Internal Oversight Services oversaw the institutional review. Of course, there had to be a fall guy. And who was closer to the investigation than Vermeulen? A typical case of shoot the messenger. It was enough to make Vermeulen want to throw in the towel. The fact that he didn't was due to two unexpected developments.

First, Suarez believed him.

"I'm sorry, but I have to suspend you again," Suarez said. "You did disobey a direct order to return to headquarters. I know why you did it, and if it were up to me, you'd stay here and keep working. But," he shrugged, "it isn't. Up to me, I mean."

That surprised Vermeulen more than anything. Suarez had never shied away from picking a fight. He was the consummate organization man who couldn't abide Vermeulen's go-it-alone-whatever-the-cost attitude. Vermeulen figured that Suarez's desire to keep him inside was out of concern for what he might do on the outside, despite the gag order that was issued to all employees.

But he was wrong. The next thing Suarez said blew his preconceptions apart. "How can they expect us to do our jobs when they cozy up to the likes of Portallis? You let the private sector do our work, they will line their own pockets. That's why it's called the 'private' sector."

Vermeulen opened and closed his mouth.

"This isn't about you, Vermeulen. You are and always will be a thorn in my side. This is a matter of principle. The United Nations has a job to do.

It's the only organization that can do this job. We shouldn't sub-contract our responsibilities."

Vermeulen wanted to give the man a hug, but restrained himself. Instead, he thanked him. Suarez had stated succinctly what Vermeulen often struggled to put in words. Here was the reason why he continued to fight battles that more often than not ended in a draw. There was only one organization that could tackle global issues with a global perspective. It was maddeningly complex, it always favored compromise over decisive action, it took forever to reach a consensus—often after it was too late—and it served as a stage for the grandstanding of minor functionaries who had been retired from their own countries. And yet, it also supported the work of people like Aisa Simango and millions like her around the world. It provided a forum where they could meet and exchange experiences. It collected reams of data without which the world would be traipsing in the dark. And it was the organization he worked for.

The second surprise was Tessa moving in with him. She arrived two days after his new suspension, when the balm of Suarez's support had worn off and he'd gone back to grousing about his lousy employer. She showed him all the materials they had received from LaFleur. Once he saw them, he knew he'd done well. Not because the bad guys were behind bars, but because those documents could not be unseen. The world had to grapple with what Portallis had schemed, even if his people mounted a full-court press in his defense.

"I don't know how they can write this drivel," Tessa said after a magazine published a puff piece on Portallis. "They should be untangling his byzantine finances and getting to the bottom of GreenAnt Investments. Instead, they publish stuff that was probably written by his publicists."

The byzantine ownership structure of GreenAnt Investments helped Portallis immensely. His name didn't actually show up anywhere. The law firms in far-off places that were listed as owners refused to reveal who'd hired them. His lawyers blamed it all on LaFleur.

"Who'd even believe that LaFleur concocted this scheme on her own?" Tessa said. "That's just absurd. She ran a small office of his foundation. There's no way she had that much control."

"I know," he said. "I wish I'd have had more time in his office. The emails and the article with his annotation just weren't enough."

"It wouldn't have made a difference. Lucky for you the butler denied you'd ever been there. Otherwise you'd have to deal with a trespassing charge. No, I'm just pissed off that everyone gives him the benefit of the doubt when it's so patently clear that he's an evil crook."

All he could do was nod.

The experience of living together in his small apartment was an entirely different matter. When Tessa first saw his fridge, she groaned. "Mustard, pickles, soy sauce packets, and beer. How can you live like that?" She went shopping and stocked it with healthy food. He had his doubts. She just shushed him, reminding him that being suspended without pay meant he couldn't eat out all the time, most certainly not at that Chinese place where they put who-knows-what into their General Tso's chicken.

It didn't help that he basically was out of a job while she was busier than ever. He offered to read her drafts, but she nixed that idea. They walked on the Highline occasionally, now that the weather was nicer. Their first spat came one evening after Tessa found out that Portallis's lawyers had threatened the *Observer* with a libel suit. The paper didn't have the resources to match the deep pockets of Portallis and decided to stop publishing the remaining information and to remove the old articles from its website. Tessa was livid.

"Just find another paper to publish it," he said.

"Do you have any idea …" she stopped, shaking her head.

"I'm just saying—"

"What? That he won't sue the next paper to take up the gauntlet? The biggest story of my career just evaporated and all you can do is say, 'Find another paper?'"

She packed up her stuff and moved to a hotel.

The next morning, Suarez called to tell Vermeulen that the suspension was over; he was reinstated. "But don't expect a commendation. Just do your job and keep your head down."

Vermeulen went to Tessa's hotel. He bought a bouquet of tulips at one of the corner stores. The concierge spent more time on the phone than it should take to announce his visit. But in the end, he revealed her room number. When he got to her door, he expected to find her waiting for him. She wasn't. He knocked. And waited. He knocked again. The door opened a crack. He could see the swing bar keeping it from opening further. Taking one tulip from the bouquet, he stuck it through the crack. She took it from his hand, closed the door, and then opened it all the way.

"I'm sorry," he said.

She said nothing. He stood there, the flowers still in his hand.

"I got my job back," he said and handed them to her.

"That's great." She took the tulips. "At least you'll be out of my hair. But we need a bigger apartment."

Photo by Joanna Niemann

MICHAEL NIEMANN GREW UP IN A small town in Germany, ten kilometers from the Dutch border. Crossing that border often at a young age sparked in him a curiosity about the larger world. He studied political science at the Rheinische Friedrich-Wilhelms Universität in Bonn and international studies at the University of Denver. During his academic career he focused his work on southern Africa and frequently spent time in the region. After taking a fiction writing course from his friend, the late Fred Pfeil, he embarked on a different way to write about the world.

For more information, go to: www.michael-niemann.com.

A Valentin Vermeulen Thriller, Books 1 and 2

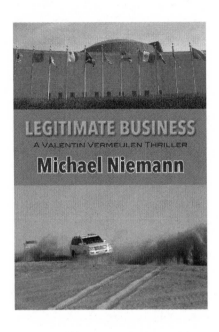

A constable with an all-female United Nations peacekeeping unit in Darfur, Sudan, has been shot dead in an apparent random shooting. The case remains closed until Valentin Vermeulen arrives to conduct a routine audit. As an investigator with the UN Office of Internal Oversight Services, his job is to ferret out fraud. It will soon be clear that he has stumbled onto a major criminal operation.

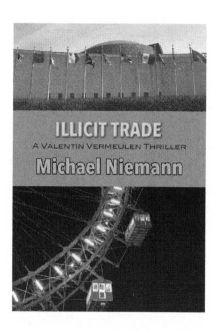

Two Kenyans who entered the U.S. with forged UN documents are killed. UN auditor Vermeulen suspects crimes worse than fraud. After riling "The Broker" in Newark, he follows the clues to Vienna. Hustler Earle Jackson soon regrets trying to con the Broker. Using the dead Kenyan's passport, he flees to Nairobi. Both men are now the targets of a vast and vicious criminal network.

FROM COFFEETOWN PRESS
AND MICHAEL NIEMANN

———— ◆ ————

Thank you for reading *Illegal Holdings*. We are so grateful for you, our readers. If you enjoyed this book, here are some steps you can take that could help contribute to its success and the success of this series.

- Post a review on Amazon, BN.com, and/or GoodReads.
- Check out Michael's website (www.michael-nieman.com) and send a comment or ask to be put on his mailing list.
- Spread the word on social media, es pecially Facebook, Twitter, and Pinterest.
- Like Michael's author page (MichaelNiemannAuthor) and the Coffeetown Press page (CoffeetownPress).
- Follow Michael (@m_e_niemann) and Coffeetown Press (@CoffeetownPress) on Twitter.
- Ask for this book at your local library or request it on their online portal.

Good books and authors from small presses are often overlooked. Your comments and reviews can make an enormous difference.

An excerpt from Legitimate Business

Chapter One

———————— ✦ ————————

Wednesday, March 10, 2010

THERE IS NO RUSH HOUR IN a refugee camp. No jobs to get to, no appointments to keep. Just waiting. Waiting to go home. The Zam Zam camp for internally displaced persons, some ten miles south of El Fasher in Darfur, Sudan, was no different. The closest Zam Zam got to a rush hour was when the food aid arrived.

Garreth Campbell drove his pickup into the camp at ten in the morning. It wasn't rush hour. The air was still a little cool from the previous night and people were milling about, waiting for something to happen. He drove carefully. No need to give anyone a reason to remember him.

The pickup was entirely unremarkable. A white Toyota Hilux, a workhorse truck used throughout Africa. White vehicles were a common sight. The United Nations, the African Union, and all kinds of aid organizations were everywhere in Zam Zam.

An armored personnel carrier waited in the distance. The acronym of the United Nations/African Union Mission in Darfur—UNAMID—was emblazoned on its side. Campbell knew it would be there. He turned left and followed a small detour past a group of tarp-covered stick and straw shelters. A makeshift fence made of dried branches stuck into the ground surrounded the compound.

The GPS unit in the cab recalculated the distance to his destination. It was a half a mile away. The female voice admitted that it had no local road information and expressed regret that it could not supply turn-by-turn navigation. The shacks and the paths between them didn't show up on the display, only a red dot indicating the coordinates he had entered.

He reached an unoccupied area the size of a soccer pitch. Thin layers of reddish sand and beige grit covered a rocky surface. Not the place where one could keep a shack standing. There were tufts of hard yellow grass here and there that would pose a challenge even to goats. At the center sat an outcropping, covered with green bushes, which looked like an alien craft on a lost planet.

Some aid organization had installed a water pump that tapped into a vein of water hidden somewhere below. Campbell parked next to it. A sign with English and Arabic script hung from the pump. The English text explained that the pump was out of order. Red plastic tape with the words 'Keep Out' was strung around the pump. The signage had done its job. No one was waiting to pump water.

He lifted a long bag from the truck. It contained an M24 rifle with a Leupold scope and a bipod. A sniper rifle, effective range a half mile. Accurate to a quarter inch over a 300-foot distance. He took the rifle from the bag and inserted the five-round magazine.

Behind the pump and hidden by the bushes was a ledge, a perfect rest for the bipod. He knelt, positioned the rifle, and levered a match-grade hollow-point round into the chamber.

Two minutes.

He focused the scope on a spot six hundred yards away, where two paths intersected. A bit of a stretch, but doable. He took a deep breath, held it for seven seconds, and exhaled slowly, taking eight seconds. Repeated three or four times, it slowed his heartbeat sufficiently.

Zam Zam took its time.

The sound of a large diesel engine starting came across the shacks. It had to be the armored personnel carrier. The engine died again.

He waited.

A crowd appeared near the intersection. Campbell expected about twenty people. There were more, maybe twenty-five, all men. The commotion had attracted some passersby. What else was there to do?

He watched. And waited.

The men surrounded two women in colorful camouflage uniforms wearing blue berets. One was shorter and had her hair tucked under the beret. The tall one had clasped her long black hair at her neck. Campbell heard snippets of sound and saw hands gesticulating. The two women stood back to back, pointing their pistols at the crowd. A very defensible position, given their circumstances. They knew what they were doing.

Campbell scanned the faces through the Leupold scope. The distance made them unreal, like faces on a TV with the sound turned off. He wondered if drone operators had a similar feeling before they pushed the button that blew up some terrorist's truck.

The defensive posture of the two women worked. The crowd around them backed off. Some men on the outside turned to leave.

He stopped waiting.

The scope came to rest on the forehead of the old man, just under his dirty *kofia,* who stood closest to the two women. Campbell pulled the trigger. The bullet made a crack when it left the barrel. A fraction of a second later, it hit the old man in the head and killed him instantly. He levered the next round into the chamber, moved the barrel a fraction of an inch, and pulled the trigger again. The second bullet raced toward the tall policewoman. She'd turned just a bit, and the bullet hit her neck rather than her head.

The moment of absolute surprise ended with the second bang. Pandemonium broke out. Some in the crowd dove to the ground, others ran in panic, while the rest stood frozen with fear.

He chambered another round and aimed for the head of one of the young men who stood still. The guy went down. Three hits in four seconds. He stopped shooting.

His heartbeat sped up. It always did, afterwards. He'd never been able to figure out that sensation. Was it the release of tension? Or was it something deeper, darker? He used his breathing technique again.

The distant diesel engine started again. It was time to leave. He pulled the magazine from the rifle, folded the bipod, and slid the rifle back into its bag. Two of the ejected casings glimmered in the sun. He pocketed them. The third casing had bounced off a rock to somewhere. No big deal. He walked back to the pickup. The door was still open. He shoved the bag into the cab. The tape and the sign at the water pump were no longer necessary. He threw them into the cab and drove off. From the corner of his eye, he caught sight of a girl. For a moment their eyes connected. Nobody else took notice of the pickup.

* * *

CONSTABLE PRIYA CHOUDHURY WAS ON PATROL with her partner Ritu Roy. They were members of an all-female police unit from Bangladesh, one of the many contingents from around the world that made up the United Nations/ African Union Mission in Darfur. When she heard the first shot, she thought some idiot was playing around with his old hunting rifle. There were plenty of idiots in Zam Zam. The cloud of pink mist rising from the head of the old man in front of her told her she was wrong.

The old man had been the leader of the crowd hectoring them, talking the crowd into a frenzy. They'd appeared out of nowhere. Usually, a gaggle of children followed her and Ritu on their patrols. Female UN police officers were a reliable source of treats. This time, grown-ups had taken the kids' place, the old man out front, shouting. Their UN-appointed translator had run away the moment the crowd formed. Amina, the whip-smart twelve-year-old girl who helped translate, wanted to stay, but Ritu sent her away. So Priya had no idea what all the fuss was about.

The old man was just skin and bones. He'd dropped to the ground and almost disappeared under the pile formed by his ratty *jalabiya*. For a split second she thought Ritu had shot him. A silly thought. Ritu had never killed anyone, and the man, although loud, had never threatened them. It was the younger men in the crowd that had Choudhury worried. They were likely to become physical. That's why she and Ritu had pulled out their pistols and radioed for backup.

They always patrolled in pairs. Their backup—Nepali police in an armored personnel carrier—loitered in the distance in case there was trouble. The Nepalis hadn't come. She'd heard the engine start and die again. That happened far too often. The running joke in her unit was that the APCs were just for show. Half the time they began their patrols late because the damn things didn't start.

The crack of the second shot turned the stunned silence into a crazy free-for-all. People running, diving to the ground. Choudhury scanned the surroundings, trying to locate the shooter.

"Did you see where the shot came from?" she shouted over the din.

Ritu didn't reply. She wasn't standing against Choudhury's back anymore. Choudhury turned and saw her friend lying on the ground. Blood formed a dusty puddle around Ritu's head. She dropped to the ground and crawled to her friend.

"Where are you hit?"

The answer was no more than a gurgle. She saw why. A ragged hole in Ritu's neck spurted blood that fed the puddle.

The third shot barely registered with Choudhury. From the corner of her eye, she saw a young guy fall to the ground. She couldn't worry about him. Her hands were already pulling the first aid kit from her pack. She pressed a bandage against Ritu's wound. It turned red immediately. She took another one, pressed it against the wet one. It turned red too. She kept pressing against the soaked bandages.

"Ritu, stay with me. You hear me. Help is coming."

Ritu's eyes were full of fear.

Choudhury pushed the call button on her radio.

"Police down! Police down! I need immediate medical evacuation. Repeat, I need immediate medical evacuation."

When the medics finally arrived, Ritu's blood had stopped flowing. There was none left.

Made in the USA
Columbia, SC
30 November 2017